The Evacuee Summer

Katie King

ONE PLACE. MANY STORIES

HQ
An imprint of HarperCollins*Publishers* Ltd
1 London Bridge Street
London SE1 9GF

This paperback edition 2018

1

First published in Great Britain by
HQ, an imprint of HarperCollins*Publishers* Ltd 2018

ISBN: 978-0-00-825757-6

MIX
Paper from
responsible sources
FSC™ C007454

This book is produced from independently certified FSC™ paper
to ensure responsible forest management.

For more information visit: www.harpercollins.co.uk/green

Printed and bound in Great Britain by
CPI Group (UK) Ltd, Croydon, CR0 4YY

The Evacuee Summer

Chapter One

The day that Milburn came to Tall Trees rectory seemed to take forever to arrive.

And no sooner had Milburn been installed in the freshly whitewashed stable and given a metal pail of cool water to drink from, than there was an enviable trumpet of flatulence from underneath an extravagantly lifted tail, followed by an impressively large mound of droppings deposited in the corner of the stall, combining to make the children crowded over the stable door giggle in glee.

Milburn's little chestnut ears flicked nervously forwards and backwards at the unfamiliar noise they were making.

The Rev. Roger Braithwaite, Tommy's father, announced in a proud voice, 'Just what the vegetables need', to which his wife Mabel replied in a tone much less proud, 'Don't be such a daft 'apporth, Roger – it's got t' rot down first.'

Nobody said anything for a moment or two, and then Tommy asked Roger in a deceptively innocent voice, 'Phew, phewee! Pa, do ponies fart a lot? And do they do much sh—?'

'Tommy!' his mother quickly cut in.

Milburn turned to peer at Tommy with such a comical look

of shock that the children could only laugh with more abandon than they had already.

The fun and games had begun a few days before.

'We're going to have a pony and trap,' Roger had announced grandly, bustling back to the crumb-strewn breakfast table after answering the telephone. 'What do you all think of that?'

Everyone who lived at Tall Trees looked at the rector in bemusement as the thought of him driving something as old-fashioned as a trap was comical. As wonderful a clergyman as he was, they all knew that the general practicalities of life, and Roger, were not easy bedfellows.

Roger pretended not to notice the joshing expressions of those sitting around the kitchen table, reminding everyone instead that although he was able to keep a car, petrol ration-ing meant it wasn't for everyday use. And probably no one needed reminding (they didn't!) that he kept losing the bit of the engine he'd regularly remove – was it the distributor cap? Roger couldn't remember – when he left the vehicle immobi-lised at night in accordance with the authorities' instructions that all vehicle owners take something out of the engine when parked up, in order to make it as difficult as possible for Jerry to use if he were to invade. It was a good thing to do, obviously, but it was trying for everyone to keep tabs on where Roger had put the 'thingymebob'.

Every single one of them had, at various times, helped Roger find something that he had put down somewhere and promptly forgotten about, usually because he placed his woolly, or his newspaper, or a tea towel on top, or because it had got buried by the muddle of papers on his overflowing desk in the study. More than once Peggy had found herself sitting down at the kitchen table only to jump up again immediately when she'd eased herself down on top of Roger's favourite Swan fountain pen, the one he used to write his sermons. Only the week before she'd sat on his horn-rimmed reading spectacles that had been missing for over a day. Of course Mabel was always on at Roger to be more tidy, seemingly oblivious to the fact that she was just as bad at failing to put things in their proper place. In fact, it was only Peggy's eye for detail and workman-like attitude for sorting things out, and using the scullery as a hiding place for the mountains of washing, that prevented the large, stone-flagged kitchen descending into chaos.

'So, from now on, for ordinary parish business it's going to be pony- (as opposed to horse-)power, with the car being reserved for real emergencies. What do you all think of that?' Roger asked the table, encouragingly.

'Madness.' Mabel's reply was eloquent in its brevity. She knew her husband well, so she didn't think much more needed to be said.

'I don't like 'orses much,' said Tommy, not that he really knew anything about them but this didn't daunt him, 'anyways, not as much as machine-guns like the…', the words dying on his lips under Mabel's stern look. She was trying to encourage her eleven-year-old son to think a bit less about weapons than he did, but it was an uphill battle as the Tall Trees boys did love to make competitive lists of guns or bombers or tanks, and they would spend hours carefully tracing photographs they saw in the newspaper and colouring them in.

Gracie added her bit with, 'I've never taken to them – 'orses – either. Their big yellow teeth put me right off.'

'Sounds like their mummies haven't made them brush their teeth,' joked Connie as she, quickly followed by her twin brother Jessie, bared her teeth, pulling her lips back with her fingers as far as she could, which of course the other children had to copy immediately too, accompanied by lots of sniggering.

Roger, Mabel, Peggy and Gracie dramatically rolled their eyes up to the ceiling, which made the youngsters do it all the more.

Despairing of the table manners of her niece and nephew but not wanting to spoil the moment, Peggy was surprised too about the pony arriving. Tall Trees was a very splendid rectory certainly, with massive windows and generously proportioned rooms. Although a sizeable amount of the large garden had been given over to the chickens and the vegetable plots, she supposed there was still quite a lot of lawn and patches of grass a pony could nibble. But this wouldn't get around the fact that Harrogate was a bustling place and it seemed odd to Peggy for Roger to be contemplating having a pony and trap in a relatively built-up area. Then she reminded herself how spacious, grand and grassy Harrogate had seemed when she and ten-year-old Connie and Jessie had arrived to their new billet on their evacuation from London the previous September, so used were they to Bermondsey's tightly packed terraced streets and the River Thames flowing silently out to sea only a stone's throw away from where they lived. 'How did the offer of the pony and trap come about?' Peggy asked Roger.

A farmer called Mr Hobbs was fed up with an extra mouth to feed that wasn't earning its keep in these straightened times, Roger explained, and so following a sermon he'd given one Sunday that managed to speak about the value of Shank's pony, and Apostle Paul on the road to Damascus (Roger having been inordinately proud of a joke he had been able to construct around these two things), Mr Hobbs had offered Roger the pony and trap on loan to use as an alternative to the car when out and about his parish.

'I thought at once of our unused stables just across the back yard and so I just heard myself replying "what a wonderful offer" and "of course we'd love to have the pony and its trap",' Roger said.

Mabel shook her head as if to say that Roger had very possibly taken leave of his senses. But there was a twinkle in her eye and Peggy didn't think Mabel was really put out by what Roger had agreed.

'I suppose my acceptance might have been hastened by having already had to bicycle to old Mr Bennett at dawn – he's on his last legs, poor chap, and there'll be bad news soon – and then go straight over to see Mrs Daley as her own brood and their evacuees have all got chickenpox. And all before breakfast, might I say, which was a lot of pedalling on the boneshaker, I can tell you,' mused Roger, 'and I thought of a pony and trap, and sitting there thinking up ideas for my sermon, and it seemed a good thing…'

Peggy knew how heavy Roger's ancient bicycle was, and she saw his point.

Mabel didn't look so sympathetic. ''Onestly, Roger, what are you like? Well, you kiddies shall take care of t' pony,' Mabel told the children, 'an', you all mark this, I'll send 'im back the first sign o' trouble, you see if I don't.'

'Deal!' they yelled in chorus, clearly delighted with the furry new arrival, and the long summer holidays stretching ahead not too far away.

Mabel had taken charge of getting everything ready for the pony, and after school she had set the children to cleaning out one of the shabby old stables and slapping a new coat of whitewash over the ancient brick walls. After, that is, they had dealt with a veritable festoon of cobwebs that needed pulling down. Connie turned out to be the only one without any fear of the host of understandably now tetchy spiders, much to the embarrassment of the boys, Tommy and Jessie, but Aiden too. He was a Harrogate lad in Tommy's class and was also staying at the rectory where the boys all bunked up together in a huge but always messy bedroom. This meant that Aiden's parents could rent out his room as there had been such an influx of people to the area since the war had begun.

Next, Mabel made the gang swish the tail end of a bar of red Lifebuoy carbolic soap about in piping-hot water from the kettle on the hob that had been poured into a couple of metal pails until the water looked opaque and medicinal. Then the children happily sloshed it about in the stall to thoroughly disinfect the floor, before using a stiff broom to swoosh the dirtied water outside. Then they neatly piled some bales of straw and hay, which had arrived while they were at school, into the stall next door, all the boys except Jessie trying to show how strong they were for the benefit of the girls.

The two buckets they'd used had been scrubbed and rinsed to within an inch of their lives to remove any smell of the Lifebuoy, after which Connie and Aiden chased each other around with the buckets half-filled with clean water trying to splash each other. Once the children were worn out, the buckets had been allowed to air-dry, as had an old zinc dustbin with a tightly fitting lid that had also been disinfected and would keep vermin out so the pony's hard feed could be kept clean and dry. Afterwards, even Mabel couldn't bring to mind anything else that needed doing.

This wasn't like Mabel at all, and so it wasn't a surprise to anybody that she put her thinking cap on and looked around for other jobs to do. Eventually, Mabel found, in an old lean-to near the chicken coops, some ancient and rather cobwebby items of grooming kit that looked as if they dated from well before the last war, in fact prior to 1910 was likely – which was the last time the stables had been occupied by horses instead of only mice and spiders – and so these elderly brushes and a currycomb had to be washed and disinfected too, and then left in a patch of bright sunlight to dry.

None of the evacuees had ever done any feeding or grooming of horses or ponies, although Connie and Jessie had sometimes helped the milkman, with his horse-drawn milk cart, to deliver the glass bottles of creamy milk to houses in Jubilee Street if they were up early enough on Saturdays (which wasn't often as the milkman and his horse with his muffled hooves did plod along the twins' home street very early in order to be in time for as many breakfasts as possible).

'Oh, I don't know,' said Roger, 'but I don't think we should worry too much about our lack of equine knowledge. I can always speak to the pony's owner if there's anything we're uncertain about, and I'm sure that as long as the pony has its scran and nobody is ever too loud, or mean, or boisterous near him, then everything will be dandy.'

The only girl evacuee, besides Connie, at Tall Trees was Angela, who had been in Connie and Jessie's class at school back at home in south-east London. Sadly, Angela was in a wheelchair following an unfortunate run-in the previous Halloween with a car driving without headlights in the black-out. All the same, Angela was determined to pull her weight as far as the pony was concerned, and after she heard Roger say that he didn't know much about ponies, she persuaded Tommy – the strongest of the children, as there were a lot of kerbs and inclines to navigate – to push her in her wheelchair over to the library so that she could bone up on horse care.

Angela was very thorough in her research, despite Tommy's recurring refrain of 'I'm bored' whispered to her in ever-shortening intervals between his stints of messing about in the road outside the library, despite the stern 'shush' hissed in his direction by the librarian. Angela made careful and copious notes on feeding and how to rub down and what the various parts of a pony's feet were called, feeling this was the least she could do as she had had to watch from her chair as the others worked to clean out the stable, knowing that Tommy's suggestion that she be gaffer was just to make her feel less of a sore thumb.

Shyly, Angela showed Peggy her jotter once they were home that evening. Peggy had been her schoolteacher a while back, and she was impressed by the diligent way that Angela had written her notes. 'Goodness me, that looks useful,' Peggy said, and Angela allowed herself to smile when she added, 'That pony is going to have a lot to thank you for, and you are going to be kept busy checking that the others are doing everything properly. Well done, Angela, really well done.'

The night they had arrived in Harrogate, nearly nine months earlier, Jessie had named his new grey teddy Neville in honour of Prime Minister Chamberlain. Jessie's Neville was the brother bear to Connie's black and white panda Petunia, the knitted bears being a surprise, hidden by their mother in their luggage as a treat for them to find when they came to unpack their belongings in their new billets.

Jessie wondered if they would be allowed to give the pony a new name when he arrived. 'If so, we could call him Winston maybe?' he asked, seeing as Winston Churchill had recently become Prime Minister.

Connie used her most strident voice to butt in quickly, 'Gi' over, Jessie, Winston's a terrible name, and you know it. What about Winnie? Much better.'

Jessie shook his head in disagreement, and so did Tommy, the two boys then doing such a dramatic thumbs-down in unison that, predictably, it had Connie leaning over to aim a swipe at them.

But she grinned coyly when Aiden weighed in on her side with, 'Clever, very clever, Connie. Winnie is Churchill's nickname, to which you're adding the sound a horse makes, and so it works two ways.'

Peggy hid her own smile as she could see that Jessie was the only one who knew for definite that Connie's momentarily perplexed expression, quickly turning into something more self-congratulatory, concealed her surprise at Aiden's suggestion that Winnie was a clever melding of meanings. To those in the know, it was nothing more than a happy accident, as Jessie would have safely bet his favourite sixer conker that his sister would never have heard the word 'whinny' before. Connie's pursed lips and immediate widened eyes back at her brother, flashing the signal to keep quiet, instantly confirmed this to her family, and probably most of the others also if they cared to think about it.

To cover up Connie's uncharacteristic failure to say something smart-aleck, Aiden went on quickly, 'I like Raffy, after t' RAF, but Shrapnel's mint too.'

'Spitfire!' yelled Tommy, a bit too enthusiastically, 'or Hawker, or Hurricane. I know, Trigger!'

'Well,' said Angela, ' I think we should wait until the horse arrives and then we can come up with the best name that suits him.'

But everyone else had been too busy thinking up names to hear Angela and to let the subject rest as she suggested.

The boys' thumbs-down appeared in quick succession for the suggestions of Brown Jack (in honour of the famous racehorse – Roger's idea), Dobbin (Mabel's, said as a joke, although she then reminded everybody that the pony might already have a name and therefore wouldn't answer to anything else, and perhaps they should consider the old wives' tale that it was unlucky to rename a horse), and Sugar (Connie's second-favourite name, apparently, reasoning that since rationing, sugar was never far from anyone's thoughts *and* horses were known for liking sugar lumps).

The children were becoming overexcited by now, which was usually the fast track to somebody ending up with their nose out of joint, and sometimes even in tears. A little reluctantly, Peggy called an end to the debate, declaring it was time for the children to clear the table and do the washing-up, otherwise there'd be no ponies for them at all.

With deliberately loud sighs to show they weren't happy, nonetheless the youngsters obediently began to see to their chores, with only one under-the-breath whisper from someone of 'Sugar? That's a dog's mess name,' to which Peggy had to quickly say 'Connie, that discussion is over now, remember?' to stop her niece seizing the moment to defend her suggestion and thereby almost definitely extending the conversation on the blessed names until it degenerated into a right old ding-dong of a squabble.

Chapter Two

On the Saturday, once they had finished their morning chores to Mabel's satisfaction, the children hung around waiting for the new arrival.

They swung on the garden gate, causing nearby butterflies to flutter furiously into the air when the plants at the edge of the drive were disturbed. Then the children had a competition throwing chips of gravel from the short drive in front of the house, down the length of the rear garden, to see who could hoof a chip the furthest. And when Tommy won and started to show off, further disturbing the hens who had been set to panicky clucking by a stray chip that bounced off their zinc water trough, Aiden and Jessie had to wrestle him to the ground so that he didn't get too above himself.

It was a baking-hot morning right at the end of May in 1940, and it seemed an age before the children heard the unmistakeable sound of a pony's metal horseshoes on the tarmac of the road outside, clip-clopping in their direction, and then slow down to turn into Tall Trees.

''E's a right little tinker, make no mistake,' said Mrs Hobbs, the homely farmer's wife, as she pulled the pony to a halt once she had driven into the back yard and hefted herself down to the ground with a dramatic sigh and a final lurch that made the wooden trap creak as if it were about to do itself a mischief.

The children supposed she was talking about the pony and not any of them.

For the moment nobody could think of anything to say, but Mrs Hobbs didn't seem to notice, adding before too long, 'Milburn needs watchin' as 'e'll nip yer if yer not careful. An' 'e's prone ter gettin' oot if 'e thinks there's somethin' more interestin' goin' on elsewhere or 'e thinks 'e can get away wi' it. 'E don't kick often, but 'e means it when 'e do, so mind yerselves an' yer all watch out.'

The children all took a step backwards.

The soft-eyed pony looked bigger up close than when turning into the yard, when the looming appearance of both the comfortably rounded farmer's wife and the battle-weary trap had dwarfed the hairy-looking beast.

Roger bustled out of the kitchen, wiping his hands dry on a holey and faded tea towel that had once proudly extolled the virtues of Harrogate, followed closely by Mabel. Roger paused too and looked suspiciously at the pony who tossed its head insouciantly in his direction as a reply – or was this a challenge? And then Roger stepped back cautiously in a pantomime version of the way the children just had, although not before a little fleck of foam from the corner of the pony's mouth from camping at the bit, flew through the air and landed ominously on Roger's hand.

Only Mabel moved forward to pat the pony's stocky neck, and the pair eyed each other seriously as if each were weighing up an opponent. 'The children 'ave 'ad a scrabble o'er t' name,' Mabel announced to Mrs Hobbs.

The chestnut blinked solemnly in acknowledgement of what the rector's wife had said.

'We'll 'ave 'e back if yer can't cope, course, bu' 'e's too small fer t' plough or much else that's useful on t' farm, an' our girt chillen are t' big fer 'e now an' we 'aven't time t' go up 'ill an' down dale funnin' aboot in t' trap, an' so yer's doin' us a niceness puttin' 'e up 'ere. An' 'e'll pay yer back as 'e's a worker. Once 'e's mind's on it, that is,' Mrs Hobbs went on as if Mabel hadn't said anything as to the pony's name, the last comment having a faintly threatening ring about it nonetheless.

The farmer's wife looked towards the pony, and then Mrs Hobbs turned to stare at everyone else, before she sighed as if one of them had been found wanting and Milburn shook a shaggy mane as if to deny all association with the sigh. Mrs Hobbs sighed dramatically once more and then swiftly demonstrated how the tack came off, and was put on again; told them what the difference between hay and straw was; and how any hard feed (which he wouldn't need before the cold weather came) should be given after the pony had been allowed to drink. Then Mrs Hobbs addressed the way the trap was connected to the harness and how the trap could be upended when it wasn't in use to stop it rolling around; after which she outlined in theory the way the pony should be made to go faster or to stop, or to turn left or right. Then she reminded them again – and this was really important, she insisted – that water should be offered before food, and not the other way around to avoid any danger of colic; while if the pony did get colic they'd need to use a drench, which always caused problems. (Everyone looked very serious at this, especially Milburn.) Finally, Mrs Hobbs produced a hoof pick from a pocket at the front of her floral pinny and the children gasped when they saw how the pony's generous feathers were grasped and then pulled upwards, so that its feet could be lifted up one at a time to rest on Mrs Hobbs's bent leg in order that each hoof could be picked, with mud and gravel being scraped out.

From somewhere low down, Mrs Hobbs muttered at last as she leant over, her corduroy trews now stretched dangerously over her ample posterior, ''E's bin shod yesterday an' 'e answers to Milburn up at t' farm, but yers all call 'e what yer wants, 'e won't mind, I dare say.' The pony's expression seemed to dispute not minding about the name, and then there was a decisive shake of a long, mole-coloured nose as if to drive the point home. ''Is feet'll need doin' every day, an' mark yer do it or you'll be in fer trouble. As long as yer remember to take 'e t' smithy every two months at least, an' more if 'e's on roads a lot as 'e'll need t' shoes kept up and they get slippy otherwise. Yer could drive a bus beside 'e, 'e's so quiet in traffic,' finished Mrs Hobbs.

'Sounds like t' pony is goin' t' 'ave new shoes more often than us,' said Mabel in the sort of rueful voice that made the adults think about the clothes rationing that was just about to start, and made the children understand anew that nobody was to expect much in the way of treats these days.

Aside from the clothing coupon issue, Roger appeared nothing short of pensive in any case; clearly he hadn't realised that a pony might be spooked by large vehicles near it, and they could all see that he had no idea what to do in the event of the creature taking fright.

Luckily everyone was distracted from these gloomy thoughts by the sound of an approaching vehicle and then the toot of a horn from a van idling out in the road.

Mrs Hobbs thrust the reins at Mabel, and said goodbye to the pony with a firm slap to its rump that caused it to bunch its quarters and clamp its tail flat down, and then with no more ado than a gruff 'cheero', the farmer's wife bustled out of the yard at Tall Trees to get her lift back to the farm without so much as a backwards glance.

The pony watched her leave, and then turned deep-brown shiny eyes with long eyelashes towards Mabel as if enquiring whether some sort of rather unamusing joke had just been made.

Once the vehicle had driven away there was a long silence, broken only by the clucking of the hens over at the other side of the garden, and then the pony pawed the ground once with a front hoof.

Jessie spied a tiny spark shoot out as the clink of a metal shoe struck a flint in the yard.

'I don't think any of our names so far suit him,' said Angela. 'What about Lightning?'

The pony was thickset with a large belly slung between short but strong legs, and a bushy tail that almost touched the ground, while a wiry mane and forelock gave a top-heavy impression. As ponies go, it neither looked very fast, or very lightning-like. And to judge by the roll of intelligent eyes the pony didn't think much of Lightning as a name.

'I know t' farmer's wife kept callin' the pony 'e, but I think it's a girl, Angela, and I've always believed Lightning seems better as a boy's name,' said Aiden tactfully.

Making sure he kept a good distance, Tommy leant down and looked under the hairy belly, before moving around to the rear to peer under a slightly raised tail and then he hooted, 'That's a lass all right!' to which Mabel muttered, 'I'm not even goin' t' ask 'ow yers know that, Tommy ...'

So the pony was definitely female. Jessie, who hadn't been quite sure he'd be able to tell the difference between a girl pony and a boy pony, fancied he saw a look of relief flit across the bright eyes now turned in his direction from beneath the golden forelock.

'Well, that cuts out Brown Jack, and Winston then too,' Connie pointed out quickly so that she could keep her advantage in the Great Naming Debate. 'My two of Winnie or Sugar both work well for a girl horse though, don't you think?'

'You should describe her as a mare,' said Jessie, 'and technically she's a pony as she is not tall enough to be a horse, given that she'd be measured in hands of four inches, although of course there is a saying that all ponies are horses but not all horses are ponies ... ' He shut up when he saw the bored expressions on his friends' faces, with Tommy waving a hand in front of his mouth as if stifling a yawn. All faces other than Aiden's, that was, as he looked quite interested in these technicalities that somehow Jessie seemed to know, despite only occasionally have patted the milkman's horse and just the once having stroked the shoulder of a huge, gentle-giant Shire horse with hooves the size of plates and extravagant white feathers fluffing down to the ground, that had been pulling a huge dray to bring a delivery of kegs of beer to the Jolly, the public house nearest to Jubilee Street, where they had grown up in south-east London.

'Well, let's give her a chance to get used to her stable, and then we can think about it over lunch,' said Roger in a voice that he tried to make as rallying as he could, but which everyone could recognise was distinctly dubious. 'You boys, are you strong enough to push the trap over to that bit of the yard out of the way? I'm sure you are! We must remember to take the pony out of the trap when we have got her and it into a position where it won't be in the way of the car, in case I need to drive off quickly in an emergency, as we don't want to be pushing the trap around the yard every day and I especially don't if it's in the middle of the night.'

His words were lost as Tommy had set about organising himself, Aiden, Jessie and Connie (Connie being right now, an honorary boy) into lugging several bales of hay (or was it straw?) from the trap to add to the others already in the spare stall, and then manhandling the now much lighter trap to where Roger wanted it to be.

Mabel passed her husband the pony's reins, and in Roger's hands the determined creature promptly hauled him over to the small patch of grass at the edge of the back yard, where she determinedly stuck her nose down and grabbed several quick munches.

'Milburn!' Mabel said sternly, and both Roger and the pony jumped, Milburn raising her head with such a start that it caused her harness to jangle, and then she opened her mouth dramatically to show all of them her yellow teeth and a crud of partially chewed grass, before she dragged Roger in the direction of her open stable door. She seemed to know just where to go.

'I, er, er – I'll just put her inside, shall I? Inside her, er, er, stall. In here, that's the ticket.' His voice got quieter as Milburn towed him through the door. 'Now, how again does this thing come off?' Roger added as he gazed helplessly at the pony's tack.

'It's called a bridle and what you are holding are the reins, Mrs Hobbs said,' Jessie clarified. 'Can I take it off her? You just undo that strap under that big bone at the top underneath her chin and pull the whole thing forward over the ears, holding it at the top of her head. You have to do it smoothly and gently so as not to damage her eyes and teeth. And Mrs Hobbs said, I think, that the pony is used to people standing on her left when they do this and so that might be why she is lifting her lip at you.'

With relief Roger almost threw the long leather reins to Jessie and made a hasty exit from the stall, but not before a soft velvety forehead the colour of butterscotch gave Roger a firm push as he brushed past.

The rector gave what could only be described as a squeak, a little later followed by, 'I'm, er, sure I'll get the hang of it by the end of today. I shouldn't think it's too difficult. Looking after one small pony, that is. Putting on and taking off her bridle, cleaning her teeth and so forth. Feet! Silly me. I mean cleaning her feet... hooves, I mean. No, no, not too tricky at all, I expect.' He paused. 'Does she need her teeth cleaning too, do you think? Goodness, her teeth *are* big, aren't they, and so I very much hope not.'

Milburn neighed loudly in reply, her belly quivering, making Roger jump visibly for the second time in only a minute or two.

The children tried not to laugh too conspicuously, while Mabel allowed herself a broad grin.

They all knew already who the boss was, and it certainly wasn't Roger.

19

Chapter Three

Several streets away, Peggy was making heavy weather of heaving the battered old perambulator she shared with Gracie back towards Tall Trees, despite it being such a lovely day and the sunlight showing the golden tones in Peggy's shiny hair to best effect. Her green-sprigged cotton summer dress felt looser than it had even a few days before but Peggy barely noticed, although once upon a time she had been very proud of her trim figure, her tiny waist being the envy of sister, Barbara.

While Peggy had slimmed right down since her pregnancy, baby Holly, now a lively five and a half months, had at last almost caught up with other babies of her age, despite being born two months early. Now, as Peggy pushed her through the sun-dappled shade of the tree-lined street, Holly was cheerfully kicking her crocheted blanket away from her now plumply dimpled legs.

Peggy had been helping out at June Blenkinsop's teashop, as she did most days. She and June had been talking only that morning about the rapid increase in customers now that the toasted teacakes and pots of tea that June had been serving in a colourful array of delicate china teapots had just about totally given way, due in no small part to Peggy's staunch encouragement, to a menu of simple but filling hot meals of the meat-and-two-veg variety, and tea served in small metal utilitarian teapots to workers from six in the morning until gone ten at night. Such was the demand from people who were often juggling paid shift work alongside voluntary but nonetheless crucial war roles, that June's business was thriving. As if to prove the saying that every cloud has a silver lining, the outbreak of war had turned June's café into a rapidly expanding business, with a growing rota of cooks and Women's Voluntary Service (WVS) helpers, that meant it was going from strength to strength.

And now it looked as if the business could expand even further as Peggy was in midst of looking into setting up at least one, although ideally two, mobile canteens that could be driven from place to place. After nearly nine months of almost no bombs dropping over England since the war had begun, the newspapers were increasingly claiming the long-expected German aerial offensive must at last be drawing near, and so if the anticipated bombs were about to rain down on them all then mobile canteens would be a godsend in fortifying those who had to deal with the aftermath of such terrible events, and this had got Peggy pondering.

'June, I've thought more about the mobile canteens as you wanted, and I think we could make it work. I've totted up some rough figures, we could use the café's kitchen for the prep and we'd need to sort some metal mugs and plates, but I think we'd get these through the NAAFI suppliers. I think we'd get an old vehicle donated from somewhere like the railways. James…' Peggy had said to her friend earlier as they sat at a table with cups of tea during a swift twenty minutes after the morning rush and before lunchtime really got going. 'Yes, you can take that look off your face! *James* said that if we got a van or something bigger, he thought some of the recuperating men at the hospital could help convert it to a canteen.'

June ignored Peggy's mention of the handsome young doctor at the new field hospital as she said that, actually for the plates and the vehicle and so forth, it might be sensible if she had a word with the people at the authorities she'd be dealing with over expanding her business. 'They'll maybe have a stock of old vehicles set aside that they've requisitioned for this sort of thing,' June added, 'and I think too, if we get this off the ground, then the WVS and maybe the ATS (Auxiliary Territorial Service) will step in with volunteers.'

'I was talking about it the other day and Gracie said she was keen to be involved, especially if she can drive the canteen,' Peggy mentioned.

June and Peggy thought a little further on what Peggy had just said, before they shared a raised-eyebrow look even though they were both very fond of Gracie, a young single mother who also lodged at Tall Trees along with baby Jack, after which Peggy added, 'Seeing how Gracie rattles that pram around with poor Jack inside, we'd definitely better have metal plates and mugs if she's going to be driving.'

Peggy and June talked through a few potentially profitable fundraising ideas and the discussion had ended with June suggesting that Peggy might like to consider going into a formal arrangement with June as regards the café. This would mean that rather than Peggy simply manning the café's till as she did at present, perhaps the two women could arrange something as bold as a proper partnership, with legal papers drawn up as to each woman's responsibility. June had even gone as far as suggesting they rename the business, with 'Blenkinsop and Delbert' being the obvious choice.

Peggy had been so taken aback at June's generous offer that she hadn't known what to say, and had been left gawping with her mouth open and closed like a fish. The offer also implied that Peggy would be in Harrogate for some time to come, and while she understood this in the intellectual sense, in practical terms she always felt as if it wouldn't be long until she and Holly and the twins were back in the crammed streets of south-east London that were so close to her heart, and she could go to see Barbara for a pep talk whenever she was feeling a bit down, which had sometimes happened since Holly's arrival.

When, after a while, Peggy still hadn't said anything, June had had to suggest that Peggy think about it for a while and then they could talk about it again when she didn't feel to be quite so much on the back foot.

'I hope you don't mind me saying, Peggy,' June added as she stood up and adjusted her apron ready to go back to the café's kitchen, 'but you don't seem quite yourself today…'

June Blenkinsop had hit the nail on the head. Peggy absolutely wasn't herself. No, not at all. The partnership discussion with June had been very flattering, naturally, and it had given Peggy a lot to mull over as she had never thought of herself as any sort of businesswoman. But she'd been a schoolteacher in Bermondsey for nearly a decade and so it was hard for her to think of herself as anything else.

Not that Peggy could do much thinking on what June had said just at the moment, as the truth of it was that she had too much else to worry about.

Normally, when Peggy pushed her daughter along, she felt consumed with love for her, as well as a very, very lucky mother indeed. Every few paces she would look down at Holly and make a funny face or say her name, and then the two would smile gaily at each other. Holly's unexpected arrival on a snowy Christmas Eve had been traumatic to say the least, and indeed it was only the quick thinking of the children at Tall Trees that had saved both Peggy and Holly's lives. Over a month in hospital under the watchful eye of the wonderfully sympathetic young doctor, James Legard, had meant that Peggy left the hospital feeling recovered and much stronger than she had felt when she had gone in, and with an always peckish although still tiny baby in her arms. But this was understandable as Holly had arrived dangerously early.

Not a day went by when Peggy didn't remember what a very close call it had turned out to be for both of them, or the many ways in which she would be forever grateful to all concerned. Connie and Jessie, her niece and nephew, had been wonderful, and Peggy felt she might not be around today if they, and their friends, hadn't acted so quickly and in such a grown-up way when they found her collapsed.

She knew too that her husband Bill was delighted to have a daughter, especially as they had had to wait many long years before, out of the blue, Peggy fell pregnant. They had been so thrilled with the news of Peggy's pregnancy, as this had seemed to cement the cracks that had been starting to enter the marriage, cracks of frustration and thwarted hopes at their childlessness.

Bill had only been able to get away to pay them just the one visit since Christmas (and it was now spring moving into summer), catching a coach and then a train up to Harrogate one frosty morning in mid-January. After they had hugged and he had chucked Holly under the chin, he had commented on the several evacuees and their parents on the station waiting to catch the train out of the town to return home as more and more parents from the big towns and cities were coming forward to reclaim their kiddies.

But Peggy had hardly taken in what he was saying about the evacuees, so wrapped up was she in the precious sight of Holly's tiny hand firmly clasping one of Bill's giant fingers, the gold signet ring on his pinky glinting to remind him and Peggy of their marriage, and the salt tears slipping down Bill's cheeks as he gazed lovingly down at his daughter.

Just that one perfect memory of a daughter reaching for a father's finger had been worth a thousand hours of letter-writing and longings for her husband to be by her side. Peggy had allowed her own tears of joy and gratitude to well up as Bill had put his arm around her and pulled her close, kissing her brow and telling Peggy tearfully in a voice choked with gratitude what a clever, clever girl she was to have produced such a beautiful baby, and how lucky Holly was to have Peggy for a mother. It had felt a wonderful moment.

Now, Holly was lying on her back in the bulky black perambulator, looking for all the world as if she was trying to catch her mother's eye in order to give her a gummy grin.

She tried waving her small pink fists in the air and then putting one hand in her mouth, and when that didn't work, a spot of further kicking that was so energetic that her thin crocheted pram blanket slipped completely askew. The silken bow that tied on a white bootee that Aunty Barbara had knitted loosened, and Holly did her best to work it off as she was sure Peggy wouldn't be able to ignore that.

But Holly's efforts, no matter how determined the baby was, were destined to fail, as Peggy's brow remained wrinkled and her dark eyes anxious, as she stared unseeing into the distance while huffing and puffing the perambulator up the hill.

The reason for Peggy's pensive expression and clenched jaw this sunny May day was because first thing that morning she had received a cryptic card from Bill, who was still located somewhere in the UK (she thought, although Bill had never been exactly specific as to quite what he was up to) as he had intimated he was now training tank drivers somewhere near the coast of Suffolk. Or might it be Norfolk?

Peggy had felt unsettled since the moment she'd laid eyes on the card. Somehow even before she picked it up to read, it seemed to beckon menacingly at her, driving thoughts asunder of the new pony and trap she could hear the children talking about, or Gracie wanting to have use of the perambulator in the afternoon. And reading Bill's scribbled words had given Peggy no reassurance at all.

Before he'd been called up from Bermondsey for his military training, Bill had been a bus conductor on the number 12 bus that went from south-east London to the West End, or occasionally he was put on the number 63, and he'd hugely enjoyed the daily banter with his passengers. Sometimes, if the depot was short of drivers, he'd not put up a fuss if he'd been asked to get behind the steering wheel instead, even though

Bill had often said to Peggy that it was nowhere near as much of a hoot driving a double-decker as it was dealing with all and sundry as he stood in his smart conductor's uniform ready to take their fares. Once war had been declared and it became obvious to the authorities what his previous job had been, it made sense therefore to all that Bill turned his experience into helping less experienced drivers gain the knowhow of manhandling heavy vehicles. And that really was all that Peggy knew about what he did these days.

Bill was no letter-writer at the best of times, and so for Peggy to receive a card from him, the second in a week, was unusual to say the least. In fact it had never happened before.

The card merely said: 'Peggy, we need to have a word – I will telephone you on Sunday, Bill'.

In fact it was so out of character for Bill to contact her again so soon after the last missive that now she was unable to dispel a niggle of worry that had multiplied and grown over the morning so it was now a seething mass squirming uncomfortably just beneath her ribcage, increasing in intensity with every passing hour. She couldn't stop chewing over the fact that on Bill's card there had been etched no 'love', 'fondest wishes' or 'missing you', or even 'thinking about our dear Holly', the last of which was a given in his communications these days. Most concerning though was that there hadn't been the whiff of even one 'X' either, not to her, and – unbelievably – not to Holly.

Something was up, Peggy knew as surely as eggs were eggs.

And she was just as certain that whatever it was that had provoked Bill to contact her so soon after his last card (which had arrived only on the previous Monday and had been gaily

27

filled with casual chatter about card games and japes to do with the NAAFI, before sending love to her and Holly, with a multitude of kisses) was likely to be something that she wasn't going to like in the slightest.

Peggy rarely experienced the sensation of a twinge of piercing worry as she was naturally quite a calm and resourceful person, but whenever she had had such a stab of anxiety in the past, it had always proved to be the precursor of something extremely trying at best, and downright infuriating at worst.

As she manoeuvred the perambulator into the drive at Tall Trees and headed toward the back yard (they all tended to use the back door to enter the house through the kitchen rather than the imposing front door that scraped heavily across the stone flags of the hall), Peggy was so deep in her thoughts that she didn't even notice the upended trap in the corner of the back yard, its wooden shafts pointing up to the sky as if to announce it was keeping its own special lookout for enemy aircraft high above them in the endless blue sky. She and Holly had left Tall Trees to head for June's teashop that morning before the children had come down to breakfast, and since then she had completely forgotten about the new arrival.

The small chestnut mare, only just big enough to be able to angle her head upwards so that she could look over the rather high half-door (clearly made for a creature larger than she), thoughtfully watched Peggy bounce the pram across the bumpy yard.

She almost let out a neigh just in case Peggy had a stray carrot lurking in her pocket, but there was something so distracted about Peggy's demeanour that the whip-smart pony quickly divined it wasn't worth bothering.

Peggy shoved the brake on the pram down with her foot and gathered Holly into her arms, not noticing the delicate blanket hadn't been grasped too as was usual, or that there was now a bootee amiss.

Holly didn't appreciate not being the centre of her mother's attention, and she gave a little cry just as a reminder that she was there and that she was looking forward to her lunchtime feed.

Peggy didn't say the soothing 'shush, poppet' or 'there's my girl' that Holly expected, or give her a jiggle to make her laugh, or swing her high into the air.

Instead her mother's face remained stony as she clutched Holly a little tighter and concentrated on balancing her in her arms along with her handbag and a lentil 'surprise' in a tin pie-dish that she had bought from June for their supper later on, whilst also trying to open the kitchen door.

There was only one thing for it, and Holly filled her baby lungs to capacity so that she could produce the first in a rapidly escalating series of loud wails that no mother could ignore.

Laying her ears flat against her head, Milburn dipped her head back inside the box and dropped her nose down to inspect her empty bucket just in case she had missed a morsel. She couldn't compete with that racket and she wasn't going to try.

Chapter Four

The next day arrived, which was Sunday, and the sense of excitement from the previous morning still held strong amongst the children, not least as there was due to be another arrival at Tall Trees.

Larry was moving back up to Yorkshire to take up residence with them once again, and everyone was looking forward to it as the atmosphere just hadn't felt the same in the rectory since he had departed several months earlier.

Larry had attended Jessie and Connie's school back in Bermondsey, and so the previous September he'd been evacuated up to Harrogate along with the twins, Angela, and indeed the rest of their school too.

Larry had had a chequered time in Harrogate, having been bullied at first and then later moving to Tall Trees where life settled for him a little. But with the Phoney War dragging on and on, his mother Susan had arrived at the end of January to take him with her, back to London.

Once Larry had been waved off on the train Jessie and Connie had been very subdued for the rest of that day. Although they suspected that Larry might be going back to a rocky situation inside his family home, as his father was known for being a lout, they couldn't help but wish that they were also on the train heading south with the prospect of seeing their own mother, Barbara, and father, Ted, very soon and moving back into their two-up two-down in Jubilee Street in Bermondsey to be a proper family again. Harrogate and Tall Trees was fine as far as it went, the glum faces of the twins seemed to say when they were alone together, but despite all that Roger and Mabel did to make them feel settled, it just wasn't their *home*, was it? And they did miss their parents terribly. Peggy knew what they meant – she had mixed feelings about their evacuation too.

Unfortunately for Larry, the situation he found back in London turned out to be every bit as unpleasant as he'd feared it would be. Peggy knew that Larry's father, Trevor, had been banned several times from the Jolly, and other public houses too, but business was business and somebody such as Trevor did spend a lot of money, so a temporary ban was more a rap on the knuckles for poor behaviour rather than anything permanent.

Peggy had taught Larry back in Bermondsey, and she had once had a worrisome run-in with Trevor in the street a day after she had encouraged Larry to take a storybook home so that he could finish off the chapter he'd begun reading aloud in class and had been very taken with. A clearly tipsy Trevor had demanded aggressively, even going so far as to poke Peggy in the arm with a ragged-nailed nicotine-stained finger, to know if she could be so good as to explain why it was that she was wasting Larry's time with something so pig-ugly useless as a piece of make-believe. Peggy tried to say that *The Family from One-End Street* had a lot to recommend it, and that Larry's engagement was excellent news.

Trevor hadn't been having any of it, with the result that the next day Peggy had had to say to Larry during morning playtime that perhaps it would be a good idea if he tried to get all his reading done in the classroom during the day and not take any storybooks home again. It was no surprise to Peggy that Larry never willingly picked up a storybook in her classroom again. She had always felt bad that she hadn't stuck up for Larry more, but, although she would never admit this out loud to anyone, she had felt scared and intimidated by the gruff tones and beery stench of Larry's father.

Once Larry was back in London Peggy suspected that, older and wiser, he'd be less tolerant of Trevor's evil moods. Peggy's intuition proved correct and Larry's mother had telephoned Mabel from the Jolly – it was actually the first time Susan had ever made a telephone call off her own bat – when, clearly at the end of her tether, she had asked in a quavering voice if there were any way that Larry could come back to Tall Trees for a little while? Mabel confessed to Peggy that she'd thought she'd heard a muffled sob, before Larry's mother added in a tight voice, 'Only until things settle at 'ome, that is, you unnerstan'. I'm sure it'll calm directly.'

Roger and Mabel had been very generous in welcoming a gaggle of strangers into their home, and after a sticky period where their good intentions had been tainted by son Tommy's vindictive response to the arrival of a lot of strange-seeming children from London arriving at Tall Trees, eventually an easier equilibrium had been established. The atmosphere lightened further once Aiden Kell and Larry had moved in. And then Angela had arrived a couple of months later to make the ensemble complete, and although her wheelchair meant she couldn't share Connie's bedroom upstairs, she had fitted in with no trouble.

Tommy's large bedroom had been made into a dorm for the four boys, and although they could be loud at times and the bedroom always looked fearsomely untidy, Mabel having to shut the door on it every time she walked by despite her high tolerance for clutter, there was something about the dynamic that made the lads all rub along together without too much ribbing or outright argument under the new regime, and so Larry had been missed when he had gone back to London.

Connie slept in her little box room at the far end of the corridor to the boys' room, while Angela was in a snug on the ground floor, not far from the large kitchen.

The two bedrooms on the second floor, up above the other bedrooms and high in the eaves, had Peggy and Holly in one, with Gracie and baby Jack in the other. Having to navigate so many stairs obviously wasn't ideal for the new mothers, but once they had moved into Tall Trees proper, across from their previous room above the stables during the cold weather, somehow they had never moved out of the main house and back into their old lodgings. As Gracie joked, all the stairs helped them get their figures back double-quick after the babies had arrived.

Tall Trees was definitely a full house these days, with or without Larry, and Peggy sometimes felt there were just too many people jammed together under the one roof, but then she would chastise herself for being so uppity as she knew that few evacuees had been welcomed the way they had by Roger and Mabel. There was a war on, after all, and there were many far worse places to be than in a large and trifle chaotic rectory, with chickens in the garden providing daily eggs, and constant fresh greens from a sizeable vegetable patch that they all took turns in digging out (Peggy thought that was the term) and planting up.

With a bit of luck they'd all be home for Christmas, Peggy sometimes sighed to herself when stuck in a queue for the bathroom. Then she would remember she had thought precisely the same thing the previous autumn; and look how that had worked out.

Anyway, nobody was thinking much about any of this as while Roger was taking his Sunday morning services at church, the atmosphere back at the rectory was one of excitement about Larry returning.

There were crisply ironed sheets on his bunk, and a clean folded towel on the pillow.

'I know, let's put somethin' in Larry's bed ter gi' 'im a surprise later,' said Tommy to Jessie, once Aiden – who could be a bit of a killjoy, he was so sensible – had gone down to feed the hens along with Connie.

'What about Connie's hairbrush? Nice and bristly if you're not expecting it.' Jessie's eyes twinkled at the thought.

'Sweet,' said Tommy, and then he kept watch on the landing corridor while Jessie crept into Connie's bedroom to retrieve the brush.

Carefully, they pushed it down Larry's bed with an old coat hanger so as not to disturb Mabel's hospital corners of the sheets and blankets, making sure that the bristles were left pointing towards the pillow so that Larry's toes would find it when he slipped into bed later. Finally, they covered the small mound it made with the towel.

'A good job done. After all, Larry'd be upset if we didn't do something like this to welcome him back,' added Jessie gravely, as he and Tommy stood back to admire their work.

The children couldn't wait to see what Larry would make of them having a real flesh-and-blood pony to hand. He was totally unused to animals, which naturally made Mabel's cat Bucky, a giant black and white tom with ears carefully scalloped from his many presumably victorious fights, especially affectionate around him, much to Larry's embarrassment. But Bucky was persistent, and even after Larry had gone to London had continued to wait for him, nestling on his bed each night with his forepaws turned towards each other and tucked under.

Eventually the greeting party for Larry assembled ready to walk over to the station, although Connie had made a bit of a fuss about being unable to brush her hair properly and Angela had had to lend Connie her hairbrush in order that they wouldn't be late.

There had been a debate about whether Milburn could come with them to the station and the children had tossed a halfpenny. The vote had gone in Milburn's favour and it wasn't long before Jessie was standing in the back yard holding the hemp lead rope to Milburn's halter as the pony carefully nosed his pockets, hoping a treat was there. Connie and Aiden stood alongside but they'd made sure they were out of harm's way, just in case Milburn went to nip or kick, as although she'd been sweet enough when the pair of them had taken her out for an hour's grazing earlier on some road verges, they didn't yet fully trust the small mare.

A minute or two passed as they waited for Tommy to hoist

Angela's chair over the lip of the back-door step, so that they could all, Milburn included, head over to the station.

As the children trailed through the back yard Peggy was in the kitchen with a serious look on her face and, despite the heat of the day, was feeling cold and a bit shaky. Ten minutes or so earlier, she had put Holly down for a nap in a deep drawer that had once been the bottom one in a dark-wood chest, but which was now used by either Peggy or Gracie if their little ones needed a nap while their mothers were preparing food or sitting together to have a natter over a cuppa, and now Peggy was pensively sipping on a cup of tea, staring out the kitchen window. She felt tense as she waited for Bill to telephone her, and she had slept poorly. Nonetheless, it was impossible not to notice how well the kiddies looked and how brightly Milburn's butterscotch coat shone in the sunlight.

Peggy's squirm of apprehension went into wriggling over-drive with the posh-sounding ring of the telephone on the desk in Roger's study, and she hurried to answer it.

She was almost certain it was Bill on the end of it, even though if it was, he was ringing earlier than she expected, but as she picked up the receiver she still didn't know whether she was ready to hear what he might have to say.

Chapter Five

There was no getting around it. From the anticipatory clank of her husband dropping his large copper pennies into the money slot at the bottom of the apparatus in the public telephone box, something sounded off. There was a metal creak of a door hinge in need of an oil, and Bill's very first word – a solitary but strangely formal 'Peg' – told Peggy that without a shadow of doubt something most unsavoury was about to be revealed.

Standing in front of Roger's desk, Peggy had leant forward and pulled out his chair, but as she heard the delay that told her that Bill was taking his time feeding his pennies into the slot, she thought better of sitting down. She decided that with a bit of luck, if she stayed standing she might be braver facing whatever unpleasant news it was that she was about to learn.

It felt as if she might be teetering on the edge of a deep, dark abyss. Peggy wasn't sure why this was, but she supposed she hadn't been married to Bill for such a long time without knowing him inside and out. And there was something so off-key beckoning to her from that one word of greeting that a precipice seemed undoubtedly to be widening below her, calling her into its depths. She couldn't say she was totally surprised, given the lack of love and kisses on the postcard that he'd sent her, but still...

The downbeat tone of his 'Peg' had cast aside any sign of his normal irrepressible cheeky cockney banter. If Peggy were honest, Bill had never been much of a looker but he'd always had the gift of the gab and had been the sort of chap who could charm the birds from the trees, and so Peggy had been seduced all those years ago by the extent to which he'd made her laugh much more than by his looks.

Now it was worrying that all echoes of this cheery repartee that she'd once loved so much had given way to something that sounded clamped down and oddly wary of her. In fact, such was the contrast, that if her husband hadn't greeted Peggy by name, she doubted that she would have believed it was him.

'Peg?' she heard Bill say again into the pregnant silence between them, almost in a dry-throated whisper this time. 'Are you there? Peggy?'

She took a fleeting instant to think of Holly, and the love and strong bond she had with her sister Barbara, and the kindness she had found since arriving in Harrogate at the rectory with Roger and Mabel, and with her new friend June. It was an emboldening moment.

'I am here, Bill,' Peggy composed herself and answered quietly with carefully enunciated words, and then she paused, once more allowing the silence to billow softly around her.

She heard Bill swallow in reply, and for an instant she imagined the dip and rise of his prominent Adam's apple giving a small punch under his shirt collar.

'Holly and I have been waiting for your call,' Peggy filled the quiet, deliberately mentioning Holly as she wanted to remind her husband that there were two of them up in Harrogate who were dependent upon whatever it was that he wanted to get off his chest.

She heard Bill take another mighty swallow and then the clink of him putting something made of glass down on something metal. His swallowing sounded round and deep, and it has been immediately preceded by a faint smacking noise almost as if his lips were retreating from a kiss, and it was a sound that told Peggy that he'd swigged directly from a bottle, and that he hadn't poured whatever it was that he was drinking into a glass. For all the world it sounded as if the beverage were alcoholic, and so Peggy guessed Bill was dosing himself with Dutch courage.

This was out of character, as although Bill did enjoy a pint now and again he was actually normally only an extremely moderate drinker. In ten years of marriage Peggy had only seen him veer slightly towards what she and Barbara called merry on a couple of occasions. Never once had she seen him drunk or stumbling around through being in his cups, and nor had she ever spied him imbibing alcohol directly from any sort of bottle, as he could be a bit priggish at times as regards the proper way of doing things, looking down on this sort of what he would call 'low' behaviour.

'Peg. Peggy,' Bill repeated.

His slight slur on the 'Peggy' told her he was definitely was more than vaguely tipsy.

Oh dear, this wasn't good at all.

'Bill, is there something you can sit down on?' Peggy was relieved that she sounded calm as she spoke these intentionally domestic-sounding, caring words, not that she felt particularly caring right at that minute, but she was starting to feel that for her to claim the moral high ground could only be to her advantage.

For the first time in their marriage she didn't want her husband to know quite how she was feeling – which was rattling – even though she really had the most peculiar feeling cresting and then pulsing through her, and her hands and feet had become suddenly icy cold.

Peggy thought she heard a soft bump that she took to be Bill leaning back suddenly against the wall of the public telephone box. Just for a second she fancied she could smell the distinctive paint the telephone service used to paint their boxes and that always seemed to linger.

She gathered herself together. 'What is it you want to say? Why don't you just come out with it? I'm sure you'll feel better afterwards, Bill.'

'Peg, I've been a bloody fool. A right bloody fool, I've been.' There was a further glugging noise, and a small belch. 'She's called Maureen, Peg. Maureen, she's called'.

Peggy blinked in crossness at the way Bill kept repeating himself, rather than getting straight to the point, but she didn't say anything – ''an she were right fun, an' I were stupid an' daft. An' one thing led to another an', well, er, yer know! Yer must know what I'm tryin' ter say, Peg.'

'I can't say that I *do* know, Bill,' replied a prudishly tight-lipped Peggy.

Heavens to Betsy! she thought to herself when Bill didn't reply to her immediately. Not only was he breaking to her some pretty dreadful news she was now certain, but he was doing it in a really cack-handed manner.

'Bill, why don't you put it down to me having given birth to *our* baby not so long ago, that dear little baby girl that we so wanted and had to wait such a while for' – Peggy paused deliberately for added drama – 'and this means that my mind might not right now be as good or as sharp as it once was. And so, I'm afraid, my dear *husband*, that you're going to need to spell it out to me, quite what it is that that you have been up to.'

She could hear Bill shift his weight around in the confined space almost as if the words she'd emphasised had kept pushing him in the chest. And then he made a strange noise as if he felt strangled. It was obvious that he wasn't enjoying this conversation in the slightest. Good.

Peggy imagined Bill as clearly as if he were right before her, standing in the public telephone box with the telephone receiver wedged between chin and shoulder, and a bottle of beer in one hand while with the other he supported his weight by leaning on the metal that made the wall at the back of the box as he stared down in shame.

Well, at least abject shame was the look on his face that she hoped was there.

The foreboding silence grew and throbbed between them.

And then there was a damp croon.

With a start Peggy realised that her husband was sobbing.

Once, her heart would have gone out to him, but now she couldn't believe these wet sounds to be anything other than mere crocodile tears. Any last shred of respect she had for him evaporated, as she felt Bill was crying only because he must have been caught out somehow, doing something he shouldn't have been doing – surely this had to be the case given that he was ringing her yet only describing what had gone on with huge reluctance – and certainly not because he felt he'd made any sort of terrible mistake. It was likely he'd have been happy with the state of affairs if there hadn't been some sort of incident or accident, Peggy told herself, and then she berated herself for thinking of the situation as in any way an accident. After all, there was absolutely nothing accidental about what Bill had been up to if he was having to apologise to his wife like this.

So Bill bloody well should be weeping, Peggy thought. She drew her shoulders back and noticed in a mirror hanging on Roger's wall that the reflection of her normally generous lips revealed that they had unintentionally closed in on themselves, shrinking to a harsh line that was aging and distinctly unattractive. Peggy narrowed her eyes as she tried to think of the most hurtful retort she could make, and the mirror-Peggy frowned threateningly back. It wasn't a pleasant sight.

'Be a man, Bill. You owe me that at least, surely? No *true* man would keep me guessing at anything else you need to say to me.'

It wasn't very strong as insults go, but it was the best that Peggy could come up with at that moment.

Peggy would never have believed even a few minutes ago, before she picked up the telephone to Bill, that she could experience such an emotional chasm stretching and growing between them, or that it could feel so treacherous or so cavernous.

It was hard to credit how once they had been so very close that Peggy had occasionally felt as if one took in a breath, then it would be the other one who would expel it.

There had been hiccups between them in recent years but

42

probably not more so than most couples had to endure, Peggy had told herself on more than one occasion. But with her much longed-for pregnancy, she had wholeheartedly believed that she and Bill had safely navigated choppy waters.

Bill rallied. 'Maureen works, er, worked, at the NAAFI as a volunteer, an' we'd 'ave the odd drink an' then that became mebbe a bit o' a laugh on the odd evening in the local pub. I didn't see any 'arm in it at first, 'onest I didn't, Peg – yer 'ave ter believe that.'

With a vehement shake of her head, Peggy didn't think she did have to believe that at all.

Bill couldn't see her reaction, of course, and so he ploughed on. 'But one day 'er sister were away an', er, well, I took the opportunity of mitchin' off camp an' then – an' I still don't know how it really 'appened – I found myself stayin' over wi' 'er as she was very persuasive,' he said very quickly in a voice now higher pitched than was usual.

'When was this?' Peggy made sure her words remained low and slow, and she fancied she could feel Bill's answering wince racketing down the telephone cord straight to the old-fashioned Bakelite handset she was grasping so tightly. She felt compelled to know all the sordid details of what Bill had been up to.

'She were fun, an' 'er 'air reminded me of yours, Peg. An' she fair set 'er cap at me, all the lads 'ere said so. It were first on Bonfire Night that we, er, um, um, yer know, Peg … yer *know*! An' I suppose that I then jus' kept on seein' her as mebbe I thought I could get away wi' it as I were missin' you right badly. But it were only if I could wrangle time away from the camp – yer know wot I mean – an' she were 'ere and you weren't, an' yer know that I never liked sleepin' alone.' Bill had to feed some more pennies in at this point, and Peggy took the opportunity to wipe under her eyes.

His voice rang out again, 'I didn't want to as such— ' Peggy snorted with contempt at this point 'but she were insistent, although when I got back from 'ers on Christmas morning to find that yours an' my little love 'olly had been born, and you'd 'ad such a fright, I thought enough's enough, an' I didn't wan' ter see 'er any more, an' I told 'er so. But Maureen wouldn't let me go, an' then she threatened ter telephone you "to put you right", an' so then it were easier ter go along with it fer a while at least, while I made up my mind what to do. Er, you weren't there an' anyways I thought you'd never find out.' Bill sighed dramatically as if he was in physical pain, and as if by mere chance life had dealt him a bad set of playing cards.

And then finally he confessed in a very small voice, 'An' now she's 'avin' my baby.'

If Peggy had thought the news of Bill having sexual relations with another woman was the worst thing she could hear, it was now hideous to discover that with the news of his forthcoming bastard offspring came a new depth of hurt and despair. She couldn't believe that Bill could have been so stupid or so cruel.

Suddenly Peggy felt even hotter than she had before, and then deathly cold. Her belly slid icily lower, and for a fleeting but nonetheless terrible moment her mouth flooded with saliva and she thought she might vomit. She struggled to regain her equilibrium.

This was the worse of all possible outcomes.

Of course she had grasped already that sexual relations with another woman was what Bill had been up to. But to hear him

44

actually put into words that he had made another woman – his floozy! – pregnant provoked a totally animal response from somewhere deep within her that was unlike anything Peggy had ever experienced.

She thought about what her husband had just told her, and then she realised with a huge jolt so powerful that it was as if she had just stuck one of her fingers straight into a live electric plug socket, that she and Bill had only been apart for a mere two months before he had given into temptation despite the wedding vows they had solemnly made to each other, vows she had always been proud to hold dear.

How could he?

She would *never* have done that to him.

How *could* he, the rat, the pig?

She hated Bill right at that moment. Loathed, and detested, and – well, she couldn't think of any other word to describe what she felt at that moment – just absolutely *hated* him.

It was a hatred that felt pure and strangely fortifying.

If Bill had been standing in front of her, Peggy felt almost as if she might have leapt at him and tried to hurt him physically with her bare hands, marking indelibly the body that in the dark she had once enjoyed running her hands over so much, such was the abject rage that immediately began to thrust furiously up and down and through what felt like every cell of her own body, her pulse thumping with a beat faster than it ever had, surpassing even its most delicious throes of passion.

Peggy knew she verged on the unhinged as she began to shout, but she was suddenly beyond caring. 'Did you not for one moment think about your own wife and baby, who have both been missing you and longing for you, Bill? The woman

– me! – whom you made a solemn vow, standing before our friends and families in church, to honour each other come what may, or our child who was conceived after *such* a long time, a baby that you said that you were so happy about and that was the light of your life? Is this how you want someone to treat your own little girl, our dear Holly, when she is all grown up? Is what you've done the sort of behaviour and the type of person you wish for her to marry, a shallow and selfish man who is unable to keep his trousers done up? I was reluctant to come to Harrogate, but I did it because *you* were insistent and I wanted to keep *you* happy, and now I wish I'd just stayed at home as keeping you happy clearly isn't worth a bean.'

Peggy paused and looked downwards towards the quivering hem of her skirt caused by her trembling knees, and then she continued bitterly before Bill could say anything in his own defence. 'That little tart. That horrible stupid little tart. Maureen? Maureen... *Maureen!* What sort of name is that? And you're no better than she! You're a pathetic excuse for a husband, Bill Delbert. What could that trollop Maureen have ever seen in you? And what did I see in you? You tell me now, this very minute, Bill Delbert, precisely when that stupid strumpet is having *your* baby?'

Peggy was close to screeching, unable to control her emotions in any way, although in this maelstrom of feeling she remembered guiltily for a split second that once she'd actually had a very nice friend at teacher training college called Maureen and so actually really she had nothing against women with the name, other than this particular piece of work, of course.

Then Peggy realised with a whump that almost made her

physically crumple, forcing her to grab the back of Roger's desk chair in support, that at the very moment she herself had been close to rapture with a burst of sunshine springing from her heart at seeing a tiny Holly reaching innocently for her father's finger when Bill came to meet his daughter for the very first time, the truth of it was that her supposedly loyal husband was nursing, close to his heart, the dangerous viperous secret of his infidelity and another woman opening her legs for him as she beckoned to him from under the covers. And so a precious memory that Peggy had believed was good and pure had been, in a crushing twinkling of an eye, tainted and besmirched for all time, leaving her flattened and despondent.

Peggy felt a shriek of anguish building in her, but she forced herself to hold it in, although her hand holding the telephone was vibrating violently with the effort.

'I noticed Maureen were plump round the middle a few days ago an' she says she's got three months to go.' Bill sounded glum as he went on regardless, and as if he'd given in.

Then Peggy did the mathematics in her head, and suddenly her need to know any further grisly details of the affair evaporated into a puff of nothingness. She understood that Maureen had almost definitely already been pregnant when Bill travelled to Harrogate to see Holly. It may be illogical, but the very idea of him playing the doting daddy in Yorkshire having already fathered somebody else's baby was nothing short of abhorrent in Peggy's eyes.

'Well, you've made your bed, Bill Delbert, and now you have to lie in it. For your information, I shall take care that you never see Holly again,' Peggy declared.

Bill let out what she could only think of as a howl, and

an instant later Peggy heard the sound of shattering glass as presumably her husband had in temper flung his beer bottle furiously to the concrete floor of the telephone box.

'Holly is innocent and untainted by anything,' Peggy went on resolutely, as if Bill were standing there eager to hear what she had to say. 'She certainly doesn't need to be contaminated by somebody as morally reprehensible as you, not now, and not ever, Bill. Do you hear me? *Do you hear me?!* And as for myself, *I* hope never to see you again. I don't care what it costs, and I don't care if I have to work for the rest of my life to pay it off and I don't care how people will look down on me for being divorced. Your monkey business with that MaureenFromTheNAAFI tart is going to cost you, and I'm not thinking about money.

'Our treasure is Holly, and as far as you are concerned she's been thrown to the wolves by you, and there's no return from that. I really hope that MaureenFromTheNAAFI gave you the very best time ever between the sheets, as if she didn't, well, words fail me.'

It was very unlike Peggy to veer onto such coarse territory, but she wanted oh so badly to shock Bill.

'She didn't, Peg, she were nothing like as good as—' he said weakly.

'Tough, Bill. Tough.' Peggy's tone was brutal as she cut him dead.

She willed herself not to sob, but to avoid the risk she didn't give Bill the opportunity to say anything else.

As, surprisingly softly, she replaced the handset on the telephone, Peggy heard Bill's last-ditch plaintive appeal sound increasingly tinny as she moved the handset from her ear and put it back in its place on the base of the telephone, his 'But I love yo—' being sliced off decisively.

She stood head bowed and statue-still at first. But it wasn't long before Peggy started to sway from side to side, and she had to grab hold of the edge of the desk to steady herself, as wave after wave of fresh emotion swept over her, and then washed back through what felt like every fibre of her very being.

And then with a long clamped-down shriek of what felt like agony Peggy picked up the closest thing to her, which was the leather desk tidy in which Roger kept the pencils that he used to draft his sermons, and she hurled the whole lot with as much force as she could muster against the wall, the pencils cascading to the ground and then bouncing merrily around, with Roger's carefully sharpened lead points shearing off the pencils as they smashed against the stone flags of the floor.

The crash was a surprisingly loud noise that cut across the calm of Tall Trees and wrecked the peace.

But Peggy couldn't hear anything now, such was the rushing of blood in her ears. Keening desperately, she continued to rock both left and right.

She picked up the pile of scrap paper on which Roger would write and she rent it this way and that, virtually growling with the effort of ripping it into tiny unusable squares, and then with a final shove of her elbow she cast the telephone and handset off the desk, the loud crash and the strange hawk of the telephone's ring of surprise at such harsh treatment finally quelling Peggy's temper.

Exhausted, she sank down onto Roger's desk chair, with

the chaos of his desk settling askew on the floor around her, and bitter sobs shuddering her slim shoulders and setting her curls a-quiver as she leant forward on her folded arms and howled, wishing herself to be any place but where she was.

Roger and Mabel, who had been inspecting the vegetable patches on their way back from church and had only just come through the kitchen door, came running, their faces panicked at the unusual sounds erupting from within the study.

However, when Roger saw the state Peggy was in, he stayed on the other side of the door and stood aside to make way for his wife, as he beckoned Mabel forward in place of himself.

He knew Mabel would be much better at the helm of this situation than he.

As the older woman crouched down to clasp an exhausted Peggy to her breast without saying a word, Peggy gave into ugly, animal noises and a fresh avalanche of tears.

A worry-faced Roger was left to creep into the office as silently as he could, stepping behind the women so that he could replace the receiver on the telephone as he always felt panicky at the thought of a parishioner in distress being unable to reach him, although he left the telephone on the floor, after which, without catching the eye of either woman, he hotfooted it to the kitchen in order to deal with baby Holly.

She had been rudely woken by all the kerfuffle in the study and was keen to let everybody know this, bellowing with all the strength she could muster in her little lungs in tandem with the throaty blubs of her distraught mother just across the passageway.

Chapter Six

Over at the train station Jessie and Angela remained outside with a bored-looking Milburn, while the other children headed onto the platform to wait for Larry.

After Jessie had gently teased Angela that he and Connie thought that maybe Tommy had a bit of a soft spot for her, Angela went very pink, leaving Jessie to guess whether she might reciprocate these feelings.

Angela noticed Jessie's expression reveal all too clearly that he was pondering what she and Tommy thought about each other, and so as a distraction she quickly reminded Jessie again of lots of the things she had learnt in the library about ponies, which seemed to make much more sense now that they had Milburn standing in front of them

When she had run out of useful titbits to share, she was relieved to see her tactic had worked, as Jessie said that he wondered if Milburn was well behaved when ridden, as he rather fancied a go.

At this Milburn gave Jessie what seemed like such a look of disgust, followed by a shake of her head that jangled the metal bit in her mouth and set her springy mane and forelock bouncing as if to say No-o-o-o at the very thought, and both children couldn't do anything but laugh.

'She's good, isn't she?' said Angela, and Milburn nodded.

'Yes, she seems to be,' Jessie agreed, although the moment was immediately somewhat spoilt as Milburn swiftly dipped her nose into the wicker basket of a passing woman and nimbly lifted out a greaseproof-paper-wrapped sandwich, much to the ire of the woman and the embarrassment of the children.

Jessie wrestled the package from Milburn's mouth, and then he offered it back to its owner, who took one look at the slobbered paper and the indent of the pony's teeth and said crossly, 'Those were fer my Bert, but 'e won't want them now, will 'e? An wot'll he 'ave fer his dinner now, an' 'e's on blackout checkin' after? T' pony had better have 'em, I s'ppose, an' mind you keep more control of 'im in future. There's a war on, you know.'

The affronted woman stalked away, and Jessie and Angela exchanged glances and then as one they looked accusingly at Milburn, who was concentrating very hard on the package in Jessie's hand.

'I suppose I ought to have paid more attention to Milburn,' admitted Jessie, sounding a little guilty.

'Poor Burt,' said Angela, and the mere mention of him made the children hoot.

Jessie unwrapped the sandwiches, which had reconstituted egg as the filling. He and Angela gave the top one to Milburn, who snaffled it greedily, but they decided the bottom one wasn't *too* squished for themselves to eat and so they shared it quickly, keen to finish before the others came back.

They talked then of the posters they could see up, seeing the irony of a poster urging a visit to the Yorkshire dales smack bang alongside a poster of a British Tommy questioning 'Is your journey really necessary?' Angela angled her chair slightly differently so that she could see the other side of the station's entrance, where there was another poster urging people to bring their own cups and glasses to railway refreshment rooms as they were often running short, but the children couldn't find much to interest them or to joke about in this last poster.

After what seemed hours, there was the sound of an ancient puffing billy chugging slowly into the station, at which Milburn held her head very high, her small ears so pointed towards where she could hear the unfamiliar sound coming from, that their darker tips looked to be almost touching.

As the sound of the final burst of steam from the train's engine gave way to the noise of doors opening and the passengers alighting, Angela started to say, 'It won't be long before Lar—' when Connie's unmistakeable voice rang out in a loud and high-pitched yelp that sounded as heartfelt as it was hard to interpret.

It was such an unexpected outburst that Jessie immediately felt queasy as these days, like so many other people, he tended to overreact to any unexpected shock, knowing that it could herald bad news, and he swung towards Angela, whereupon the children stared at each other with worried faces.

Then Jessie sprang forward as he dropped the lead rope to Milburn's halter so that it dangled in the road. Uncaring and with his thoughts of paying more attention to the pony completely forgotten, he fairly pelted towards the station platform to run to his twin's aid.

Angela apprehensively watched him go, and then as he raced inside and turned towards the platforms she saw him halt suddenly, his mouth open in obvious shock. Her heart lurched more stomach-churningly than before, and a rising panicky feeling made her tingly and jittery.

Jessie ran forward again abruptly, but not before Angela had seen his face break into a tremendous grin as he stretched both arms out as wide as they could go.

He *does* seem very pleased that Larry is coming back to Tall Trees to be with us all, thought Angela, the sickly feeling quickly dissolving and falling away.

It wasn't long before the reason for the excitement of Connie and Jessie became clear.

Barbara and Ted had come all the way to Harrogate on a surprise visit to see the twins, and to catch up with Peggy and Holly too, of course. They had travelled up to Yorkshire from London on the train along with Larry.

Neither of the twins would remove their arms to let their parents go from their hugs, they were so excited to see them.

Barbara and Ted had spent a weekend with them at the end of January, as their train tickets had been funded for that journey by the government.

Understandably, since then it had felt a very long four months for the ten-year-olds to be without their mother and father, instead having to make do with letters, and – joy! – on Easter Sunday, even a telephone call made from the Jolly for Barbara and Ted to say they hoped that Mabel's Easter Egg hunt of hand-decorated hard-boiled eggs hidden in the garden was going to be fun.

'My, look how you two have grown!' said Barbara now, as despite having a shopping basket hooked into her elbow, she managed to put an arm around both of her children to pull them close.

'You're nearly as tall as yer ma, both of yer!' Ted added, standing close. He was naturally a more reserved person than Barbara, but the tremor in his voice gave away how happy he was to see his children, and then he allowed himself a gentle pat of hello on each of the twins' shoulders, just so that they knew how deeply he cared for them.

Jessie and Connie were both too overcome to do anything more than grin at each of their parents with glee, as they both turned around to hug their father too, their eyes shining bright with the unexpected thrill of what had just happened.

Jessie, who was more observant than Connie, noticed a few wrinkles at the corners of Barbara's eyes that had not been there before the war, and some white hairs glinting in Ted's short hair. He thought too that both of his parents seemed a bit smaller and very slightly shabbier than they had before, but Jessie was wise enough to know that maybe he had grown a little and that these days nobody could buy new clothes for best as often as they had done previously, and so most people were making do and mending to preserve outfits and shoes for as long as possible.

Barbara and Ted felt just as overcome, although they were making a better fist of hiding their exuberant feelings. They really missed having their children at home, but Ted was convinced that the bombs would soon be falling on London and so Connie and Jessie were much less likely to come to physical harm, or worse (although that didn't bear thinking about) if they stayed billeted in Harrogate. And although Barbara probably would have brought the children back to Bermondsey if it had been left up to her, she trusted Ted's opinion and knew that he wouldn't be so insistent if he didn't really believe that Jubilee Street was going to be very vulnerable to aerial attack.

Angela had no option other than to wait for them all to walk back to her, while she sat marooned in her wheelchair on its wheels as she noticed how alike Peggy and Barbara were, and how Jessie favoured his father's colouring.

Milburn's lead rope was still hanging downwards but the pony hadn't taken the opportunity to test her freedom and instead had edged over so that she was standing beside Angela, casting curious looks towards the new arrivals. Then the small mare shook her nose forwards and backward several times as if she rather approved of Ted looking strong and muscular in his Sunday-best suit and Barbara smart and pretty, with the sunshine highlighting her freshly pin-curled hair.

'Blimey!' yelled Larry, the second he spied the pony. And then a little more quietly but with an unmistakeable tone of wonder in his voice, 'Blimey O'Reilly.'

Milburn looked as if she were pretty much thinking the same thing as Larry headed towards her.

'Larry, language please,' Barbara reprimanded.

She might as well have saved her breath as Larry looked around at his pals with a massive grin and then simply repeated 'Blimey!' again, although this time in the most excited tone of all, as if he were thinking of all sorts of things they could all get up to now that they looked as if they might have the cheeky-looking Milburn with them as a partner in crime.

Milburn's mischievous glint in her eye seemed to say that yes, she agreed with Larry, and that they only had to say the word and she'd be ready and willing for all manner of fun and frolics over the summer. Whatever japes they could think of would be all right with her, yes sirree.

Larry appeared to everyone as if he had grown taller too, although his scrawnier frame, sunken cheeks, shadows smudged under his eyes and generally a more put-upon demeanour were a far cry from the bonny boy who had left them at Tall Trees earlier in the year.

As Tommy went to grab hold of the handles to push Angela's chair, Aiden picked up Milburn's rope, Ted divided everyone's luggage between his two hands, and Larry seemed unable to take his eyes off Milburn. And then he said as if he hadn't uttered anything a matter of seconds ago, 'Wot the bloomin' 'eck is that?'

'It's a pony, dimwit. A pony,' said Tommy, laughing. 'And when Father isn't using her, she's ours to do with what we want.'

'Blimey. Blimey O'Reilly.'

'Lang—' said Barbara, and then gave a defeated smile. 'Oh, what's the point!'

Ted laughed and pulled Barbara close to him for a moment, and then they broke apart, eager to hear what the twins had been up to.

And with that, the odd mismatch of people trooped back to Tall Trees.

Mabel and Roger knew already that Barbara and Ted were coming to visit, although they hadn't given as much as the tiniest hint about this to anybody else, even Peggy, as Barbara had telephoned the previous afternoon to say that she was terribly sorry for the short notice, but she wondered if it were all right if she and Ted could stay over for a day or two at Tall Trees.

Mabel told Barbara how wonderful it would be and that the twins, and Peggy, would be over the moon.

Then there had been the usual friendly argy-bargy between the women over the financial arrangements, with Barbara offering a payment and Mabel refusing, and Barbara insisting, and Mabel refusing, and so forth, after which Barbara had begged Mabel and Roger to keep their visit a surprise.

Mabel had agreed, but actually it proved to be a trickier thing to keep quiet about than she had expected.

For first thing that morning Mabel had almost been caught by Peggy carrying fresh sheets and clean towels across the back yard on her way to sort out the generously proportioned room above the stables that Peggy and Gracie had once shared and where Barbara and Ted would now be sleeping.

A quick-thinking Mabel had had to dart into the pantry to hide as Peggy then spent what felt to Mabel to be an inordinate age standing just on the other side of the pantry door in the kitchen getting herself and Holly ready to leave the house and head over to June Blenkinsop's. At one point, Peggy even asked Holly if she should take June the bag of currants she had for her that were – naturally – in the pantry, causing Mabel's heart to do a flip, and then a double-flip as if in answer.

Holly didn't say anything in reply – well, that wasn't surprising given her tender age – but she did let out a cheery gurgle.

At last Mabel was able to breathe an audible sigh of relief when Peggy decided that the dratted currants could wait for another day as June probably wouldn't be doing any of this sort of baking on a Sunday as she'd be concentrating on getting large trays of cottage pies and Lancashire hotpots ready for the coming week. Finally Peggy got around to pushing the pram out through the back door and weaving it through the yard and onto the garden path to the road.

This was a huge relief because, try as she might, Mabel hadn't been able to think of a convincing reason why she was hiding next to the large bowl of eggs from their hens at the bottom of the garden and a hessian sack of potatoes with its top rolled over so that the teddies were easy to get to. And Mabel knew that Peggy would almost definitely have smelt a rat of the Barbara-and-Ted-arriving variety if she had caught her sneaking about in the pantry with an armful of clean laundry and no plausible reason for doing so.

Now, as the others would all be making their way back from the station, Mabel only just had time to find Peggy a handful of clean hankies following the telephone call with Bill, and to make her cup of tea. She'd sneaked a surreptitious peek at a soggy and spent Peggy, and couldn't decide if Barbara's imminent arrival was a good or a bad thing. It could go either way, to judge by the look of her, Mabel thought.

Peggy remained closeted still in Roger's study with a desolate expression on her face, staring with unfocused eyes into the distance, obviously dazed and emotionally exhausted after her unheralded display of temper following her highly wrought outburst.

Although Holly had been bawling, Mabel wasn't sure that Peggy had even heard her daughter's cries, as for the very first time her doting mother hadn't raced across the corridor to attend to her, and this neglect had made Holly wail even more loudly.

Now, across the way in the kitchen and jollied along by Roger, Holly had finally ceased crying although she remained restless and a little snivelly, her eyelashes still wet with tears, following such a rude awakening from her nap caused by the clatter of things hitting the floor in the study.

Once the baby's wails had abated, a too casual-seeming Roger replaced Holly back in her sleeping drawer and then quickly made himself scarce, leaving Mabel to pick the baby up again when Holly started to grizzle, as she did almost immediately.

Mabel had no choice other than to walk around the kitchen, jiggling Holly in her arms as she showed her what was in the kitchen cabinets, and the eggs and potatoes in the pantry, in an effort to prevent her from returning to her full-blown wailing of a few minutes earlier.

Holly was surprisingly heavy for such a little thing and she obviously wasn't very convinced that what was in the various cupboards was very much for Mabel to boast about, and so Mabel was relieved to hear the sound of those returning to Tall Trees heading across the back yard.

The baby immediately stopped grumbling, at last fully engaged in her surroundings, and quickly swung her head with interest towards the door from the back yard into the kitchen to see who might be about to come in.

Mabel could hear Aiden pulling the bolt to the stable door across and then encouraging Milburn inside as he told Larry where the hay and straw was, and she saw Tommy push Angela's chair to the back door. Mabel noticed the Ross family huddled together as they gave Tommy room to help Angela inside.

For a moment Mabel wondered at Ted Ross allowing Tommy

to push Angela what looked like all the way back from the station to judge by Tommy's pink face, but then she thought that actually for Tommy to have a bit of responsibility and to do something for somebody else wasn't necessarily a bad thing, the episode to do with his bullying and the orchard affair being still rather a raw memory for all the Braithwaites, although the other children never seemed to refer to it.

Barbara bustled into the kitchen, which was smelling deliciously of the barm cakes baking for their dinner and Barbara could see what looked like a giant mixing bowl with bread dough proving on a warm part of the range.

Connie and Jessie stayed out in the yard in order to tug Ted, once he had set all the luggage down, good-naturedly across the yard and over to see for himself where Milburn was housed. Barbara undid her headscarf with one hand as with the other she plonked the wicker basket full of small thank-you gifts for Mabel – some homemade biscuits, a couple of new tea towels, a vest for Tommy and some hankies, several pork chops, some juicy-looking carrots and a very late dark-green Savoy cabbage that the caterpillars had only had the merest chomp on the outside leaves of – down on the rather battered kitchen table that had obviously seen many years of faithful service.

She and Mabel smiled in greeting at one another, and then Barbara raised her eyebrows in a quiet query as to where her sister Peggy might be.

Mabel put a finger in front of her mouth to signal silence, and then with Holly still in her arms she edged over to her guest and then stage-whispered in Barbara's ear, 'She'll be jiggered, Barbara. There's jus' been an awful ding-dong on the telephone not more than twenty or so minutes ago betwixt her an' Bill. She's 'avin' a quiet moment jus' at present in t' study wi' a cup o' tea to set 'erself to rights, but there no denyin' it were right bad. She'll be glad yer 'ere.'

'Oh my goodness!' Barbara hissed quietly back. 'That's unlike them. Poor Peggy... I can guess what he's done, I suppose.'

Mabel said she hadn't asked Peggy what the row was about, but she thought she'd heard Peggy moan the name Maureen as she had sobbed in her arms in the aftermath of the argument.

Then the two women shook their head at the thought of what was happening to a lot of couples during their enforced separations. Many relationships were suffering badly, and both of them were pretty sure that Peggy wouldn't be the only woman in the land who had just had a big barney with her husband over another woman, while many men away from home drove themselves to distraction with dark thoughts of what their wives might be getting up to back on the home front without them. It wasn't an ideal situation, no matter how one tried to look at it.

Barbara then saw that Holly was looking curiously towards her aunty and waving an arm in her direction, opening and closing her fingers, and so Barbara whispered to Mabel, 'May I?'

With a rather relieved smile Mabel promptly handed her over, and after deeply inhaling the familiar scent of the young baby and then gently touching Holly on the head with her lips in a feather-light caress of hello, Barbara clutched her affectionately to her chest and went to find her sister.

She was taken aback a moment later to see how large and black the pupils in Peggy's eyes appeared, and how pale her face was.

Peggy was totally still as she gazed with unseeing eyes out of the study window and down towards the hen coops on the far side of the garden, with the undrunk cup of tea by her elbow, and she didn't notice that it was her sister who had come into the study.

It was only when Barbara said gently, 'Peggy, my darling, whatever's happened?' that Peggy turned to face her.

For an instant Peggy's brown eyebrows wrinkled in incomprehension and she looked confused as she gazed at Barbara.

And then she simply flung herself at her sister, leaving Barbara only a moment to move Holly out of the way. As Peggy broke once more into sobs, Barbara was able to feel hot tears on her neck as Peggy held her close in a vice-like grip. Barbara stood still as a rock and pulled her sister close.

The sisters didn't say anything for a while, as Peggy was too upset to speak, and Barbara thought it best that this new wave of emotion be allowed to crest and then die of its own accord.

After a while Barbara contented herself with repeating 'Sssssh, there now, there now. Sssssh, there now' in the same way that she had comforted Jessie and Connie when they were colicky as babies.

Holly made some adorable snuffling noises and reached pudgy fingers towards her mother's hair, but Peggy didn't look at her and so Holly turned towards Barbara with a puzzled expression, causing Barbara to give her a jiggle of acknowledgement with her other arm and a smile, as she knew the baby would be feeling unsettled at these unfamiliar goings-on and the strange sounds coming from her mother.

When Peggy's grip on her sister had reduced to less of a stranglehold, Barbara said, 'Peggy, dear, we'll have a long talk very soon, I promise. I want to hear all about it, really I do. But first why don't you have a lie down and have a little rest? Take Holly up with you as to me she's looking as if she still needs a bit more of a doze after her lunch, and then I'll come and find you when I've got everyone else sorted and have caught up with Connie and Jessie. How does that sound, dear?'

Tiredly, Peggy untangled herself and then nodded a damp and exhausted smile of agreement, before she quietly slipped upstairs with her daughter cleaved tightly to her bosom. She felt done in, and now she could hear Connie and Jessie's happy voices outside, she wanted to make sure that her tear-marked face wouldn't dampen the party mood that was sweeping the rest of Tall Trees with Larry being back with them, and the pleasure of the unexpected visit from Barbara and Ted.

With a concerned expression, Barbara watched the sway of her sister's disappearing world-weary steps with a tremendous pang of sympathy and trepidation, and then she sighed in empathy before she consciously made herself look happy as she turned to retrace her steps outside and find her husband and the twins.

Chapter Seven

Ted was full of surprises, it seemed.

'Mother, you'll never believe it,' squeaked Connie breathily, her cheeks red with excitement as her mother joined her family. 'But Father can drive a trap! And he's going to teach us. He knows all about ponies, and he's going to teach us *everything*!'

'Oh, he can drive a trap, can he?' Barbara raised an amused eyebrow in the direction of her husband, who winked in response. This was news to her, as was Connie's use of the formal-sounding 'mother', but she supposed this was a sign of Connie getting older as perhaps 'mama' or 'mummy' seemed babyish, especially in front of the other children.

Ted grinned back at Barbara, causing her to shoot him a rueful, only half-amused grin in return. He'd never mentioned to his wife that as a child he had helped out at the local coal merchants, so much so that by the age of ten he had been allowed, after much begging, to take the reins on the delivery cart whenever he wasn't at school.

Barbara prided herself on knowing all there was to know about Ted, and to learn this news so hot on the heels of discovering that something dire had happened with Bill that Peggy had had no idea about and therefore had been unprepared for, she felt now slightly peculiar and wrong-footed by Ted's admission, harmless though it was.

The children were mightily impressed with Ted's insouciant wink, however, to the extent that they were all pulling a variety of comical faces as they tried to outdo each other in the winking stakes, with Tommy and Larry trying the hardest, but Tommy getting the eventual thumbs-up from the others for a particularly showy double wink at the same time tipping his forefinger to his brow.

'Okay, you lot,' Barbara interrupted their fun, 'let's go in for some food as I believe Mabel is setting the table and has the kettle on, and then we'll see if Roger minds Ted taking you all out later in the trap.' Barbara sounded quite firm as she looked around at the children and pulled her best delicately scalloped beige cardigan together over her chest as if she meant business.

As one, Ted and the children all looked a bit crestfallen as they had clearly wanted to go out in the trap right away, but then they realised that Barbara wasn't saying a firm no as such, but just that Roger had to give his seal of approval first.

Tommy summed up their thoughts with, 'Let's go in an' see Pa – 'e's always ready for 'is dinner, and I'll bet 'e'll like a bit of teachin' too 'ow t' 'andle t' trap proper.'

And indeed when Roger learned that Ted had some experience with horses and would be very happy to spend a bit of time showing them what to do with Milburn, there was an unmistakable sigh of relief bubbling up from below his white dog collar. He'd not yet tried to go out in the trap on his own, not least as he wasn't sure he could quite remember how to put the harness on Milburn or how to attach the trap to all the harness gubbins, although these were admissions that he didn't particularly care to make in front of all the children.

Dinner was eaten hastily, with no one mentioning anything about Peggy and Holly not being there, most probably because it was only Barbara and Ted who noticed, and they contented themselves with acknowledging the absence of the two Delberts with the exchange of silent but nonetheless telling looks.

There was a scrag end of mutton stew Peggy had prepared the evening before, that was surprisingly tasty as she was picking up some good tips for flavoursome food over at June Blenkinsop's, and Mabel had eked it out to make sure there was enough as of course she couldn't say to Peggy that her sister and Ted would be joining them, seeing as this was a surprise. It was served along with fluffy dumplings and the unexpected gift of the Savoy cabbage to go with the runner beans that Roger was very proud he'd grown.

Once everyone had wiped their plates clean with a still-warm barm cake and sat back replete, Barbara announced that she wasn't going to partake of the pony and trap session, which made the twins put on deliberately dejected faces in an attempt to get their mother to change her mind. But Barbara held firm, although she tried to sweeten the pill by saying that for this meal, as a special treat, the children could be let off their table-clearing and washing-up duties as she would put the kitchen to rights and everyone else could go out into the yard to practise tacking up Milburn. 'Go on, out you scoot, and leave me to it,' she said, waving a tea towel around as if to scurry them outside.

'Please come and watch Daddy with us,' said Jessie. Barbara noticed the 'daddy'.

'Oh, we *so* wanted to show you Milburn,' Connie wheedled.

Barbara wavered for a moment but then she thought of Peggy, and held firm, their pleas being to no avail.

'I've seen her and she's a very eye-catching pony, right enough, and I'll be there tomorrow when no doubt you will want to repeat it all again. I'm sure Milburn won't mind if I watch you then. And I promise that tomorrow I will even let you drive me along in the trap, if it's still sunny and Ted thinks you know what you're doing,' said Barbara. 'But right now, there is something else that I really need to see to instead, and so you all vamoose.'

The children knew that Barbara never reneged on a promise and so they decided to make the best of it as it was really good to have Ted there to spend some time with. Mabel stepped in to ease the moment further with a vigorous call of 'last one out there's a sissy' ringing in their ears as she bolted out of the back door before the children, with Roger hot on her heels. The children all scampered off happily enough to watch, along with Milburn's quizzical expression, Ted untangle the harness as he muttered that they must hang it up properly when not being used, and not leave it in a heap like they had as to do so was to risk the leather perishing, before reminding them how it should be put on the pony.

When she had sorted out the kitchen to her satisfaction, which was a much tidier and cleaner satisfaction than Mabel, or even Peggy, would have deemed acceptable, Barbara made a fresh pot of tea that she placed on a doily-covered tray along with two cups and a small jug of milk. She put a couple of plain biscuits that Gracie had made on a side plate and popped that on the tray too.

As Barbara carried the tray out of the kitchen she could hear her twins laughing out in the yard as Roger attempted but failed to get Milburn to open her mouth so that he could put the bridle on. The familiar sound of them enjoying themselves brought a rush of happiness to Barbara's chest.

Barbara climbed the stairs right to the top of the house and tapped on Peggy's door, and was greeted with a husky 'come in'.

Holly was sound asleep in a large but battered crib that looked as if it had had the pleasure of nursing many children from babyhood through to them being ready for a 'big' bed.

Looking distinctly bleary, a blinking Peggy watched her sister put the tray on top of a chest of drawers, and then a bit reluctantly it seemed, she pulled herself up to sitting position and gratefully accepted the cup of tea that Barbara poured for her.

Barbara tried not to look too obviously at the darkly shadowed puffy bags under Peggy's eyes, or her dry and cracked lips, her rumpled cotton summer dress that was hanging too loosely on her slender frame, or the constant twitching of a muscle in one of her eyelids that was punching out a tiny SOS of distress. Peggy did look a mess and a wretched sight but her sister thought it kinder not to say.

'Peggy dear, I'm so very sorry to hear that you've been through the wars today,' said Barbara sympathetically in the sort of voice that she knew her sister would take as an invitation to talk about what had caused such a ringing disagreement between husband and wife. She perched on the edge of the bed with her own cup of tea in her hand as she looked towards Peggy with her eyebrows raised in encouragement.

'It was horrible, just horrible,' said Peggy, as she stared without focusing at Barbara's face before turning to look mournfully down at the tea softly swirling in her cup.

'Another woman?' Barbara said softly. What else could it be, she thought, to cause such a maelstrom of emotion in the normally so level-headed Peggy.

'Another woman,' her sister agreed morosely.

Barbara wasn't sure what to say. She'd always found Bill to be pleasant enough company although, try as she might (and she had tried very hard over the years), she had never believed him to be quite good enough for her sister.

Once or twice Barbara had thought Bill had looked as if he'd had a roving eye, and just before he and Peggy had married all those years previously, bolstered by two port and lemons one Saturday night at the Jolly, Barbara had even been so bold as to say outright to him, 'I do very much hope you're going to be true to Peggy, Bill; she deserves the best, and she absolutely doesn't need some dog of a husband who's going to be hard to keep on the doorstep.'

Bill had replied in such an earnest voice that Barbara found herself somewhat mollified, saying that he knew he wasn't worthy of someone such as Peggy, but if she would deign to marry him then he'd never so much as even look at another woman or do anything at all in Christendom to make her unhappy, God strike him down dead if ever he did.

Thinking about it later, Barbara hadn't quite been placated but she had allowed the matter to lie, and over the ensuing years a lot of time had passed without any obvious shenanigans on Bill's behalf and so gradually she had done her level best to think well of him.

Then, when Bill and Peggy hadn't easily been able to have their own children, Barbara had started wondering about him again, fuelled at this point by Ted telling her that there had been the odd rumour heard in the Jolly about Bill and a fancy-woman flying around the docks.

Still, Peggy and Bill had seemed to weather that particular storm, helped no doubt by the announcement of Peggy's unexpected pregnancy with Holly after ten barren years of marriage. And at the time Barbara was pleased that she had kept quiet, at Ted's advising, over Bill's reported peccadillo. She thought he might have well overstepped the mark once or twice although not necessarily in a really serious manner, and therefore she hadn't want to upset Peggy with no firm evidence to back up the allegations. And once the pregnancy had been announced Peggy had seemed so full of happiness that it would have been a desperate shame to ruin her unadulterated joy, and although Barbara had scrutinised Bill carefully, he never gave so much as a hint that he wasn't just as thoroughly delighted that he and Peggy were going to be parents.

However, this time around, Barbara thought now, the cat seemed to have been well and truly set amongst the pigeons.

'Why don't you get it all off your chest, Peggy? I'm sure you'll feel better if you do,' Barbara cajoled. She still had no idea precisely what it was that Bill had done, and she was keen to know more.

'I feel a fool, Barbara, such a total fool. While I've been stuck up here, away from you and Ted, and far from home and all that I know, looking after our dear Holly and washing

71

and feeding her, and bringing in some money working at June Blenkinsop's, and trying to do the right thing by your two as well, and never suspecting a thing about what Bill might be up to, he's clearly been living the life of Riley.' Peggy's sentences jumbled into one another, but she didn't seem to care although Barbara wished she'd get to the point. Then Peggy sighed dramatically and took a sip of her tea, before adding with a sarcastic tinge to her words, 'She's called Maureen, and she was working in the NAAFI, he told me. And he's been seeing her since November, although apparently he wanted to end it at Christmas, although somehow he never did. And now she's having his baby, and only has three months to go.'

Peggy swallowed, making a strange swigging noise in her throat that caused her to pause what she was saying, and despondently she looked down at her cup and saucer once more. Barbara rubbed Peggy's arm that was closest to her in sisterly support, expecting a fresh outburst of sobs.

The forthcoming baby would be the clincher that Bill had passed a point of no return as far as her sister was concerned, Barbara knew.

Peggy remained dry-eyed to her sister's surprise, although her voice was quieter when she was able to continue, 'Barbara, I'm ashamed to say I more or less told him to go to hell, and then I said to him that he'd never see Holly again.'

'Of course that was what you said at this news, Peggy! Any woman would have told him that. I would have, make no mistake, and then probably gone a whole lot further as well.'

'But who's going to suffer, Barbara? Not Bill, as he'll be back in MaureenFromTheNAAFI's bed quicker than a rat can get up a drainpipe, I've no doubt, as he's not the sort to stay on his own if he can help it, and I'm pretty certainly he'll have found a way to sneak off camp to be with her whenever he can. She's obviously keen on him, and so his nest is already feathered, even if it doesn't feel like that to him just at the minute. And I'll get over him – I'll make sure of that as otherwise I'll let his actions punish me every day and I refuse to do that. Obviously my heart feels shattered to smithereens, and I despise him for what he has done to me and Holly. But the thought we meant so little to him will help, and so I think if ever I waver I'll remember how little he cared about us and so I'll hold firm,' said Peggy.

'No, it's little Holly who'll pay the price, don't you think?' she went on. 'The poor little mite is going to grow up knowing that while many brave and honest men will die in this war, a louse like her father is very probably going to come through it unscathed and end up living with some other family that he'll have had after her, and with him completely forgetting that he already has a daughter. I'm old-fashioned as I do think a child needs both parents, but it's not going to be the case for Holly as he's a canker that needs to be removed from our lives, and so the poor dear thing will never know what it's like to be loved and cherished by her very own father. That breaks my heart more than anything Bill Delbert could ever do to *me*, I'll tell you that for nothing, Barbara.'

Now the tears arrived, and in torrents.

Her sister shuffled a little further up the bed and put both her arms around Peggy, who leant her head down and sobbed so violently against her that Barbara felt the bounce of her sister's head against her breastbone. 'It's not fair, Peggy, you're quite right. It's not fair. But you will be able to give Holly enough love for two parents, I know you will, and with you by her side she couldn't ask for better,' Barbara said as reassuringly as she could. 'And Ted and I, and Connie and Jessie, will never be far away, you know.'

After a while the sisters drew apart to stare dolefully at one another, and then in perfect unison they turned to look over at the old crib holding the peacefully sleeping baby girl who looked as if the only care in the world that she had right at that minute was whether to nap with her white knitted bootees on or off.

Chapter Eight

Milburn had a distinctly put-upon expression on her long face by the time Roger had been fully tutored by Ted in the proper way of putting her harness on and then how to connect the trap to the harness.

The children tried to help Roger by exuberantly calling out instructions (many right, but some unintentionally wrong), but this only further confused him, especially when Mabel tried to say what she thought he should do too, with the result that he kept getting in a pickle, and inevitably would do the various leather straps up either too loosely, too tightly, or in the wrong way. And once Roger had finally got the harness on, only a bit askew, he then had difficulty in backing Milburn into the trap's traces as he kept walking her backwards as if around a corner rather than keeping her moving in a straight line.

But Ted was very patient, as was Milburn, and suddenly the penny dropped, much to everyone's delight, and Milburn wrinkled her velvety nostrils with what looked like relief.

Understandably, the children had started to become bored while Roger fiddled about and so they had started to do things like trying to push each other in the back of the knees, so that – if the timing were right – the unlucky recipient would be plunged forward and, if the timing was perfect, right down to the ground. As the boys were wearing short trousers and Connie a cotton summer dress Gracie had adapted for her from one of her own, it was likely that there'd be an array of bruises on the back of their legs that the children would be able to compare next morning.

'Oi! Watch it!' Ted had to be firm that that sort of behaviour was never to go on around Milburn, as it was the sort of thing that could lead to the pony getting unintentionally spooked and then somebody ending up hurt, he explained.

'We didn't mean anything,' said Jessie.

'I know, son, I know,' Ted replied, 'but none of you are used to big animals an' yet yer 'ave to do their thinking for 'em.'

Connie and Jessie looked at their friends with frowns, each twin seeming to forget that they had been happy to try to sneak up behind their pals to do likewise only a mere matter of moments ago. But their unhappy expressions reminded the others that their father hadn't been in Harrogate long, and already he was having to lay down the law, which risked spoiling a nice day, and so for a little while all the children felt suitably chastened.

'I'm sorry, Daddy.' Connie sounded so contrite and in fact her saying she regretted anything was so out of the ordinary that Aiden immediately apologised too and then went and stood by Connie to show solidarity with her.

On the final run-through Roger managed to do it all very adequately with – best of all – no reminders from any of those watching him. And so it was then that with a smile, he stepped well away from Milburn to take a theatrically low bow, with one hand behind his back and the other swooping extravagantly towards the ground as he made a flurry of quickly delivered feathered waving gestures as if he were a nobleman bowing to his queen, and he was rewarded by an enthusiastic round of applause from his audience. Even Milburn tossed her head up and down, and whiffled her whiskers, as if she were agreeing with everyone that Roger had achieved a success of heroic proportions.

Ted asked Jessie to take hold of Milburn's bridle just above the bit to keep her steady while he and Roger climbed up into the trap and took their seats on the driving bench. The ever-sensible Aiden passed up the whip to Ted, taking care to wrap the rope bit of it around the whippy bit and to move slowly in order not to startle the pony, as he'd been instructed.

'I'll drive Milburn round the block to see 'ow she goes, an' then you take over, Roger,' said Ted, and then he looked towards the children. 'An' you lot, you can walk wi' us if yer likes, but keep jus' behind us, out of 'arm's way, an' no messin' about or shoutin', mind. We don't know whether she'll spook easy an' so let's not ask fer trouble.'

Milburn lifted a front leg and stamped it down as she champed on her bit and tugged at the reins, clearly eager to be on her way.

With that, Ted neatly manoeuvred the pony through the yard and out onto the road, with Aiden and Jessie paying especially close attention to exactly how he managed to do this. They wanted to be doing it themselves before too long, and if they could grasp the technicalities before the other children, then so much the better. Larry and Connie followed, but Tommy stayed behind with Angela, offering to change the pony's water and clean out her stall ready for when she came back.

Roger said a distracted 'thank you' to his son for thinking ahead and sorting Milburn's stable, then immediately found himself gazing benevolently around as he sat beside Ted, before he turned back to smile at the children and give them a quick salute, looking as if he was enjoying the sun on his back on this lovely balmy day. Then, much to the twins' amusement, Roger obviously remembered that he should be watching Ted more closely and so he tried to concentrate on what Ted was saying with a suitably attentive face.

After a while, Ted said 'giddy up' and gently touched Milburn with the whip on the flat of her broad back, and she broke into a smart trot. Ten minutes later the children were red-faced with the effort of racing along just behind the trap.

Next, Milburn was slowed down to an amble, before being made to walk out briskly, then to trot again, and turn left and right, and pull up from a trot to a dead halt, all of which she did as if she were an old hand. Finally Ted took her to a busier road, where there was some traffic moving along, to see what she was like near cars (not that there were very many as petrol rationing was biting), and buses and larger vehicles.

The game little chestnut did everything she was asked to do with the minimum amount of fuss, and she didn't flinch or even flick an ear in the direction of the traffic. Ted said 'good girl' several times in appreciation, getting a twist of her ears in reply to him.

Back at Tall Trees, Ted halted her with a 'whoa!' and the application of a gentle pressure on her mouth, and then he handed the leather reins across to Roger, who took the gathered loops up cautiously and held them in the way Ted instructed, although he said he hadn't enough hands just at the moment to cope with the whip as well, and so Ted said he'd hang on to that and that he really didn't think Milburn needed it as she seemed to be very willing.

'You need to make her think you know what you're doin', and then she'll do what you want. She's got a bit of spirit but she's a nice pony, an' you'll 'ave the 'ang of 'er in no time,' Ted promised.

Roger hoped that would indeed be the case, and then he clicked his tongue against his teeth in the way he had seen Ted do, and rather to his surprise Milburn began to walk forward on this command as if he were an old hand too in the pony-driving stakes.

Mabel had come out to see them off and she held up her hands in silent applause, and Roger couldn't resist a little smirk in her direction, at which Mabel gave a dismissive downward wave of her hand, with a jolly call of 'Gi' over, Roger!'

This time they were out for quite a while longer, during which time Roger picked up the rudiments of driving the trap quite quickly, mastering the firm tones needed for the hups, walk-ons, giddy-ups and whoas much more easily than he or anyone else had expected, indeed so much so that the children quickly became bored again as there was a lot of walking, trotting, turning and stopping, and categorically no drama at all. Then Ted announced that it was getting on and Milburn had probably had almost enough, although they were going to give her a step out into the country before they brought her back to Tall Trees, and so while Ted didn't mind giving each of the children a turn at driving the trap tomorrow, what he could say was that it wasn't going to happen today and that the children should probably make their way home without them, to see what Tommy and Angela were up to.

It had been brewing for a while, but at this confirmation of nothing in it for them any longer, the children soon lost the last remnants of interest and, challenged by Larry to a race, they peeled off to gallop home as quickly as they could without even the tiniest moan of disappointment.

It was a much happier-looking Roger who drove the trap back into the yard half an hour later, and then untacked and sponged down a now sweaty Milburn, before popping her back in the neatly mucked-out stall that Tommy had got ready, all executed without a hitch.

He and Ted stood back to watch her drink, and then nodded at each other in the way that men sometimes do when they feel a job has been well done.

When Roger and Ted went into the kitchen it was to find Mabel, Peggy and Barbara all looking engrossed as they leant over the kitchen table.

Peggy got up to give Ted a hug, and he tried not to show his shock at the sight of her blotchy face and her bloodshot eyes peeping at him from underneath their swollen lids.

Peggy gave Ted a weak half-smile and then turned again to the kitchen table, which was covered with a swathe of white cotton fabric delicately sprigged with red, pink and blue summer flowers, and soon the women had their heads bent close together once more as they tried to pin the fabric to a pattern for a summer dress for Connie and eke out in the spaces around this enough material for a summer blouse for Peggy. It was like they were doing a very complicated jigsaw puzzle.

At the end of the table was piled a new pair of grey short

trousers for Jessie and a grey shirt, while there was a newly knitted cardie for Connie that Barbara had knocked together in a striking shade of magenta three-ply.

In order to leave the women to it the men made themselves scarce, heading out to inspect the chicken coops and decide where the pen for a porker might go, if Roger brought one to Tall Trees.

Then Connie and Jessie called the dads over to see Milburn. They'd found Mabel's large tom cat, Bucky, crouched on Milburn's back, purring loudly and paddy-padding with his paws for all he was worth. Milburn seemed vaguely affronted and the angle of her ears seemed to say that it was a very warm day and she really didn't need a hot-water bottle of a furry friend nestled on her loins although she wasn't bothered enough to stop pulling hay from her hay net, nor did she do anything to dislodge Bucky.

Over in the kitchen there was now the not wholly pleasant smell of some bones bubbling in hot water in a sizeable saucepan on the hob. The bone-boiling went on every few weeks even though every single person at Tall Trees would moan about the distinctive and rather grim smell. But the resulting liquor would be later added to some diced ham hock, leeks and carrots, and left to set solid to make some brawn for supper on toast later in the week. To get rid of the aroma the back door had been propped open, with a curtain Peggy had made of dangling pieces of wool and string and other bits and bobs that she'd weighted at the bottom with wooden cotton reels, positioned across the top of the doorframe, to keep the flies out. As Bucky found the dangling reels irresistible to play with – and no amount of shooing would keep him away for long, which meant constant running repairs to the curtain – a persistent pair of fat bluebottles had made their way inside through the latest gap and were lazily flying in squares around the ceiling light.

The women were ignoring the smell of the bones, and the bluebottles, as they needed to use the kitchen table as it was the largest in the house. Although Barbara worked during the daytime in a haberdashers and normally Peggy was very practical, it was Mabel who proved to be by far the best at making the two patterns fit on to the available material, although the wrestle with this piece of summery material was threatening to turn into a manful struggle that she wasn't totally certain of winning.

Barbara had been given the cotton remnant by one of the other ATS women whom she volunteered with several nights a week, and she'd been delighted when she'd seen how big the piece of cloth was. Now she was even more pleased that she and Peggy had something useful to talk about that wasn't to do with Bill's upsetting news.

As they all stared down at what they were doing on the table, in a determined effort at keeping Peggy's thoughts occupied away from Bill and MaureenFromTheNAAFI, Barbara described what daily life was like back in London with the war on, even though she knew she'd said some if not all of this to Peggy on other occasions and that Peggy wasn't really listening to her anyway, while Mabel kept feeding Barbara questions so that the conversation didn't dry up.

'It's so strange on the buses late on in the day, and on the trains too,' Barbara said. 'When it's dark they have blinds that are pulled down and blue lights inside that don't really give out anything more than a murky dark haze where you can hardly see anything. And the conductors don't call out the stops any longer so goodness knows how strangers know where they are, which is the point of course, but still... It's really easy to knock into people, but on the whole everyone is very good about it, and it's rare to hear anyone complain.

'And Ted and I went up to Piccadilly the other day, didn't we, Ted, and the big statue there had been boarded up and covered with advertisements for War Bonds, not that we've got any spare money to buy them. And meanwhile Ted said it was very strange at the Jolly a couple of months back on the day when the two IRA bombers were hanged, as a couple of patrons dared to say they were pro-Irish, and there was nearly a fight.'

'Well, one can see how incendiary that would be, when everyone else is looking to back the war effort, and the Irish are doing exactly the opposite,' said Peggy more than a trifle half-heartedly, although she was clearly trying her best to concentrate on something other than her row with Bill. 'Well, I know they say they're neutral, but how can anybody be neutral these days. I bumped into Dr Legard the other day – you remember him, Barbara, as he came to our bonfire party here? – and he was saying that he'd heard that people who are too despondent, and dare to say so publicly, can now be taken to court.'

Barbara did indeed remember the rather striking doctor – he'd saved Peggy and Holly's lives, of course, but Barbara had noticed and been impressed by him well before that, as he'd been the first to twig that there was something awry with Peggy's pregnancy back during a previous visit Barbara had made to Harrogate, when they'd thrown a small children's party to mark Bonfire Night or, more accurately, Bonfire Afternoon seeing that nobody could do anything with illuminations or fireworks once it was dark because of the blackout.

The usually talkative Mabel was concentrating deeply on the patterns still and so was uncharacteristically quiet for a while. But once she had finally managed to shoe-horn all the required pieces of tissue paper for both garments onto the cloth, she set Barbara and Peggy to cutting the now pinned patterns, while she described at length her plans to bring young Gracie into the WVS, and then a whole range of ideas that she had had about useful things for the League of Friends and their work with local hospitals.

Mabel went on a bit too long about this, and cutting a trifle rudely across her monologue (although Barbara would never have dared to acknowledge this on such a cataclysmic day for her), Peggy said that there was one thing James had mentioned they were very short of at the hospital, and that was some sort of homemade drawstring bags for the wounded military men to keep their personal items safe and in one place.

Roger looked up from organising the shoes that needed polishing and said, 'Ah, interesting. Remind me to make a note of it to mention at tomorrow's services. I'm sure many parishioners would be interested in helping out.'

'You should ask for donations of old material and have a look in the jumble box at the church hall,' added Mabel, 'as with so many children in the house you've a ready-made army of "volunteers" living right under your nose, Roger.'

'Can you imagine the faces of Aiden, Tommy, Larry and Jessie if they have to learn to sew? Priceless!' he chuckled.

'Bribe them, as that will work most likely,' advised Mabel. 'Say that t' first boy t' make five useable bags will win a prize of, well, I really don't know, but I'm sure you can think of summat, Roger.'

'I'm sure I will be able to. Perhaps being able to choose the piglet we are going to put under the apple trees, or not having any chores to do for a week,' he replied.

Peggy was staring off into the distance, and Barbara thought she very probably hadn't heard much of this last bit of the conversation.

There was a pause, and they could all hear Ted, once more back in the yard, talking to Milburn as he leant in over her stable door.

Then as she began to cut the patterns, the long scissors making a rhythmic chopping sound on the wood of the table as she went, Barbara said, perhaps erring a bit too much on the casual side, 'Peggy, you probably ought to have a word with James to see what size would be ideal for those bags.'

'Oh, I think it's just for a few bits and pieces like tobacco and matches, maybe a letter or two, and a pen, and so the bags needn't be too large,' answered Peggy in a distracted way as she moved to fill the kettle. 'I doubt anyone would mind what size they are.'

'Well, we don't want to make them too large and thus waste material,' Barbara answered, 'and it would be foolish if they were made too small simply because nobody checked.'

Roger and Mabel caught each other's eye, and slightly raised their eyebrows but Barbara's blank but nonetheless articulate glance in their direction told them in no uncertain terms to keep their counsel, at least while Peggy was in the kitchen.

But Barbara needn't have worried as the children came in as one and looked expectantly at Mabel. They were clearly peckish, and keen to know when they would next be fed, and so Peggy said distractedly above the children's chatter, 'Oh, maybe you're right, Barbara – I'll try and remember when I next bump into him.'

Chapter Nine

Roger went back to church for evensong, and as it was bath night which was always a bit of a palaver, Mabel served an early tea of a large Woolton pie, made with fresh vegetables from the patch the children looked after in the garden at Tall Trees, under the guidance of the verger at Roger's church, who seemed to be able to coax things to grow in the most unlikely of places, in this case Mabel's old ornamental rockery, which had had only the most rudimentary of clearances, with just the largest stones being heaved to one side.

Mabel had sliced and diced the vegetables, and had added several handfuls of porridge oats and a thickened vegetable stock to bulk it out, all covered in a golden shortcrust pastry topping. To go with it there were fresh garden peas that Roger had nursed along, shelled by Angela, plus Mabel had served what she described as her 'legendary potato surprise', pronounced sur-preeze she claimed, the only surprise being, Tommy joked, that it was made of potatoes and *nothing* else. Immediately his mother pointed out that she had added a little milk and some tiny daubs of margarine dotted on the top to help it brown in the oven, which meant it wasn't 'just potatoes', and then she had to laugh when Tommy good-naturedly rolled his eyes. She knew what he meant, and she had to agree with him.

Still, with lots of salt and pepper, it was a much more appetising meal than many were sitting down to, everybody knew, and so nobody dared to comment that it was anything other than moreish.

Ted had been very clear with the twins when they'd left Bermondsey the previous September that they were to eat whatever was put in front of them, with no arguments, and for either of them to leave any food on their plates would definitely not be acceptable under any circumstances, whether they liked what they'd been given to eat or not. The twins had been quite fussy eaters when they were small, but they left London knowing that those days had to be in the past now, and generally they had tried their very best, with only fried tripe proving a complete stumbling block and, once, even Mabel had to agree with the twins that her attempt at serving half a boiled calf's head with white sauce was a mistake never to be repeated again.

'Ma, do yer mean we don't 'ave to 'ave calf's 'ead no more?' Tommy had dared to ask. 'Or yer goin' t' practise cookin' it like mad?' Mabel had used her best withering look before she shook her head, and the children all laughed in relief, with Connie saying, 'Mishap avoided!'

Although Peggy barely ate anything of the Woolton pie, both Ted and Barbara were very gratified to see the twins guzzle down everything put before them with no quibbling, a far cry from the slightly picky, vegetable-shy appetites they had demonstrated less than a year earlier.

As a special treat because Barbara and Ted were visiting,

there was even a bread and butter pudding (heavy on the bread, light on the butter and raisins) to follow, accompanied by some thinly made but still tasty Bird's custard. When the children were at last allowed to get down from the tea table, they were all feeling as if their eyes had been bigger than their tummies, and very full indeed seeing that, unusually, they'd just had their second cooked meal of the day, while even Peggy looked to have perked up a little, now that she had eaten something hot and sweet.

After tea, while Tommy, Aiden and Larry drew lots to see the order in which they would get into the same water for their weekly bath, Ted and Barbara retreated to the parlour with Jessie (who was hoping he might be able to avoid a bath this week) and Connie, so that all the Rosses could have a little time on their own, as they had used to do.

They didn't get up to anything special, other than Jessie show his parents a code he was working on so that he and the other boys could leave secret notes for each other at school, after which they all played a hotly contested Snap tournament with Ted's playing cards, which he'd remembered to bring, and then dominoes and some other board games, before all cramming onto the two-seater couch, the twins perched on the arms and leaning against the parent next to them, as they listened to the nine o'clock news from the BBC on the wireless. Then the twins were told to have a quick top-to-toe wash and jump into bed as the next day was a school day, and so they mustn't be late to go to sleep.

Angela was still awake when Connie and Jessie went past her ground-floor bedroom on their way upstairs, as since her injury she had been a poor sleeper, exceptionally prone to nightmares, so Mabel was sitting with her, reading to her from a battered and dog-eared copy of *Swallows and Amazons*. But although Connie wanted to listen to Mabel read too, she was herded up the stairs alongside her brother by Barbara.

Once Connie and Jessie had settled down, and their parents had returned to the parlour, Peggy came in with cups of weak cocoa for Barbara and Ted, although when they asked her to join them, she said she was tired and so was going to head on straight up to bed herself.

Left alone at last Barbara and Ted could talk about the twins. It felt very odd to see them so much more independent than when they had left Bermondsey, as well as taller and stronger (although Jessie still looked to be small for his age and he definitely seemed younger than his sister at times, with Barbara pointing out to Ted how Jessie had said 'daddy', but Connie had preferred 'mother', and Ted saying Connie had reverted to 'daddy' when he had told the twins off).

Naturally, before too long, the conversation turned to Peggy and Bill, and Barbara went through everything Peggy had said at least twice. 'And she knows how expensive getting divorced is, and how everyone at home will gossip, and so I don't know what she'll do,' Barbara wound up.

Ted didn't seem to have much of an opinion either way, which was, in Barbara's view, much too reasonable, and indeed downright irritating when he refused to condemn Bill totally, and she sighed strongly in disapproval, even shuffling away from her husband a little on the sofa.

But Ted remained firm, closing with, 'I'm sure that if things 'ad gone on as before an' Peggy and Bill 'ad been able ter stay at 'ome, it would all 'ave worked out otherwise for them an' Bill would never 'ave strayed. But it must be strange to be away from 'ome and wi' other men, an' some women can be right determined on a chap if they feel that's who they want.'

'Well, I don't agree,' said Barbara petulantly as she stared at the old-fashioned carpet in front of the small sofa on which they were sitting. 'And how would *you* know, Ted, what other women are like?'

Ted took the sensible decision to keep quiet as he knew Barbara could be fiery when riled.

They both stared at the carpet, and after a while Ted poked his elbow into Barbara's side. She huffed, but then she poked him back with her elbow, at which he put his arm over her shoulder and drew her close, whispering, 'Well, I don't know, do I? It's jus' what the lads say at the Jolly.'

'Just you make sure it says that way,' said Barbara, and then she changed the subject as she felt her point had been made. 'I don't know, Ted, I'm pleased that the twins seem to have settled so well here with Roger and Mabel, but I can't help feeling we're missing out on such a lot, don't you think? Jessie is code-mad, which he never used to be, and he's getting a bit of Yorkshire about him as he speaks, isn't he? While I can see too that it won't be long before Connie finds herself starting to develop as a young woman as she's not quite the beanpole she was.'

'Barbara!' said Ted, looking uncomfortable. He hated talking about anything to do with 'women's things', and Barbara realised that this meant he felt awkward therefore with her even encouraging him to think about how much Connie had grown, and this was without Barbara having stepped into any territory to do with adolescence that Ted would have described as 'saucy'. 'Surely not? She's still a little girl, not yet eleven…' he faltered.

'Well, I'm not saying anything major is going on just now. But I can see that it will do at some point, and that this all might not be too far away for either her or Jessie. All I am pointing out is that I think things will be happening to Connie that her own mother should be around for, and as good as Mabel and Peggy are, it's not going to be the same for Connie without me to speak to, especially seeing how keen she is on Aiden, although I'm sure that is still completely innocent and so I don't want to say anything that will spoil it for her,' Barbara said reasonably. 'And of course the same goes for our Jessie too, although not the Aiden bit! There will be things to do with his own body that will be facing him that a father needs to prepare him for, otherwise he'll be getting the gossip from school and probably scaring himself to death, and so it's a shame that you are not with him more to help him understand what is going to be happening to him. Look at Tommy and Aiden, for instance, they are big strapping lads, and have you noticed that Tommy almost looks as if he has the first hint of a moustache coming through, which says to me that a lot more is probably changing than just a bit of facial hair.'

'Barbara!' breathed Ted again, although this time in an even more shocked tone, his cheeks, earlier ruddied by the sunny jaunt out in the trap with Roger and Milburn, paling rapidly at the thought of what his wife was driving at. 'Oh…'

Barbara smiled and shook her head. She could see that Ted wasn't going to be ready to have the birds and the bees talk with Jessie on this visit, but she needed to let him know that he couldn't keep telling himself that he would do it one day but not quite yet.

'You're not going to be able to put it off for too much longer, Ted,' she said with just the tiniest hint of iron in her voice, 'and so I think that you must prepare yourself that if you get a good moment to broach what you need to say to Jessie about all the changes his body is going to go through, and how babies are made, then you should take the plunge.'

Ted's face was so stricken at this that Barbara had to work quite hard at not laughing out loud.

Chapter Ten

The next day was Monday and the twins had to attend school in the morning, along with the rest of the children from Bermondsey, while the pupils who came from Harrogate were on the afternoon school shift for the week, and so Barbara and Ted walked the twins to school well before the first lessons would start, as they wanted to have a quick word with their teacher to see how the twins were faring.

Angela and Larry were also on 'earlies', but they were going to set off a bit later, with Larry pushing her there. Angela was only doing two hours a day in class at the moment, as following her head injury she found she got a headache if she tried to concentrate on anything for too long, and Larry hadn't yet returned to school officially and it probably wasn't going to herald the end of the world if he were a little late. James's advice was that Angela be eased gently back into her normal routine as he didn't want to risk the sort of setback that would see her have to return to hospital for further recuperation, as his field hospital, which had been set up for wounded servicemen and had only taken Angela because they had at that point been quiet and he had the best expertise in the area with head injuries, was becoming busier by the day with soldiers and naval men, and Air Force pilots who'd been injured now rapidly filling the wards after being returned from abroad. Luckily for Mabel and Roger, who was always over-committed at the best of times, Aiden and Tommy could pop over to the school to collect Angela after her two-hour stint and take her back to Tall Trees, after which they would share an early dinner together, before the boys would head back to school for their 'lates' session with the other children who'd been born and bred in Harrogate.

Peggy had said to Barbara and Ted that so many London children had returned to the city that she thought the early and late system was all but finished, and that at some point soon the children would be merged into classes that were taught together, although for now the dwindling class sizes could only be good for the twins, as it meant they were getting more attention from their teachers.

The last time Barbara had been to the school had been six months earlier, and on this Monday morning once again she was impressed by the four-square look of the solid building, with its boys' entrance to one side, and the girls' at the other. The window frames around the tall windows looked relatively freshly painted, and the playground was clean and tidy, with none of the stray bits of rubbish that had always collected in the nooks and crannies of the run-down outside area at the Bermondsey school the twins had attended. Once inside though, the difference between the schools didn't feel so marked with the parquet flooring having the same sound as Barbara and Ted walked to the classroom, and there being a similar smell in the air of grubby hands and none-too-clean hair of some of the pupils, while the sound of the children gathering for the lessons was also the same.

As always happened, these sounds and smells brought back happy memories, and Barbara and Ted smiled at each other. The first time they had met was when they were in primary school, when Barbara had given Ted a lesson in using a blade of grass carefully split for a nail's width and then pressed between two bent thumbs and blown into as a means of making a loud whistling noise.

As expected the news from the twins' teacher was that Jessie was doing really well at school in his lessons, and everyone was very pleased with him. He had a real aptitude for puzzles and problems, and the teacher was encouraging him to play some chess at lunchtimes and to do crosswords. Jessie was still shy when left to his own devices with the other children in the playground who weren't part of his Tall Trees coterie, but he was starting to come of out his shell a little (especially when talking about codes and ciphers), and this was deemed to be excellent progress.

It was a different matter with Connie though, which saddened Barbara and Ted a great deal, although they weren't exactly surprised. They knew all too well that Connie, although whip-smart when out of the classroom, had always struggled once she was sitting behind a desk, never having enjoyed her letters and being the sort of girl who much preferred being read to than to do any reading herself. The teacher's voice was sombre as she explained that Connie's attention was amongst the poorest in the class, her sums full of crossings-out, and her ink-splodged handwriting appalling and looking as if she were still in kindergarten. And as for her reading out loud, poor

Connie was probably two years, if not more, behind where she should be, to the point that she would do anything to get out of standing up in front of her class with a book to read from. She was good at remembering things said out loud to her, apparently, but that seemed to be about the only thing she excelled in, in the classroom.

Barbara wasn't sure what to say, and neither was Ted. Connie had wiped the floor with the rest of her family at cards the previous evening, and then again in the games of Ludo and Lookabout, so either the rest of Ross family was unbearably stupid – which didn't seem to be the case given the high praise heaped a minute or so ago on Jessie – or maybe there was a resilient streak of naughtiness in Connie that meant she just wouldn't knuckle down and pay attention when she was in the classroom.

Looking out of the window at Connie who was currently holding court to a group of school pupils, both boys and girls, with everyone apparently eagerly hanging on to her every word as she gesticulated in a lively way to illustrate whatever it was that she was saying, Barbara knew she shouldn't feel disappointed, although she did.

Connie had always had poor reports from school, and Jessie really good ones, and so it was unrealistic to expect that anything would have changed just because Connie was living several hundred miles away, Barbara acknowledged. Connie was a healthy, bright girl who made friends easily and who had a bold, resourceful streak that served her well. Jessie, although a model pupil in the classroom, was much more introverted, and was all too ready to step aside so that Connie could be the spokesperson for both of them. In fact, Barbara thought that

Connie could reason and structure an argument in favour of her doing something or other with a speed and alacrity that many adults would be jealous of and that completely diverted attention from her lack of prowess with paper and pen.

But it was galling, all the same. Connie was letting herself and by association the whole Ross family down, and Barbara wasn't happy.

Once everyone was home from school that day, as promised the previous afternoon, Ted took Milburn out in the trap again, this time for the children to have a go at driving the pony.

During the afternoon, before Aiden and Tommy had got home and while the others had done their homework, Ted had led Milburn to the edge of the town, and allowed her to graze on the verges and hedgerows. Barbara and Peggy, and baby Holly, had gone to June Blenkinsop's, and so Ted had a welcome hour or so to himself.

It was warm and sunny, and the rhythmic sound of Milburn pulling herself mouthfuls of grass made his eyes feel heavy. Ted sat down on the verge with his back comfortably propped against a dry stone wall, the lead rope in his hand, enjoying the clean air and the smells of the hedgerow, and he tried to concentrate on the butterflies he could see fluttering nearby and the intermittent drone of bumblebees going about their business.

When he woke up about thirty minutes later it was to find Milburn stretched out beside him, having a snooze in the sun as well, while a concerned woman with a pram was staring down at them both.

'Thank 'eaven,' she exclaimed when she saw Ted open his eyes, 'I thought summat bad 'ad 'appened, an' I weren't sure wot t' do.'

Ted and Milburn both scrambled up quickly, apparently equally embarrassed to have been caught napping out in the open, and after Ted had apologised for scaring the woman with the pram he quickly led Milburn home, deciding not to tell Barbara what had just occurred as she would certainly think it extremely bad form to be caught sleeping outside in broad daylight like that, especially as some people might – shamefully – have thought he was sleeping off a drinking session, which of course was very far from the truth.

Quite a while later, after Barbara had made both Jessie and Connie read to her, and once Tommy and Aiden had returned from the lates at school and joined the others for a barm cake with a scrape of margarine, just to keep the wolf from the door until their tea at six, all the children, except Angela, had a go at putting the harness on the patient pony, and Ted was pleased to see that they all managed to do it without a hitch.

Ted noticed Angela looking downcast, and so asked if she wanted to have the first go at driving, and her face lit up. She was lifted up into the trap by Ted and she proved a natural, and actually probably the most intuitive of all the children at controlling Milburn, although Aiden was pretty good too, it had to be said.

Ted thought he'd have a word with Roger as this could be a way of giving Angela a little independence and she could have one area in her life where she wasn't totally reliant on other people helping her move around.

They'd gone through the back streets almost right over to the other side of Harrogate, and it was time to turn for home.

Ted felt confident enough of Milburn, who hadn't spooked once that afternoon or the day before, to let the boys now bundle themselves into the back of the contraption rather than having to walk alongside, and so while Tommy and Larry were facing forwards as they watched what Connie was doing, Aiden and Jessie were sitting cross-legged with their backs to their pals as they looked down the road the way they had just come.

A few minutes passed and then Aiden and Jessie watched a group of rough-looking larger lads scramble over some railings edging what looked like a park and then arrange themselves in a line behind them, none of them taking their eyes off the old-fashioned pony and trap.

These boys – 'Them's the 'Ull lads,' said Aiden in a low voice to Jessie – were staring unblinking at the retreating trap with undisguised dislike.

Jessie noticed how they all stood with their feet firmly planted apart and their hands bunched and their elbows slightly bent as if they were inviting fisticuffs. Not one of them said anything and not one of them did anything other than frown menacingly in his and Aiden's direction, but this was almost more threatening than if they had done something more overtly aggressive.

'Look at these evacuees from Hull.' Jessie didn't dare take his eyes off the other lads as he hissed this command over his shoulder, and alerted Larry and Tommy with a couple of well-aimed jabs of his elbow backwards, who quickly turned around and stared back.

Connie and Angela were oblivious to the silent drama going

on behind them as they were both sitting on the driving seat alongside Ted, Connie having her first go at taking Milburn's reins. The girls were chatting fervently about this and that as if they'd forgotten about Ted being beside them, and to his surprise Ted found himself rather enjoying this ringside glimpse into the girlish chatterbox world of what Miss had said at school earlier, what was annoying about no longer being in Bermondsey, and who was sweet on who.

It was a different story at the back of the trap. As the four boys from Tall Trees looked down the road towards the Hull scallywags, who stared back with a clear aggression, it seemed as if some sort of unspoken gauntlet had been thrown down, and picked up by the other side. There didn't seem any obvious reason why such a challenge had been proffered or accepted, but Jessie and his friends just took it as what was going to happen.

'Blimey O'Reilly,' said Larry under his breath.

'Bugger,' Tommy added. The four boys nodded as one.

Connie drove the trap around the corner and the Hull contingent could be seen no longer.

But none of those in the back of the trap were under any impression that this was the last they'd see of that motley Hull crew who had stood so confidently and united as they had issued a wordless invitation to battle with the boys from the rectory. It was a grave thought.

Chapter Eleven

Two weeks later and well after Barbara and Ted had returned home to Bermondsey, Peggy continued to feel as if almost her whole world had been rocked off its axis.

Her body ached constantly from chin to toe, and she nearly always had a nagging headache. She felt worn out during the day, yet unable to sleep at night, waking with a feeling of exhaustion that somehow managed to eclipse that of the day before. Thoughts of Bill and Maureen tumbling in the sheets together raced unbidden through her mind at the oddest of moments as she lay in the dark, and although sometimes they were oddly exciting, more often than not she couldn't help but keep going through all the signs she might have missed, and then berating herself for even caring when it was obvious that Bill hadn't given a jot.

Well, maybe it wasn't as simple as all that, she'd think at other times. Bill had telephoned on numerous occasions, and he had written to her most days. But Peggy steadfastly refused to speak to him, even though sometimes she really wanted to, and she made sure she sent all his letters back with 'Return to Sender' in firm letters on the front.

Barbara said that Bill had contacted her too, asking her to

persuade Peggy to open up a means of contact, but Barbara had said back to him, in a curt note, that she trusted Peggy would do the right thing, and if Peggy couldn't see her way to a telephone conversation or a letter, then Barbara certainly wasn't going to do anything to convince her otherwise. Bill then tried telephoning the Jolly on a Thursday night to speak to Ted, but Ted said sharply he wasn't going to get involved and it was Bill's mess to sort out.

Mabel advised sticking to a routine as the best way forward, and so Peggy made sure that however unhappy she felt she turned up every day at June Blenkinsop's, no matter how little she believed herself able to contribute to the war effort there, and she would always do her very best to smile warmly at the customers in the café. But the number of times she gave customers the wrong change, or couldn't add up what they had had to eat, or said it was cottage pie on the menu rather than the Lancashire hotpot that was actually being served when she was asked what was on offer that day, or vice versa, told both Peggy and June just what a low ebb she was at. June told her to shelve the idea of the mobile canteen for now as it was quite clear that Peggy had enough on her plate already.

Peggy didn't feel heartbroken any longer – she'd cried too furiously on that dreadful Sunday of the telephone call, and she was still livid with Bill for that – but she felt more that she'd been tipped upside down by her mistaken belief in a marriage that, now they had their darling Holly, had been cleaved together in a way that with Bill at her and her daughter's side, they could weather any storm.

The long and short of it was that she believed she had been

publicly made a fool of, and this, Peggy discovered, hurt almost as much as Bill's casual infidelity with MaureenFromTheNAAFI.

But depressed and glum as Peggy felt, it wasn't all bad.

Every day seemed to bring with it something new that Holly could do, which was a complete joy. Peggy never tired of watching the tiny girl look about curiously, eager to absorb more and more of what was going on around her, or how Holly would, if laid on her front, put her little towelling-nappied behind in the air and waggle it about, followed by putting her hands on the ground close to her shoulders as if she were about to lift her shoulders up. This, Mabel said, meant that she'd be crawling before too long, and that Peggy would never get a moment's peace then as Holly would be into everything, and so Peggy had better make the most of the time before Holly made herself mobile.

Peggy didn't feel capable of 'making the most' of anything just at the moment, but Holly was such a happy, good-natured baby that it was hard to stay miserable for all the hours in the day, Peggy found, when Holly was all too ready with her gummy but adorable smile. And she found that she didn't often have any more down-at-the-mouth thoughts as she had sometimes had in the months following Holly's birth, although of course by now these feelings had become inextricably confused with the high emotions that Bill's revelation had provoked.

Everyone at Tall Trees continued to rally round, all trying to help Peggy as best they could.

Gracie was there most of the time with her baby Jack, when she wasn't stopping over at the Kells' house if Jack's father Kelvin were home on leave, and she would keep Holly amused for a couple of hours in the late afternoon once she had finished her shift at the greengrocers. If it was sunny, Grace would place both babies on their tummies on a rug in the garden where they would stare at each other as if trying to unravel a puzzle, and although Peggy would never relax enough to drop off as she lay on her bed upstairs, she did appreciate a little time on her own so that she could have a few minutes to herself where she didn't have to do anything, or even think.

And Mabel, who was privately worried that Peggy's drawn face and increasingly gaunt figure were also because she was still feeling the after-effects of her difficult pregnancy and Holly's traumatic birth, and not just because of Bill's silly antics, made sure that all of Peggy's linen was taken care of, and that Peggy had an egg for breakfast each morning, freshly gathered by Tommy from the hen run. Roger religiously cleaned Peggy's shoes each night and made sure the perambulator always looked spick and span, while Angela and Connie would spend ages at teatime trying to amuse Holly.

Jessie was hard at work on an ABC book for Holly, which he was making from a spare roll of old lining paper that Roger hadn't pasted up when – some time ago, it had to be said, well, actually it had been before Tommy had been born – he had done his last lot of wallpapering at the rectory. Jessie had been ribbed about the book he was making by Larry and Tommy, who'd called him 'a big girl', but Jessie ignored them, and made several trips to the library with Angela, much to Tommy's chagrin who didn't like it when anyone besides Connie did anything with Angela, to look up various pictures in the library books. Peggy found Jessie's thoughtful gesture of making the ABC book to be unbearably touching, especially when she saw the care with which he was sketching and then colouring in the illustrations for each letter. Perhaps she would have advised something a little less war-relevant than Jessie's choices – she wasn't sure, after all, that Holly wouldn't have preferred a colourful golly for the 'G', rather than Jessie's gun; or an apple for the Army of his 'A', or a dog for the Destroyer of 'D', but she would have bitten her tongue off rather than say anything other than, 'Well, Jessie, if Holly decides one day to join the military she's going to be streets ahead of the competition and she will be thanking you all the way as she heads to try on her uniform. She's a very lucky girl to have a cousin like you.'

Aiden had meanwhile talked June Blenkinsop into allowing him to sit on the till in the teashop for an hour or two the moment he had finished school if he was on earlies, so that Peggy could slip off back to Tall Trees. Afternoons in the teashop were the quietest times, and he was a bright and conscientious boy, and so even though he was only eleven, he was making a pretty good fist of taking the money, although Peggy would do the totalling-up for him when she came in the next day. And Larry was helping out in June's kitchen by making sure the tables were cleared and cleanly wiped, and all the used cutlery and crockery was neatly piled by the sink ready for washing up. He revelled in the title of 'bus boy', which one of the customers told him he'd be called if he were working in a posh restaurant in London, and as a surprise one evening June made Larry a 'Bus Boy' badge to wear, and Aiden one that said 'Till', which the boys were very pleased with. June paid them each a shilling a shift, and would send them back to Tall Trees as often as not with a pie made of scraps or some leftover cooked greens for bubble and squeak, which Mabel was always grateful for, but with the firm instructions from June that they weren't to show off about the money they got for each shift to Tommy or Jessie, who weren't earning and had only very limited pocket money, otherwise Aiden and Larry would both be 'out on their ear', no matter who had done the boasting.

Indeed, if Peggy thought too much about the kind thoughtfulness she was being shown, she would find her eyes filling with tears and a lump forming in her throat. This feeling of weepy melancholy wasn't confined to when Peggy was thinking of those moments, as she discovered it could creep up on her at the most unexpected of times, one day causing a customer to joke that when Peggy had asked him what he'd eaten, and he'd replied 'the curried spinach' and Peggy's eyes had gone watery, he'd had to say to her, 'Ee by gum, love, it weren't that bad!'

Like Mabel, June also worked on the principle that being kept busy would take Peggy's mind off things. She suggested that as she herself was up to her ears in meal planning and a few staffing problems at the café, it would be really helpful if Peggy could go over to the hospital to have a word with James, to see if they should carry some first-aid equipment in the event of bombing and, if so, whether the staff at the café should also have some rudimentary first-aid training.

Peggy sighed in a tired way, and suggested that wouldn't a telephone call be as good as an actual visit to find out this information? June could do that, she was sure.

June pretended she didn't hear Peggy, and so after another sigh Peggy plonked Holly back in the perambulator and popped on her own cardie as the day was overcast, and headed over to the hospital.

As luck would have it Peggy was able to catch James Legard between shifts, as he was standing outside the hospital entrance with his white coat unbuttoned and his face turned up to the cloudy sky. When she saw how pale he looked she guessed he had been working long hours and hadn't been able to be outside much, so Peggy apologised guiltily for interrupting his rare free time.

'Don't give it another thought, Mrs Delbert,' said the young doctor with a smile, as he rallied and then leant forward to look at Holly lying in the perambulator and to give her a quick chuck under the chin.

'Peggy, please, Dr Legard.'

'Well, Peggy, in that case it's James.'

Without being sure why, Peggy experienced the now all-too-familiar sensation of tears threatening, and when she didn't say anything James threw her a casual but nonetheless scrutinising look.

Then, as he didn't much like what he saw, taking hold of her elbow with one hand and deftly scooping Holly out of the pram with the other, he said invitingly, 'Come with me, Peggy. I was just going to have a cup of tea and so it will be a treat if you would join me. And I can give Holly a quick once-over to make sure everything is shipshape and tickety-boo with her.'

With that he neatly manoeuvred Peggy into the hospital foyer and down the corridor into his office, on the way asking a blue-uniformed ward sister to take care of the perambulator and then to bring in a cup of tea for himself and Peggy.

Once Peggy was sitting down, James put Holly down on her back on the narrow bed crammed against one wall. He peeped into her towelling nappy to check for nappy rash and he looked at her tummy button. Doing up the large curved safety pin holding the nappy together, next he lifted all the baby's limbs this way and that, listened to her chest with a stethoscope, shone a light into Holly's mouth and ears and eyes, clicked his fingers by each ear to see if she could turn her head that way towards the noise, and finally he waved a scrap of clean bandage all around her face about eighteen inches away to see when she would look to see it and if she could move her eyes from side to side and up and down.

'Who's a clever thing then, Holly? Who's a clever girl?' he said in the voice people often talk to babies with, and was rewarded with Holly's best grin and chuckle, at which he gave her belly a gentle jiggle with his whole hand, causing Holly to elevate the chuckle into a proper laughing sound.

The sister came in with the tea, and James plunked pillows either side of Holly to stop her turning over and risk any danger of her falling to the floor.

He went and sat down with his knees facing Peggy's. 'Well, Holly seems to be quite tip-top, which is good, and a testament to how well you are looking after her. I think she's caught up now with where she would be, had she gone to full term. But her mother is important too, and so I'm just as interested in your state of health, and how you are feeling,' he said.

At the sound of the kindness bubbling behind his voice, Peggy bowed her head, and although he was presented with the top of her head, meaning that he couldn't see her face, James guessed by the sight of her hunched shoulders and trembling tendrils of hair, that she must be crying.

'Have a drink,' he suggested quietly after a minute, gently nudging Peggy's saucer a little in her direction.

Peggy wiped her eyes and sniffed, and then she reached obediently for the cup and took a sip.

James passed across to her his clean handkerchief that had been neatly ironed and folded, and which had been nestled in the top pocket of his white overall, and then he waited patiently for her to say something.

Looking down again Peggy dabbed underneath her eyes with the hankie, and she raised her head towards him.

The light was shining through the window straight onto Peggy's face, and James could see she was exhausted and wan. There were blue veins just under the skin around her eyes, which were slightly bloodshot, and there was dry, flaky skin under her nostrils. She looked in the grip of an emotional crisis. But he thought he detected alongside all this misery, something resilient and brave in her expression too, and James found that this, in his eyes, gave Peggy the faint but undeniable aura of magnificence and feminine resilience.

'I'm not ill,' Peggy said, and James had to blink several times to break his train of thought and concentrate on what she was saying. 'And every day I thank the very moon and the stars that Holly is here, and is healthy and thriving. I thank you too, as without you looking after us on Christmas Eve neither of us would be here today, and so I do want you to know how much I appreciate your skill and quick thinking.' James's eyes crinkled at the corners at this, and he looked slightly abashed.

Peggy didn't notice though as, despite her eyes being turned in his direction, she wasn't really looking at him as she continued in a more downcast tone, 'But I've had some bad news that's knocked me for six, and I feel quite often as if I'm just done in. And even before that I did sometimes find that I didn't quite enjoy being a new mother as much as I'd expected – I can't describe exactly how I felt, only that I found myself feel very inadequate and short-tempered. I can't seem to get myself back on track. It's hard to think straight, and I have to fight very hard sometimes not to be snappy with Jessie and Connie.'

Peggy didn't elaborate further, although James gave her a further opportunity to do so. But she did twist the hanky this way and that in her hands. So to keep the conversation going, James asked Peggy if she was still feeding Holly herself, and how she was spending each day.

She replied that yes, she was still breastfeeding, and that in addition, she was helping Mabel as much as she could around the house, and June Blenkinsop too, while also trying to look out for Jessie and Connie. James commented that bearing in mind how poorly Peggy had been at the start of the year, she should remember that her body had taken a real punishing and that it would take a while for her to feel right as rain and completely back to normal, and meanwhile she was asking quite a lot of herself with so many irons in the fire, and so should she think of cutting back a bit?

'You must look after yourself, Peggy,' he said, and then nodded his head in Holly's direction, 'as this little one needs you to be healthy most of all.'

Peggy nodded in agreement, and James was gratified that her eyes didn't fill with tears once more.

Then he looked as if he wanted to probe a little further about what the 'bad news' was but Peggy didn't want to go into this, so she took up the reins of the conversation, jumping in quickly to say she had come to the hospital with June's questions about first-aid kits in places of work, and in mobile canteens (if she ever got that idea off the ground), and then she remembered to enquire about the size of the little bags to be made for the patients' possessions.

They chatted about this awhile, and at last Peggy smiled properly for the first time when James said that if Roger arranged a day with his parishioners, then he'd be very happy to come to the church hall, or Tall Trees if Roger felt that more appropriate, and do a basic first-aid demonstration, and also explain what the cloth bags would be used for and how they could be made to be most useful to his patients.

'You are kind. I'm sure this will please Roger and Mabel, and June too,' said Peggy. 'And if you were to bring a partly made bag you yourself had done, then I think the boys at Tall Trees might not think sewing to be such a namby-pamby thing to do after all...'

'Deal,' James answered, quite quickly. 'As long as you make sure that you are getting enough rest yourself and are not pushing yourself too hard.'

Chapter Twelve

Milburn was getting quite a lot of exercise these days. Roger would take the trap out on weekday mornings, and unless there was an emergency and he had need of the pony and trap later, the children would go out in it either after school or just after tea, and then when Milburn had been driven back to Tall Trees, and unhitched and sponged down, they would put on her rope halter and the boys would take her out to one of the grass verges on the edge of the town to graze for an hour or two.

Angela would stay behind at Tall Trees for the grazing bit as she would be feeling tuckered out by then and would just want to sit and have a rest, and Connie would usually opt to keep her company, Tommy now tending to stay with his pals following the sighting of the Hull lads.

The boys religiously made sure that they took the pony out to graze every summer evening, although they had something of an ulterior motive.

They'd been told that they mustn't ride Milburn as there wasn't a saddle nor a riding bridle, and so without the proper tack it wasn't safe for them to get on board (or as safe as it ever could be with a pony, as even the very best riders could sometimes fall off, Roger had pointed out).

But boys will be boys the world over, and quite often they dislike being told what to do. Inevitably, they had started giving each other a boost up to sit on Milburn as she placidly grazed.

'Go on,' Tommy would say, 'Pa'll never find oot.'

Even the normally very obedient Aiden found the lure of Milburn's broad back irresistible, and he'd reply, 'All right, just fer a while.'

'I'm next,' Larry would add, and Jessie saying, 'Me too,' with Tommy insisting that he could have the longest time on board seeing as he was last in the queue.

Milburn put up with this without a fuss, and it wasn't long before they'd barely have turned the corner away from Tall Trees before one or other of them would be sitting proudly high on top of her. They taught themselves the knack of jumping up on her back by grabbing a handful of mane and using her forward momentum as she walked along to help send them vaulting upwards as they flung a leg over her back. At first somebody would always lead Milburn, until Jessie said, 'Why don't we use the lead rope to tie to her noseband on the other side? It'll be almost like reins and we'll be able to steer better.'

This proved to be the case, although that could well be because Milburn was being kind to them rather than they were getting to grips with the nuts and bolts of riding.

Jessie seemed to have the best balance of all the boys, and therefore looked to be the most accomplished on horseback, although none of them ever dared to do more than urge Milburn forward at a slow walk. But within several days each boy could make her go forward or stop, and turn left and right, albeit with various degrees of success. They had to make sure she had a good hour at least of grazing, and when they realised that they were spending quite a lot of time riding her, they worked out a rota so that they could get up early and take her out for a hedgerow chomp before they had to have their own breakfast or Milburn had to be tacked up to take Roger out and about on his parish business.

'It'll be dark early in the morning in the winter, and at this time in the afternoon, and so this system of feeding Milburn won't then wor—,' said Jessie just after the morning grazing rota had been mooted for the first time, and then he stopped abruptly what he was saying.

He'd just realised that he'd been assuming that he and Connie would still be in Harrogate once the summer had come to an end in several months' time, when the autumn nights would be drawing in, and he really wasn't sure what he felt about that. If they were still in Yorkshire at that point it would mean that he and his sister had spent a whole year away from London – and what a long time a year was to a ten-year-old.

Larry looked across at Jessie quickly, and they shared a moment of understanding, Larry signalling with a silent look that he wasn't at all sure about wanting the evacuees' sojourn up in Yorkshire to end, bearing in mind what was likely to be waiting for him at home, which was almost definitely not going to be pleasant given how horrible his father could be. Jessie telegraphed back that he massively missed his parents and Bermondsey, but there were undeniable benefits to having a ready-made group of playmates around, and not too many house rules to follow, as they were all enjoying under the present regime at Tall Trees.

Tommy didn't see Larry and Jessie looking at one another, as he was staring at the ground. Rather to his surprise, and especially bearing in mind the scrumping debacle of the previous autumn when he hadn't been very nice at all to any of the evacuees, he realised suddenly that now he didn't want any of them to leave, although he was old enough to understand that all things must come to an end, and so it was inevitable that at some point, Jessie and Connie, and Larry, and – worst of all – Angela would have to return home to London.

Aiden was standing beside Milburn's nose and he stroked the kitten-soft area just between her nostrils. He didn't care to think of a time when Connie wouldn't be sitting across the table from him at mealtimes or taking him on at a grass-whistling contest. He'd never thought he could be friends with a *girl* – and neither had Tommy, Aiden suspected – and yet if there was something he, Aiden, wanted to share with the others it was always Connie that he imagined himself telling it to, and he thought that Tommy probably felt the same way about Angela. Who would ever have thought that when they were all standing on the edge of the experimental orchard in October?

Milburn nudged Aiden's pocket just to see if he had a spare handful of carrot peelings hidden away in there just for her (which he didn't), and so Aiden said, 'I think we ought to make a pact to have the best summer we can. It might be the only one we can spend together so let's make the most of it.'

'Yes!' said Larry. 'Let's make a serious and solemn pact, and then we have to stick together for all time. I know! It can be a blood pact!'

'All for one, and one for all?' said Jessie.

'Except you mean that we'd be The Four Musketeers, rather than three,' said Aiden, who'd recently read Roger's copy of

Alexander Dumas's *The Three Musketeers* right after Jessie had finished with it.

'Well, I suppose we'd be the Six Musketeers if we asked the girls,' said Larry.

There was a silence.

'Connie will be furious if we do this and she's not asked to be a musketeer,' Jessie pointed out.

Everybody nodded as they could see the truth of that.

There was another silence, and Milburn lifted a hind hoof towards her belly to shoo away a persistent horsefly.

'But a group of musketeers is a boys' thing really, isn't it?' Jessie added tentatively as he looked from one of his chums to another, who all appeared deep in thought.

Then Tommy nodded seriously, and stuck his hand, held as a fist, forward.

Larry smiled and quickly put his fist on top of Tommy's.

Jessie, who was on top of Milburn, leant down and put his fist on top of the other two.

All three looked at Aiden, who seemed to be poised in indecision, obviously thinking of what Connie, who could be a real firebrand when she felt like it, would say when she discovered – as she surely would, knowing Connie – that she had not been included in their musketeer pledge.

And then he came to a decision, and so Aiden placed his fist on the top of the others, with the declaration, 'A blood pact it will be then, and we can do the blood part in our bedroom.'

As they all repeated loudly in unison 'a blood pact it will be then', Milburn lifted her nose and turned her pretty head to peer from under her bushy forelock at a spot close to her shoulder where their fists were piled one on top of the other.

She shook her head as if to say 'girls have a lot to recommend them – you lot are making a mistake, a *big* mistake'.

But the boys were too busy smiling at one another, and imagining the adventures that they would be able to have together once they were bona fide musketeers, to take any notice of what the intelligent pony might be thinking.

Milburn plunged her head down to pull at the nutritious turf once more.

She might not approve, but she thought she'd better fill up while the going was good, as she sensed there might be a time coming in the not-too-distant future when she was going to need lots of energy.

Chapter Thirteen

By now, virtually all the talk in Harrogate, and in the letters Barbara and Peggy wrote to each other (Barbara, who could barely imagine what she would feel like if Ted had done the dirty on her the way that Bill had, was making sure she scribbled at least a few lines to her sister daily just to try and keep Peggy's spirits as buoyed as possible), were equally concerned with what was happening across the English Channel at Dunkirk as with the mundanities of their own daily lives.

One thing for certain was that everyone agreed that what had felt at first as if it were occurring a very long way away indeed, now felt as if it were happening virtually next door. The war, and the struggle between life and death, and victory and defeat, suddenly seemed startlingly vivid.

'DUNKIRK DEFENCE DEFIES 300,000' Tommy read after tea from a *Daily Sketch* Larry had brought home from June Blenkinsop's, once the news of the mass evacuation of British soldiers from the shores in northern France began filtering through.

And Connie managed to read to the others the *Daily Express* headline: 'TENS OF THOUSANDS SAFELY HOME ALREADY'.

'Aunt Peggy, what would ten thousand soldiers look like all together?' Connie asked.

Peggy thought about it before confessing, 'Do you know, Connie, I don't have any idea. I do know however that this number of men wouldn't be able to fit into your playground at school, even though it is a much larger playground than you had at Bermondsey. It is a lot of men though, that much is clear, and it's needed a large number of small boats to sail over the Channel to get them. The customers at June's have hardly been able to speak of anything else.'

'Just like Tommy,' replied Connie, and it was true so aunt and niece shared a conspiratorial smile.

Later Peggy and Roger spoke of how it seemed that the more the public had time to think of what was happening at Dunkirk, the more a chord was struck that reverberated across the whole nation, with the result that even though it was a retreat, somehow it felt to everybody like a major victory that everybody could and should feel proud of.

A still under-par Peggy gathered with Roger, Mabel, and the children to listen on the wireless to the BBC broadcast Prime Minister Winston Churchill's rousing speech on the subject, to the nation. As everyone was getting ready for the broadcast to begin, Gracie bustled in too with a grumbling baby Jack in one arm, although she had to beat a hasty retreat to give him a feed when he wouldn't stop creating, just as Roger finished playing with the tuning knob and began to explain to the children that Churchill was using what had happened in France to try and encourage the United States to support the British cause against Germany.

But before Roger could go into too much detail, Mabel gave a firm shush, and soon the parlour was filled with the sound of Churchill saying in his distinctive voice crackling through the tinny-sounding loudspeaker, 'We shall go on to the end, we shall fight in France, we shall fight with growing confidence and growing strength in the air, we shall defend our island, whatever the cost may be, we shall fight on the beaches, we shall fight on the landing grounds, we shall fight in the fields and in the streets, we shall fight in the hills; we shall never surrender...'

A frisson engulfed the room and although they weren't prone to this sort of demonstrative behaviour, Roger and Mabel clasped hands briefly.

Churchill had honestly acknowledged the British defeat on the French sea shores, but still somehow he made his words feel to everybody as if the war was not lost. Those held rapt in the parlour at Tall Trees, even the children, found themselves feeling they could – and they would – be heroes.

It was only Peggy who felt lost and adrift in her own world as Churchill's words washed around her, and she gazed unseeing into the space before her.

As the Prime Minister's speech continued, she barely noticed the four boys all sitting facing each other crossed-legged on the floor in their grey short-legged trousers, staring seriously at one another and then nod, before putting their clasped fists once more together in a vertical tower.

Connie and Angela were sitting on hard chairs, their heads together as they whispered to one another, but the boys' close attention to what they were doing didn't quite escape Connie's eagle-eye, although she continued to make a show of listening to what Angela was murmuring about how fond Bucky seemed to be of Milburn.

Gradually, as Churchill's inspiring words lulled a sense of

calm and confidence over his listeners, Peggy started to feel almost hypnotised, even soothed.

A new mood crept upon her, and with what might almost be a jolt, she realised that in the blink of an eye suddenly she felt bolder and more competent, and less disappointed in herself and her situation. And although she didn't realise that this was the case, she began to square her shoulders a fraction. She wasn't quite sure what was making her embrace a new frame of mind from her hangdog feelings of only a few minutes previously, but as Churchill's rousing words rang out, the closest she could have described it was that she was experiencing a feeling of being cleansed and renewed. Although their leader was talking about fighting in terms of winning the war against Germany, to Peggy it more felt like Churchill was addressing her and her alone, making a direct call to arms as regards bonding her and Holly into a unit, held fast and strong together, and invigorating their intensely personal fight for a better future.

Peggy took a deep breath. No longer did she feel she wanted to spend her time and energy picking over the whys and wherefores of what Bill had done – or, more painfully in Peggy's opinion, think endlessly on quite what it was that had made Bill want to put to one side both herself and his marriage vows of fidelity.

Instead – and it was an amazing feeling growing quickly from the tiniest seed of hope – it wouldn't be going too far to say that she felt purged of Bill's bad behaviour, and as if she had the spirit now to forge forward and look to her and Holly's future with a sense of inner strength and equanimity.

Of course, Peggy knew it wasn't going to be as simple as

this. She would feel bruised and battered for a long time, that was inevitable. But she wouldn't allow herself to feel a victim any longer, Peggy suddenly believed with the clarity of day coming from night. Bill had hurt her by what he had done, absolutely. But she didn't need to let him go on hurting her; and while Barbara had said this on several occasions to Peggy (only using different words), and actually so had Mabel, June and Grace, and even though she herself had paid lip service to this too, now Peggy understood exactly what everyone had been driving at, and what her own head had been reasoning but her heart hadn't been ready to follow.

Peggy resolved just to accept that although they had tried very hard, despite their best efforts, it had gone irrevocably wrong between herself and Bill. Now she had done her grieving for what might have been, and she should try not to dwell on it any further. It might not be a very big decision on her part, but still it seemed to Peggy as if a weight had lifted from her shoulders.

Peggy shifted the sleeping Holly from one arm to another, and she realised as she refocused her eyes and looked around, that it was only her and Roger left sitting down, and the wireless was now silent. She had lost all sense of time and place, and she had no idea if everybody else had just left the room, or if they had gone out and about their business as much as an hour ago.

She felt dreamy almost, and she startled slightly when Roger said, 'I've never heard anything quite like that. Mr Churchill is very good at his speeches. I found his words stirring. Very stirring, wouldn't you say, Peggy?'

She nodded, and for a moment felt overwhelmed,

experiencing just for a second or two the too-familiar ache of threatening tears. But even this wasn't anything to fear, Peggy decided, as it felt too, for the first time in weeks, as if they wouldn't be tears of anger, bitterness and rancour, but more as if the 'right' sort of tears were going to come. Healing and purifying tears. She took in an enriching breath and, oddly unembarrassed considering that Roger was there, let them spill from her eyes unchecked.

Presumably Roger was used to this sort of thing from some of his female parishioners, as he didn't look uncomfortable or awkward in the least.

Instead he pulled his chair closer and contented himself with smiling down at the softly snuffling Holly, deeply asleep, and then he raised his head to look at Peggy, his gaze steady but warm.

Peggy felt as if she were being looked at as herself, Peggy, for the very first time in quite a while; it wasn't an unpleasant sensation. She tried to concentrate on just the moment, and not thinking forwards or backwards, or worrying about what had happed yesterday or what tomorrow might bring.

It seemed enough just to be sitting there with caring people close to her, and a happy and healthy baby in her arms.

'We're doing it all for them, aren't we?' said Roger softly after a while, as he leant forward to tuck Holly's shawl a little more securely across her bare legs uncovered by her short cotton dress, as although the evening was still warm now that the sun had moved and thrown the room into shadow, the temperature was dropping slightly. 'Whether we are fighting on the beaches, to use Churchill's words, or within the realms of our own hearts, we are all fighting for something. You have it in you to be a wonderful mother, Peggy, so you must remember that always. I see it clearly.'

Roger smiled encouragingly and then continued, 'While it has been difficult for you in recent days concerning your marriage, you should remember to embrace too that Holly was born from an act of love. I know you're not an especially religious person' – Peggy felt a little twinge at this being articulated so clearly, as Roger was a man of the church after all, and she hoped he wasn't about to make her feel guilty for not sharing his depth of belief, or that she would plunge him into a sense of disappointment that she wasn't more enthusiastic church-wise, but she needn't have worried as then Roger ploughed on regardless – 'but it is times like these, perhaps when we have just listened to something like our Prime Minister speaking directly to all of us while we are sitting in our homes as if we had invited him inside in person, that makes many of us start to think once more of our faith, whether it be faith in our children, or in our leaders, or, in my own case, before the altar I hold so dear.

'I think that as long as we allow goodwill of all sorts to flourish in our hearts, that can never be a bad thing, and that it will give us many different kinds of strength. It strikes me that faith in our next generation is maybe as close to a real sense of grace as any of us will ever feel in this life, and when I look at a baby such as Holly or Jack I see how very special that is and how extraordinary they are.'

Peggy nodded furiously, tears welling up again, and she had to use Holly's muslin cloth, already damp from her earlier tears and which fortunately wasn't too grubby from wiping Holly's milky mouth, to mop under her eyes.

Roger sat quietly by, not saying anything more. It was an enriching and comforting silence, and as Peggy's fresh tears abated and Holly woke up and looked at her mother, Peggy understood that she was much, much recovered to how she had been only a day or so ago.

'Thank you, Roger, I er…' Peggy began.

'No thanks needed, my dear,' he said as he got up, giving her a vague pat on the shoulder as he went to put his chair back in its proper place. 'Now, I wonder where I put that lethal sloe gin that Mrs Timms gave me last summer? I think a small toast to Mr Churchill and our brave boys, and in fact the brave boys from all sides of the war, is very much on the cards, wouldn't you agree?'

Peggy stood up too, and then quickly touched Roger on the arm to stop him walking off to the kitchen to find the gin and the glasses just yet. 'Roger, I do want you to know that me, and Barbara and Ted, will never be able to thank you enough for everything you have done for us all. And we know that we can never repay you and Mabel either. You really have been most kind to us all.'

'Peggy,' said Roger gently, 'have you ever considered for a moment that perhaps it is you and little Holly, and Connie and Jessie, of course; and now Larry and Aiden and Angela, and Gracie and young Jack, who have given us Braithwaites the biggest gift of all simply by us having you, each and every one, here with us at Tall Trees?'

Peggy didn't want to start weeping again, and so she smiled and said, 'You forgot Milburn.'

'And dear Milburn too, of course – how could I forget her!

Now, where's Mrs Timms' gin? Let's hope Mabel hasn't turned into a secret drinker and hogged the lot all to herself.'

'I 'eard that, Roger!' came Mabel's ringing tones from just the other side of the open door, making Roger jump and, in a moment of pure joy, Peggy clasp Holly to her chest as they looked up to see Mabel step past the doorway en route to Angela's room, with the laundry basket and some folded bed linen, clearly intent on changing the sheets.

Suddenly it felt good to be alive. Peggy wanted to shout this out but she didn't want to scare Holly. In many ways she had Mr Churchill to thank for that, she thought, and then she wondered if many other people listening to his words had felt their lives shift just as she had?

Chapter Fourteen

Walking back from June Blenkinsop's one warm day after their stints, Aiden and Larry were worried about the sizeable number of newspapers left behind in the teashop by the end of the day.

'I've 'ad an idea,' said Aiden. 'What about if we make cards an' drop 'em off all round town t' tell folks t' gather their papers, an' then of a weekend we could collect all t' newspapers? We could do it in t' wheelbarrow, but Roger might let us use Milburn. An' when we git a good load we could lug it all t' depot.'

Larry agreed this was a good idea, and so did Roger when Aiden broached it with him and even said without any surreptitious prompting that it was perfectly all right for them to use Milburn and the trap as they would be able to collect more than if they were having to use the wheelbarrow. The government wanted all paper saved as part of their National Salvage Campaign, either newsprint or scrap, as it could be used for packaging around weapons when they were sent abroad, or bullet cartridge boxes, and some of it was even being used to eke out the concrete in the runways that were currently under construction for Britain's bombers to use. People were already saving all their papers and were using collection points, but Aiden's idea would be in Roger's opinion a service that those who were very elderly or who found it difficult to get out and about would find invaluable.

Jessie wished rather enviously that he'd had the idea, seeing how much everyone seemed to be congratulating Aiden for having come up with it.

Aside from Roger's congratulatory clap on Aiden's shoulder, Connie was sneaking looks at Aiden with undisguised admiration, and as Jessie watched them, one nudging the other's elbow and the other nudging back with their own, for the first time he understood with a feeling of what he could only think was sadness that although he and Connie would always be twins and have their very special bond together, there would be a time – and indeed maybe it was practically here already – when he wouldn't hold the closest place in his sister's heart (well, after their parents, obviously).

Jessie felt a sense of hurt for an instant as if he might be about to lose something precious, as he knew how eagerly Connie had always leaped to his defence and had tried to make sure nobody bullied or was mean to him, especially when he'd been having such a terrible time at school back in Bermondsey. He often wished he'd been able to do the same for her, but this situation never really arose as Connie always seemed to be so much better at looking after herself than he could ever be, which had been most galling to Jessie in the past. However, these days he'd noticed recently that he didn't need her to step in on his behalf quite as often as she had had to do when they had been living in Jubilee Street, and he liked this feeling of a slowly growing independence – it made him feel, while not quite brave, definitely more certain of himself and his place in the world, and so he tried to be happy that Connie liked Aiden and Aiden seemed to like her back.

As Roger gave a few useful suggestions as to how they might collect the paper, Jessie peeked again at the way Connie and Aiden were laughing together, and he wondered if he'd ever be like that with a girl, larking about with someone who wasn't his sister, with them hanging on his every word. He doubted it – he'd looked in the mirror only that morning, and had been chastened by the sight of his bony chest and puny arms – and anyway, he didn't really like girls, other than Connie, of course, although then he had to admit to himself that for a girl, Angela wasn't too bad either.

The previous week he'd even asked Connie precisely what it was that she felt about Aiden, and her reply had been, 'I like the way he makes my heart beat when he's near me, and when he smiles at something I say I like how my cheeks go pink no matter how hard I try to make them not do so.'

Jessie wondered what it would be to feel like that, but he couldn't imagine it. He was much more comfortable spending time with his pals than thinking about girls, let alone talking to them. In his opinion girls – especially when gathered together – seemed too noisy and complicated and unknowable.

Sighing silently to himself, Jessie now tried to pay better attention to the talk at the tea table, which was still on using Milburn for the mobile waste-paper collection, and the girls were volunteering to make the cards so that everyone would know about it.

'Yes!' Connie not-quite-shouted. 'We could have Tall Trees Paper Collection at the top.'

'And?' said Angela.

'Well, that's it. What more do you want?' Connie brows were moving from enthusiastic to miffed as she replied.

'Um,' stalled Angela, anxious not to invoke Connie's flash of temper. 'Maybe when the cart would be collectin', an' on which day. An' the streets we'd be goin' to.'

Seeing Connie starting to bridle, Gracie cut in to adjudicate before tempers flared by suggesting that perhaps the best thing would be that instead of having to make lots and lots of cards to post through people's letter boxes, which would in itself be adding to the waste of paper, the girls – and maybe the boys too – should make posters for a few shops, and for the church porch and the church hall, saying when the pick-ups would be, and in what streets, and that the children would ring a bell on their way around so that people could flag them down. Gracie thought for a bit and then added, 'Some people might 'ave a lorra paper now an' then, an' so you could also put t' Tall Trees telephone number in, sayin' special collections can be made "by arrangement".'

Feeling very grown up, the children cleared the tea table in record time, and as the boys polished their shoes, the girls got to work on the posters. Once all the shoe brushes and polish were back in the wooden box that lived under the kitchen sink, the boys – who had poo-pooed the idea of them joining in with the posters – concentrated on, as they saw it, the more manly task of working out the most efficient route for the collection.

Then Mabel poured cold water on the whole shebang, saying she was playing devil's advocate and were they all really convinced that it was a good idea? Was it a service that was really needed in their part of Harrogate, and were they sure that they weren't doubling up on something that other people were already doing – had anyone checked that? (They hadn't, but Roger and Gracie chipped in to say that they hadn't heard of a competing collection.) Then Mabel went on that if they got a loyal base of users, these people wouldn't like it if the children lost interest after a month or two, and they probably would, as it might turn out to be quite hard work and boring too. And would they be prepared to keep it going through the summer and on into winter if the war lasted that long?

The children sat sullenly for a while, Jessie and Connie both hoping that the war would be ending before the cold months began as they were missing their parents. Then Aiden remembered that he had read a story in one of the newspapers at the teashop about a milkman saving an elderly lady's life when he noticed she hadn't taken her milk bottle in from the day before. The milkman had gone into her kitchen, through the unlocked back door, to find that she had taken a fall and had been unable to get up because of a broken hip, and the lady had understandably been very grateful. And so he said, 'I think we'd be good at doin' it at the same time every week, an' Roger could tell us of anyone in 'is congregation he were worried about, an' we could look in on them on our rounds too. An' by t' time t' summer 'olidays are ending, maybe by then we could 'ave found a grown-up to 'elp if we're busy wi' school stuff.'

'Hear, hear,' said Roger in an approving way, as he was all for encouraging free enterprise in the younger generations. 'Capital idea.' The children smiled at him gratefully.

Mabel still looked distinctly dubious but she could see that nobody was going to agree with her. She put her hands up in mock surrender, and then couldn't resist pointing out a spelling mistake Connie had made in her very first poster.

Roger and Tommy both scrutinised Mabel, and then glanced at each other – she looked the same as always, but it wasn't like her not to be encouraging get-up-and-go in other people. Roger gave a slight shake of his head, and Tommy realised that his father was saying that it would be best not to draw attention further to this.

Connie let out a slightly anguished noise meanwhile, and sounded very grumpy when Angela suggested that she did the writing and Connie stick to decorating the posters. She'd been more than a little upset by Mabel's comment as her poor handwriting and terrible spelling was very much a sore point, and it meant that she hated to be criticised out of school as she felt she got far too much of that when she was sitting at her school desk. And with Angela also seeming a bit critical it all felt a bit much.

The boys could see the way this was likely to go and so they quickly invented something to do in their bedroom just as Connie began to say petulantly, 'Are you saying my writing isn't good enough?'

The next day, James Legard caught Larry jumping up onto Milburn just around the corner from Tall Trees, as the lads were going to walk the streets to see how many they could reasonably do in an hour, which Roger had said would be long enough both for them and for Milburn to start with, and they could increase the round at a later date if all went well with being out for an hour.

'Hello lads, is Reverend Braithwaite in? I want to have a word with him about a first-aid demonstration Peggy mentioned,' the doctor asked. And after Tommy had said yes he was, but that James would have to go down to the hen run as Roger had just gone to clean out the coop, James looked at Milburn, who was in her rope halter, and Larry sitting bareback astride her, and then he said, 'You all best be careful. That doesn't look very safe. Even if that pony is quiet as anything, you're not going to have much control if something out of the blue happens and makes it want to take off.'

Although he hadn't said as much, it was clear by his firm tone that James was saying that he didn't think the pony should be ridden without better tack on, and after James held his eye for a while, Larry gave in wordlessly and slid one leg over Milburn's rounded back and dismounted with only a single 'blimey' whispered very, very quietly under his breath.

James left them to it, and Larry and Milburn looked at each other dolefully, and even though she prodded at him with his nose as though urging him to get back on, Larry didn't vault onto her again, and neither did any of the other boys.

Chastened by the unexpected combination of Mabel and James's attitudes, the boys set off with Aiden holding the map, Jessie a notebook and pen for him to jot down the precise route, and Aiden with Roger's stopwatch that he had borrowed on 'pain of death' should it be damaged in any way, as Roger used it for summer fairs when he would usually organise some track events, which, aside from giving the winning times for that year, would be measured against the times the watch had given to race winners over past years.

Larry led Milburn, although privately he thought they

probably should have popped her back into her stall to pull at her hay net so that they could have gone on their *reconnoitre* without the pony, as if they weren't going to ride her then there didn't seem much point in dragging her along.

'Does it look a bit soppy,' Larry asked after a while, 'us leading Milburn through the streets as if she were a big dog?'

'Well,' Aiden reassured Larry, 'surely it's sensible we bring 'er as we can check the roads an' make sure they're not too slippy if she has a heavy load in the trap, an' we see if there's something she might scare at that we wouldn't think about if we didn't have 'er with us.'

Milburn didn't seem to feel it soppy. She was very good and paid no untoward attention to anything they walked her by, and Larry began to hope someone would suggest riding her again as it was his turn. But no one did and he didn't feel quite confident enough to jump on her back regardless, in case somebody would be snarky with him for acting off his own bat and not taking working out the route they would need for the collections seriously enough.

Still, the party had cheered up considerably by the time they were at the furthest point that they thought they might reach on their paper-collecting round, being halfway down a long straight street with no turn-offs.

Suddenly, and eerily quietly, the five Hull lads, just like the time when Jessie and Aiden had been sitting in the trap looking backwards while Ted had been tutoring the girls in how to drive Milburn, slithered over a wall about a hundred yards in front of them, and stood side by side with one another in an ominous line watching the group from the rectory making their way towards them.

Larry's grip on the halter rope tightened although Milburn's pace didn't falter despite her throwing her head to look at the unusual sight before her, her ears pointing sharply forward.

The Hull evacuees were all older and considerably larger than Jessie and his friends, even Aiden and Tommy, who were the biggest of the Tall Trees lot. They didn't make so much as a murmur and they didn't move, but as Milburn's clopping hooves got nearer to them, with seemingly no communication between them, as one the boys from Hull all moved their feet apart just as they inclined their heads towards their right side and jutted out their jaws, before taking two large steps forward very quickly, and suddenly stopping completely still again, standing lofty and menacing. The Tall Trees boys were unable to take their eyes away and, allowing enough time for their hearts to hammer uncomfortably, the Hull boys then rolled their shoulders slowly backwards and switched their jaws from their right side to their left.

Jessie thought these bigger boys must have practised those moves many times together as they were so perfectly timed, and although he was sneakily impressed with their foresight of working out a routine to perform without the need of any obvious signs to one another, he had to admit it was most effective at being very disturbing. He heard Aiden breathe in deeply beside him and so he guessed even Aiden, whom Jessie believed privately to be the bravest of them all, felt similarly.

'Look at t' middle one's face!' Tommy murmured excitedly in a quiet undertone, and so they all stared at the scruffy boy in the middle of the row, who was sporting a black eye and a split lip; and then they noticed that one of the other boys had scabby knuckles, as if he had hurt himself viciously punching somebody. It was a truly dispiriting sight, and none of those from Tall Trees dared to examine what combat injuries any of the other boys standing in the bullying line-up might have.

It was undeniable that these lads looked like trouble, and that they were nasty with it. They seemed mean and ready for a fight. And they were – deliberately so – standing in a really tricky spot.

The group from Tall Trees would have to make their way past them or, unthinkably, turn around and head back the way they had come. In spite of the unpleasantness of keeping going along the street and having to walk right by the Hull lot, to turn around in acknowledged defeat was a much less pleasant option as it would be an obvious sign to their aggressors that they were scared of them, which although the truth, nobody from Tall Trees felt it needed to be broadcast. They all knew too that if they did turn around, the Hull boys would smell blood and would very probably then give chase, which aside from whatever might happen to any, or all, of them in terms of being beaten up, might also have horrible implications for Milburn, who might get frightened or even injured, and this didn't bear thinking about.

And so they kept on walking although their pace definitely felt increasingly heavy and laboured. Jessie found his friends huddling closer to him, and as they came up to where the Hull boys were, subconsciously they positioned Milburn between the two factions as a sort of furry shield.

There was no musketeer camaraderie, no 'all for one, and one for all', as their threat had crept upon them far too quickly for that, leaving no time for them to rally each other. Out in the real world it all suddenly seemed more complicated than they had bargained for.

Milburn didn't help matters. Taking no notice of the posing boys from Hull, she lifted her tail as she plodded on and let out a loud gust of wind. Normally this would make everyone snigger, but not today.

The Hull lot certainly weren't laughing. They tilted their heads in unison the other way, and scowled as if Milburn had made a foul smell, which in fact she hadn't. But still not a sound left their lips. This was worse than if they had jeered and cat-called, or even issued an out-and-out invitation to a fight.

A few heart-thumping seconds later and the Tall Trees lot had managed to creep with shaking knees (well, Jessie's were shaking) past the threat. The Hull boys hadn't so much as twitched a muscle in their direction. But it was quite a long way down the street before Tommy breathed a very quiet but nonetheless heartfelt 'Bugger me', which the others all nodded agreement with.

And when Jessie sneaked a look back from about fifty yards further on, he was shocked to see that in total quiet the Hull boys had spread themselves in a line across the street and realigned themselves as a wall of antagonism shooting piercing looks at their retreating banks. They were standing in the same menacing pose as before, staring intently at the departing backs of Jessie and his pals.

As Jessie continued to stare, the biggest boy – the one with the split lip – raised two fingers in a 'V', not for victory but for something much ruder. And then as Jessie looked on in horror, very slowly this boy pointed his two fingers at his own eyes and then slowly turned his hand to point these two fingers at Jessie's eyes and silently mouth what Jessie thought might be 'fucker!' at him, although he couldn't be sure, at which point the other boys beside him each gave, again in unison, a slow single nod.

Without realising it, Jessie had faltered to a standstill. And as he gawped at this lad's hideous filthy fingers pointing in his direction, he felt almost blinded, as if the threat they posed was being launched straight at him and was finding its target deep within him.

Jessie hadn't thought he could have found these bigger evacuees more imposing than when they had been standing and staring at close quarters towards him and his friends. Sadly though, this wasn't the case at all, he discovered now with a slithering downward lurch of his belly as he realised without a doubt that this wasn't the last they'd see of these evacuees from Hull.

'I think that big one just said "fucker" to me,' said Jessie, when he had caught up with the others.

'D' yer think 'e meant 'imself, or one o' us?' said Tommy, trying to make a joke of it.

Nobody laughed.

That evening Jessie took a long time to come up with a letter that he hoped his father would find to be both reasoned and grown up, and – crucially – impossible to ignore.

Dear Father

We are all well and Mabel and Roger say hello. Milburn and Peggy and Holly are well to. But I want to ask you for some advise, and it is VERY IMPORTANT that you reply to me QUICKLY. I think I might need to box some boys soon, and so I want some tips on boxsing if you have them, and very much on the best way of punching and making them stop if the person you are fighting is much bigger than you. This is URGENT.

Thank you. And please say hello to Mother.

~~Your affectshunite son~~

With best regards
Jessie Ross

Chapter Fifteen

James arranged with Roger that he would do a demonstration of first aid in the church hall for anyone who wanted to attend.

It was a well-attended event as Roger had mentioned it at church under 'notices', plus Gracie put a card about it in the greengrocers, while Peggy stuck one up in June Blenkinsop's.

Although Britain was largely still in limbo waiting for something to happen, with no attacks yet from the Germans on the home shores, people were feeling increasingly edgy after what had happened at Dunkirk, a mood not lightened by the newspapers being packed with column inches on the high-profile sinking of several large aircraft carriers such as the HMS *Glorious* and RMS *Lancastria*, and reports coming in of Japanese offensives in China. Whilst everyone was trying to keep morale high, it was also true to say that most people – even the children – felt increasingly jittery as clearly the Phoney War they'd experienced so far wasn't a state of affairs that could go on for too much longer. Barbara was clearly feeling the strain, Peggy thought, as she had been most curt in her last letter to the twins in response to Connie suggesting that she and Jessie return to Jubilee Street, at least for a little while, and her stern words had quite upset Connie.

On the afternoon of the first-aid demonstration James arrived at the church hall accompanied by an obviously efficient but rather gruff-looking woman in medical get-up called Nurse Hampton. But before he could get down to what he was there for, first James had to deal with Tommy, who was sporting a sprained wrist that looked swollen and painful.

When James asked how he'd got it, Tommy said initially that he'd fallen off a gate they had been playing on. However, when James kept his counsel but continued to stare at him seriously with his forehead kinked in his direction, Tommy shrugged and then admitted that he and Larry had been trying to ride Milburn with one bunked up behind the other. Milburn had taken exception to this, and she had done a little bunny-hop of a buck and then had trotted off quickly, with both boys being unable to find purchase on her slippery summer coat and soon they had tumbled to the ground into some long grass, which although providing a softish landing, wasn't enough to prevent Tommy's wrist bearing the brunt of the fall for both boys.

James tutted, and said in a depressed-sounding voice, 'I warned you all about messing about too much on that pony when you didn't have enough control. If you saw the sort of injuries I see ... well, you'd take it all much more seriously. And really there are no excuses for this, Tommy, are there? Angela ran into a car when she was messing about all those months ago at Halloween, and look at how long she was in hospital and how she is still unable to walk. You all see poor Angela in her chair every day, and yet you and Larry were taking liberties with the pony, without a hard hat, may I point out, and now see what's happened and where it's landed you. It's not a serious sprain luckily and so I'm going to pass you over to Nurse Hampton to bandage, and not a peep from you as she does it, mind you, as I'm told she's very firm, almost brutal in fact.'

At the word 'brutal' James made a spectacular grimace, which made Peggy smile as she knew the doctor was deliberately overegging the pudding in the hope that what he said about the children being more sensible might hit home.

It seemed to, as Tommy immediately turned to look at Nurse Hampton, who was making a strapping noise with something that looked like webbing she was slapping against her thigh to get the kinks out, and Tommy's colour blanched a shade or two on his summer-ruddy cheeks. Aside from Nurse Hampton's possible brutality, Dr Legard wasn't the sort of person one wanted to disappoint. Tommy knew it was his own fault that he and Larry had upset Milburn and that he had been hurt as a consequence. He sneaked a second look towards Nurse Hampton, who was assessing him with a owlish expression that made the bits of her eyebrows near the top of her nose point intimidatingly together as she snapped, 'Look sharp, lad, and let's sort this bandage out. I haven't got all day to waste on the likes of you.'

Tommy glanced over at Larry as he walked across to the nurse, as if to plead for help, but Larry could only give a small shrug in sympathy. Tommy's wrist clearly needed bandaging as it was hot and swollen, and Larry was relieved that it was Tommy who had been hurt and not him, as there was a limit to how peeved James and the nurse could be about the whole thing when Roger and Mabel were standing nearby as hosts, and Tommy was their son, while the nurse might have been even more abrupt if she had had to deal with Larry.

There was a tap at the door, and a young man in Army

uniform stuck his head around the door to the church hall. James smiled and beckoned him in, and Peggy stopped her natter to June Blenkinsop about turning collars and cuffs on their blouses as the cotton started to become worn when she realised that the soldier was walking, aided by crutches, in jerky and shaky strides on what had to be, to judge by their lurching straightness, two prosthetic legs.

It wasn't long before Roger clapped his hands to hush the gossiping, and he thanked James for coming to talk to them and then, as instructed, quickly went and sat down beside Mabel because he knew people hadn't turned out to hear him, as Mabel had put it earlier, 'witter on'.

'Good afternoon everybody, and thank you for coming,' said James, looking very serious now. 'I'm going to run through the basics of the likely injuries and the sort of first aid you might need to apply if a bomb drops near to you and you go to the aid of injured civilians, which might also include fire or electrical injuries, of course. Then Nurse Hampton will advise on cleaning wounds and demonstrate three types of bandages – cotton, crepe and square bandages for slings – as well how to apply a tourniquet, and the things you can do to determine if an injured person must definitely be referred to a doctor or hospital, and when you can safely deal with an injury yourselves.

'But before we get into that, I'd like to introduce you to Private Benjamin Smith, who sustained severe injuries in a depot accident right after war was declared last September. Private Smith can tell you what it feels like to be injured and then to recuperate in hospital, and drawing on his own experiences what he feels that people can do to make loved ones who might have sustained life-changing injuries ease back into their, and your, everyday lives.'

It was quite a shocking and aggressive start to what Roger had intended as a helpful and informative session, Peggy thought, heightened by James's rather glowering expression and firm tone. To judge by the sound of shuffling chairs and the odd muffled whisper that she could hear behind her, quite a lot of other people felt similarly.

But as Private Smith hobbled across the church hall to stand by James, and remained standing even though Roger leapt up to fetch him a seat, as he described in simple and unexcitable facts what had happened to him (it had been a crush injury when a heavy crate containing metal armaments fell on him) and the precise nature of the injuries he had sustained before moving quickly on to – and this was the emphasis of his talk – how his injuries had made him feel about himself, and how he had also felt about some people's well-meaning but nonetheless distressing comments to him. Peggy began to think that Private Smith had actually been rather an inspired choice on the part of James.

The audience settled quickly and then listened with close attention. Although upsetting, it was very interesting to hear first-hand what it might be like to be badly hurt through no fault of one's own. Certainly everyone gave the soldier a very warm round of applause when he finished with, 'I wouldn't have chosen this for myself, or in fact for my deepest enemy. Every time I look down I see how my life has changed, and I'm not twenty years old yet. But I've made my mind up that I'm as much of a man as I was before my injury, just that I am without my legs, and I'd appreciate it if nobody felt sorry for me but instead banded together to help me – and, more importantly, all those who are or who will be injured far worse than me – become just as we are, with our limps and our injuries, the most useful members of the community that we can be.'

Peggy felt a lump in her throat. This young man seemed so brave and laudable that it was almost painful to witness. She couldn't help but compare Bill and his cavalier attitude to life and how he treated people against the quietly modest and upstanding determination of this young man, clearly now set on living the best and most fulfilling life that he possibly could, legs or no legs. Bill didn't come out of the comparison very well in Peggy's eyes, and as Private Smith made his tottery way to sit down on an empty chair beside Tommy (nodding with a questioning look towards Tommy's clean white bandage on his wrist as if they were now comrades in arms and seeing Tommy's shy grin back as he mimed a horse-riding accident) Peggy thought Private Smith would make somebody a lovely husband one day, and she very much hoped he had a sweetheart who cared for him just as much after his accident as she had done when he was well and healthy.

As James led the thanks for the previous speaker and then began to do his part of the talk, Peggy whispered as much to June, who smiled her support and squeezed Peggy's knee in reply when her voice wobbled as she sighed in an undertone how disappointing Bill felt by comparison. While Peggy would never wish such a heinous injury on anybody, and despite Private Smith's can-do attitude, to have lost both legs did seem a huge burden for such a seemingly kind young man, whereas her own husband could be this very minute lying wrapped in MaureenFromTheNAAFI's arms, his legs and arms and everything else intact and all too functioning. Life was very unfair at times, Peggy could only think gloomily.

James ran through some basics of first aid – if a bit of a person is bleeding, then get it elevated as soon as possible and try to staunch the bleeding; and how to check airways are clear, and so forth – before pointing his finger at Connie and Jessie and asking them to join him and Nurse Hampton at the front of the room.

'Right, we'll now see an expert in action as Nurse Hampton demonstrates the correct way to do all sorts of things with bandages,' James concluded as he bade the twins to climb onto two chairs in order that everyone could see the nurse's bandaging techniques. 'But do please remember everyone,' James added, 'never to put your own lives at risk when going to someone's aid. This is really important, especially with moving machinery or fire or anything electrical, as the worst scenario would then be that two or more people end up injured rather than one and thus stretch already stretched medical help further. So, take care of yourself, check for danger first and if danger is present and it is safe to do so, turn off electric and gas sources, or vehicle engines, or any machinery, and then you can touch people who need your help.'

As Peggy watched Connie being told by Nurse Hampton that she must pretend she'd had a head injury that needed bandaging (Connie proving quite the little actress as she grabbed her head just as if she were in acute pain, rolling her eyes dramatically), and Jessie was told he'd broken his collarbone and so his arm would need to be bound up in a sling (his acting skills a poor second to his sister's), Peggy realised that she had never thought of giving help in quite the way that James had just outlined. It seemed selfish on the face of it not to just step in as quickly as possible as valuable seconds might be a matter of life or death in heinous injuries. But the more she dwelled on it, the more she saw all the various implications of wading in regardless, most of which were likely to offer a worse outcome overall. What was it about James? Peggy wondered. She thought of herself as a sensible, reasonably practical person, and yet he had the knack of showing her how many of her ideas were perhaps not as solid or as sensible or as straightforward as she had always believed. She wasn't quite sure she liked this sensation, but she realised that she always looked forward to hearing the next thing that he had to say.

Once all the demonstrating had been finished and the floor had been opened for questions, James thanked everyone for listening so attentively.

And then from his pocket he produced a distinctly ill-sewn cloth bag. 'Before I finish, I would just like to say that any donations to the field hospital of drawstring bags about this size, sewn from whatever scraps of cloth you have to hand, will be gratefully received over on our wards. The patients need something to keep their tobacco in, and their knick-knacks and maybe the odd pair of socks or a book, or a letter or photograph from home. This is one I made last night. It's not very good, as you can see, but it will do what it needs to do, and if I can do it, then anybody can, I promise.' At this the doctor pointed a roving finger at all the boys in the audience, 'and so I would like to see everyone who is still at school make some bags like this over the summer for our patients, *boys* as well as girls, so no excuses, lads. And the person aged fourteen or under who makes the most bags by their own hand will win a prize of either going in an ambulance for a ride, or coming to the hospital for tea, with the sandwiches and maybe even a cake made by some of my patients, or else something that I can think of that might be even better. I'd love to see a boy win either of these prizes, wouldn't you Private Smith?

'And,' James went on in a louder voice as the boys gave a small cheer, 'Nurse Hampton, I dare say you'd like the girls to be top dogs though? I think the girls are going to give the boys a run for their money. Or are the boys going to surprise me? What do you think, children?'

All the children in the audience were so busy calling out who they thought would win the race to make the most bags that they just about drowned out the doctor's finishing words, 'And all bags to be at the hospital by 1st August, please.'

A still-bandaged Connie led the cheering of the girls, even standing up and turning to face the audience in order to take a pretend bow for the girls' victory, calling out cheekily 'I'd like to say it was a close-run thing, but we girls wiped the floor with you boys,' before being shouted down by the boys in the audience who, in the heat of the moment seemed to have forgotten all about sewing being something for girls or sissies, to judge by some raucous boos and whistles aimed in Connie's direction, and one expertly aimed screwed-up piece of paper thrown at her by Aiden that scored a bullseye by striking the tip of her nose.

At this point the older and calmer members of the audience began to make their way to speak to one of the three who had spoken.

Peggy was congratulated by several of Roger's parishioners

for Connie's lack of fear of performing in front of so many people, at which Peggy could only shake her head and say 'nothing to do with me' with a self-deprecating smile.

She waited for a lull, and then she went over to Private Smith. 'I want to thank you for coming to speak to us,' she said. 'I doubt there was a person in the room who didn't find what you had to say most inspiring.'

Private Smith looked a bit pink around the gills at her praise as he hoisted himself to his feet, but Peggy didn't notice as she was too busy signalling to the Tall Trees children to come and thank him.

The first thing that Tommy said once the children had all gathered around was could they have a squiz at one of his artificial legs? The children nodded enthusiastically.

'Oh my goodness, I'm so sorry!' said Peggy, clapping a hand to her mouth in shock as she would never have beckoned the children to him if she had thought for a moment they would be so forthright as regards what they had to say to him.

But Private Smith just laughed and said he'd better sit down again so that the children could get a better look as then he could put his leg up on a chair for them to see at close quarters.

He really didn't seem to mind, and after Peggy had reminded everyone only to ask sensible questions and to remember that they were to be nice and not rude, she left them all to it, noticing that out of all of them it was Connie who seemed the most interested in the intricacies of the false limb the young man was showing them, asking if she could touch it and looking carefully at the straps that attached it to the young soldier's leg very carefully.

Tommy got a bit carried away when asking questions about

what weapons Private Smith had used, although Jessie and Larry diverted Tommy's enthusiasm before he could then go on to ask the inevitable 'have you killed anybody?' with their own questions to the young Private on what sort of food soldiers were given when on manoeuvres and did they have to sleep on the floor or were they given camp beds if doing something tactical abroad.

Once she had reassured herself that Private Smith wouldn't let himself be drawn on answering questions on anything he didn't feel comfortable about, and nor would he let Tommy get too carried away, Peggy went to find June, intending to ask her back to Tall Trees for a cup of tea. But before she could do this she was waylaid by James, who said, 'How are you feeling now, Peggy? A little more rested up than when I last saw you, I trust?'

'Much better, thank you,' said Peggy, and then once she'd remembered how she'd bawled her eyes out in front of him not very long ago at the hospital, which was the last time she had seen him, try as she might she simply couldn't think of anything else to say. Remembering now how she had reacted back then to the doctor's kindness, her hot tears about her own predicament seemed such a lily-livered response to the times they were living through, and she felt acutely embarrassed and as if she had been made to seem all the more shallow and selfish after the touching and brave way Private Smith has spoken about his own plight.

Peggy looked at her feet, then flashed an awkward smile at James, before she had to look down at her sandals once more as she felt herself getting a bit hot and bothered.

James looked uncomfortable as well, and as if he couldn't

think of a way to keep the conversation going either now that Peggy had become tongue-tied. There was an awkward silence, during which Peggy longed to have Holly with her, as that way she could have covered her lack of imagination by saying something about the baby, but Gracie was looking after Holly for the afternoon as she wanted to go out later with a girlfriend, during which time Peggy would see to Jack for Gracie.

Peggy rather hoped James would make his excuses and leave her, but he didn't, and eventually Peggy managed with a bit of squeak, 'A very good talk, and a good turnout too. You must be pleased.'

'Well, hopefully nobody will ever have to use what we covered, but in these times it pays to be at least slightly pre-pared,' James replied stiffly, and then the conversation fell fallow again.

Peggy didn't know what had come over her as she was rarely lost for words. And a disconcerted James looked mightily relieved when Mabel's booming voice called him to her in order to settle a dispute about something or other to do with homemade remedies, and he was allowed to beat an honour-able but hasty retreat, although not before giving Peggy a two-fingered salute from his temple.

The instant she was standing on her own, Peggy felt relieved, and then a second later chagrined and out of sorts as she discovered she wished he was still standing close to her.

Chapter Sixteen

A couple of hours later Peggy was at the white five-bar front gate to Tall Trees saying goodbye to June Blenkinsop, who had been treated to a typically lively Tall Trees tea, and who was now heading home, clutching a brown paper bag containing some fresh eggs that Peggy had persuaded Larry to scavenge from the hen house.

The sun had moved the imposing shadow of Tall Trees' impressive foursquare frontage around, and as she leant on the gate, Peggy enjoyed the feeling of the sun on her back and the way her favourite green-sprigged cotton dress gently fluttered at her knees as she stood dreamily watching June walk down the road and then turn the corner. Peggy allowed her shoulders to drop as she listened to the boys race noisily around the garden as somebody else – was it Connie? – was giving the back yard a sweep to clear away any stray straw following Milburn's afternoon muck-out.

Nearby, there was a bush that was attracting the bumble bees, and as Peggy listened to the gentle humming of the hard-working bees and watched their furry yellow and black bodies bob this way and that as they harvested the pollen, she wondered briefly whether they should get a beehive at

Tall Trees, or maybe the churchyard might be a more sensible place to position it seeing as there were young babies at the rectory and bee stings could be very nasty, although a crop of honey would be wonderful.

It was a peaceful end to the afternoon, as Holly had had a feed and Gracie had fed Jack too, and so now the babies were top-and-tailed in the perambulator under the shade of a tree in the garden as they napped, with Connie and Angela watching over them with strict instructions to move them if the sun moved and shone directly on them.

It felt good to have a moment to herself. So wonderful in fact that Peggy allowed herself to slip her feet from her shoes and wiggle her toes as she stood barefoot on the warm stones that edged the front of the drive. She refused to think about how worn her sandals were – back in Bermondsey she would *never* have gone out and about in footwear that had so clearly seen better days, and actually they had such stretched leather that they weren't very comfy, but what could she do? and nor would she have dared to be in public with bare legs as that was very frowned upon at home no matter how hot the weather – as she closed her eyes and breathed in the scent of the garden flowers. Then Peggy put her hands on top of the tall wooden gate, which was wedged open as it always was, and slowly she leant backwards, arching her back in a luxurious stretch that took her head far enough back to feel the sun on her eyelids, while she supported her weight with her straightened arms and she kept her hips quite close to the gate. She straightened up and then bent her shoulders first to one side and then the other, after which she circled her head, dipping it down towards each of her shoulders. Peggy's neck cricked slightly and she could hear her shoulders each give a small crack as then she raised them up towards her ears in a circular motion. She was stiff these days, she thought, and no longer the nimble and flexible young woman of previously, and with a small sigh and still keeping her eyes closed she lifted her hands to massage her neck. Okay, she might be feeling older, but Peggy hoped she was wiser too. And she knew a moment or two allowing herself to enjoy such a glorious afternoon was making herself feel, just a little, healed.

Then there was the briefest whiff of a strong floral perfume that had a chemical hint to it.

'I wonder if you might be so good as to point me in the direction of Margaret Delbert?' somebody addressed Peggy in quite posh tones, cutting abruptly through her reverie and the sensation of the scent in her nose. This sounded like a voice belonging to someone very used to getting her own way.

Peggy's eyes flicked open. How cringeworthy. To be discovered enjoying with such abandon what was obviously a private moment felt wrong and as if she had been caught doing something illicit and oddly intimate. And in bare feet too!

Standing before her was a stranger who was appraising her intently. This woman had tightly curled hair as if by a semi-permanent, heavily pencilled eyebrows and ruby-red lips painted on with a dry-looking lipstick. She was wearing an expensive, well-tailored summer dress and her leather brogues were carefully polished and looked practically spanking new, while over her left arm bent across her front she'd slung what looked to be a jacket made out of the same patterned material as her dress. She wore white kid summer gloves on each hand and carried a neat leather handbag in her right hand that looked as if it had been made to partner her shoes, while gold earrings were clipped onto her earlobes and a matching, slightly too ostentatious gold brooch was glinting insistently at Peggy in the sunlight filtering down through the trees beside a décolletage exposed to just, but only just, the right side of propriety for walking around on an ordinary summer's afternoon.

While Peggy wouldn't have described the woman as pretty or sweet-looking, as the overall combination of everything added up to give a well put together and stylish although slightly harsh impression, nevertheless Peggy would have said this person standing before her was incredibly well presented and very possibly affluent, and that she had taken a great deal of care with her appearance.

Peggy had no idea who this woman was, and she was so unused to hearing her own name said in full that, for an instant, Peggy found herself wondering who this Margaret Delbert could be as she hadn't seen anyone around who would answer to that, and wasn't it funny that there was another woman with the same surname as she in this same street?

The woman continued to stare, her eyes slightly narrowing in concentration, and Peggy found herself frowning – this stare was verging on the nosy rather than the curious, and it didn't feel polite in the slightest as the two women stood now openly assessing each other.

And then Peggy's mouth opened in a soft 'O' as she realised that she herself was of course the Margaret Delbert that the woman wanted to speak to.

'Are you looking for me?' she said with a slight hesitation, and then she broke the mutual stare as she looked downwards to fumble herself back into her old sandals that very much needed a polish, without unbuckling the strap, which led to a bit of forcing of each foot inside, so that one shoe's back collapsed under Peggy's heel, although it felt like too much of a loss of face to lean down before this fashionable woman to sort it all out.

'If you are Margaret Delbert, in that case I am indeed looking for you,' said the woman. She sounded curt and determined, and as if she had an agenda that Peggy at that moment could only guess at.

'It's Peggy.'

She wondered briefly if she were dreaming as this unexpected meeting seemed so improbable. She had dreams occasionally that seemed very real and where she would be caught in public without a necessary item of clothing on, usually a hidden item of her underwear, which Barbara had told her were anxiety dreams and not naughty ones, and so it could be that whatever was going on at this moment was a variation of that particular family of worry-dreams.

The woman put her handbag in the hand holding the jacket and removed her glove, and as she stepped forward she spat 'Take that' from between clenched teeth and with her right hand she delivered a hard and stinging slap to Peggy's cheek.

Peggy gasped loudly in shock, and Gracie, who must have been in the garden on the other side of the privet hedge that Peggy was obscured by in order to take a peek at the babies and how well Connie and Angela were looking after them, called out sharply, 'Peggy? What's goin' on?'

The buzzing pain Peggy felt in her jaw – the woman had absolutely thrown her weight into the slap – insisted that the meeting between the women was no peculiar dream, and Peggy felt her cheek immediately flush and redden where the woman had struck her. She hadn't been at all prepared for such a blow and it had forced the top row of her teeth to clash uncomfortably against her lower row, and she had a faint ringing sound in her left ear. She shook her head as if to banish the ring and put a hand to her mouth, but although painful, it didn't feel the sort of pain to signify that any lasting damage had been done.

Peggy felt dumbfounded. To her knowledge she had never seen the woman before, and she had absolutely no idea who she might be.

'How dare you?' the woman said, her head pitched forward and close to Peggy's. 'How *dare* you?' Her tone was low at this point, indeed almost quiet, but it oozed venom and ill will, and the deep pitch of her current tone made the words all the more sinister. The words were expelled with such force that little tiny droplets of spittle were sprayed over Peggy's face and Peggy caught a whiff of sour breath. She couldn't help but lean back a little in the face of this woman's aggression.

'Excuse me,' Peggy tried a bit feebly to rally, 'but I think you are most terribly mistaken. I have no idea who you are or what you could possibly want with me.'

'You are Margaret Delbert, wife of Bill Delbert?' the woman questioned commandingly.

Peggy nodded and then realised with a shudder who this person had to be. How could she have been so dim not to guess immediately? She risked a glance down at the woman's stomach and, sure enough, she could see a rounded bump at the white-belted waist of her dress.

'MaureenFromTheNAAFI,' said Peggy flatly, and then could have kicked herself for addressing Maureen as such, but this derogatory running of the words into one was how she and Barbara had taken to calling her, and it had just slipped out before Peggy could stop it. She didn't like the woman, but this was a rude way to speak to her, no doubt about that, and Peggy didn't consider herself to be a rude person, no matter how provoked.

'My name is Maureen Creasey, or Mrs Maureen Creasey to you,' came the carping reply. 'And before you make any insinuations, I would have you know that I am a widow and a free agent.'

'A pity you weren't so respectful over my husband's position then as you set such store by insinuations, as he wasn't a widower or a free agent,' Peggy replied before she could stop herself. Even though there was past history lurking under the surface that Peggy would have been super-human not be antagonised by, there was something incredibly riling about this woman's imperious attitude that was nothing to do with what she'd been getting up to with Bill, that was just rubbing salt into an already open wound.

Now she was so close, and had turned slightly so that her face and scrawny neck were lit by the sun, Peggy could see that Maureen was significantly older than she, perhaps even as much as forty or perhaps a year or two on top of that. She was bony to the point of emaciation, although her extended belly looked quite large and buoyant. And although her hair had been expertly coloured and primped, when a shaft of bright sunlight fell across it Peggy could see that a significant proportion of it must be grey to judge by the variation showing through the colourant.

Peggy remembered Bill's plaintive 'her hair reminded me of yours', and she felt affronted at being compared with this dry and over-styled hairstyle. Not only was Bill stupid, but he was also clearly blind, she muttered to herself.

Maureen's face had a downy texture to it too, exaggerated by each of these minute hairs being individually coated with a fine face powder. Up close Peggy was struck by the many small crinkles in the skin around her eyes, as well as the sheer depth of the unhappy-seeming lines that fanned out from Maureen's nose towards her lips, and the first signs of nipped-in lines around her current slackly open mouth that were beckoning her lipstick to feather into. Her teeth were large and in good condition, but Peggy couldn't help but stare at them until she could convince herself that Maureen's gnashers were starting to show the yellowing of age right before her eyes.

Peggy felt that she herself had seen better days in the looks department but as she studied Maureen, she couldn't imagine for a moment what her husband had seen in her, or why such a posh woman as she had even been working in the NAAFI at all. She supposed it was to do with how people were volunteering in the war effort. Whatever, in comparison Peggy felt age on her side, which was a nice feeling, and that she personally had a freshness of attitude about her (or at least she hoped she did) that had none of the desperate feeling that Maureen was exud-ing. Bill had described Maureen as fun but this person before Peggy looked as if she would be more at home sucking a lemon than cracking a joke or even saying something nice. But all the same, if Maureen had been the preferred option to herself, for the briefest of seconds Peggy felt as if she could happily lie in front of a bus and end it all, her world seemed so bleak.

Then she reminded herself that she wasn't going to let Bill win, and she had the biggest asset of all: Holly.

'So now we both know who the other is,' said Peggy cautiously, 'I'm still at a loss as to why you have come all this way to see me. Immediately Bill told me about you and your pregnancy I severed all contact with him, which I assumed was all for the best, at least as far as the pair of you were concerned. I presumed you and he were carrying on as you had been doing and that these days you were awaiting your baby together.' It cost Peggy quite a lot to say this, but it was the truth and so she didn't see any point in trying to pretend otherwise.

'If only that were the truth of it. Don't you see? Don't you *see*! I thought it would be so, but Bill tells me all the time now that you are nothing short of a saint, and a wonder, and the best thing he's ever known. I can't compete with that, and now he hardly looks at me,' said Maureen, taking a belligerent step forward, which caused Peggy to step back as she didn't want another slap. 'He moons after you, and tells me I'm half the woman you are, and that I'm dried up and past it.' Maureen's voice was increasingly loud – where had the whispering gone of a few seconds previously? – and it had a note of anguish about it that indicated all too clearly to Peggy the very deep depths of despair that this woman had been plunged into by Bill's lack of commitment. 'It's *not* true that I'm past it, and I want you to tell him to make it right with me.'

For an instant Peggy felt the tiniest twinge of sympathy with Maureen. She clearly was frightened about possibly bringing up her baby alone, and terrified at the thought that Bill hadn't turned out to be the man she had thought he was. Join the club, Peggy thought, but then the full meaning of what

Maureen was really asking her sunk in, and she pushed these thoughts aside for ones much harder and uncaring.

'Excuse me?!' If Peggy had thought she was shocked before, it was nothing to what was growing inside her now. The damn cheek, the sheer bloody gall of this woman to come all the way to Tall Trees expecting to be able to hector Peggy into doing her bidding. Peggy felt herself losing her temper. 'Excuse me!' she repeated, much more loudly than before.

'Peggy, what's goin' on? You don't sound right,' said Gracie from somewhere on the other side of the privet hedge.

But Peggy wasn't listening to Gracie. She took a deep breath and marshalled all her inner strength.

'I think you seem to be forgetting, Mrs Creasey, that it was *my* husband that you had relations with, and so by rights it should be *me* telling you to take a running jump, baby on the way or no. And in fact Bill still *is* my husband, I'll have you know, the lanky streak of, well, you know... It's rich coming from a strumpet like you, telling me how I should be speaking to *my* husband when it was you who couldn't wait to leap into the bed of a married man who had a pregnant wife at home.' Peggy's voice was louder than she intended but somehow she couldn't seem to control it, and she could hear Connie saying to Angela that she was going to get Roger and Mabel.

Gracie had sidled up the drive to the warring women by now and she was standing protectively beside Peggy.

Then Gracie said in the rude and bolshie way that only someone of sixteen years of age can manage, 'What's this rude bint want wi' you, Peggy?'

'Don't you dare speak to me like that, you good-for-nothing little piece of skirt,' screamed Maureen at Gracie, and quick

162

as a whippet, slapped her face too. Maureen was very skilled at face-slapping, it had to be said. Peggy wondered if Bill had also been treated to the odd swipe; it would be poetic justice if he had, and she hoped it was so.

Gracie, who could be a bit uppity at the best of times, made as if she was going to leap at Maureen and do her a mischief, and Peggy had to fling herself at Gracie to put herself between the pair of them, shouting, 'Stop, Gracie, *stop* – the silly woman is expecting a baby!'

Gracie stood still and looked menacingly at Maureen over Peggy's shoulder, while she rubbed her flushing cheek. But before she could inflame the situation further with any inopportune words, Maureen lost control, grabbing Peggy's arm and shaking her as if she were a terrier with a rat, as she began to yell.

'Your husband doesn't want you! He never would have strayed if he'd been happy. You look like you'd be a sack of potatoes between the sheets, and he was grateful for everything I did with him in the bedroom. I taught him things he'd never even heard of, let me tell you, things a woman like you couldn't even dream of, and he was so grateful for it that he kept coming back for more, and then more on top of that. And then you had to go and say to him that your marriage was over, and he couldn't see his daughter, and it killed everything in him with me, and I hate you for that. *Hate* you, do you hear?! He's obsessed with you, and he won't give me the time of day. Bill doesn't know it, but what he wants is *me*!' Maureen shrieked at the top of her voice, summoning the four boys to the gateway.

There was the sound of Roger and Mabel bustling over to

them too, and a mortified Peggy could see several neighbours coming to their own front gates to see what all the fuss was about.

'And I'm having his baby, and what are you going to do about that, Miss Prissy Knickers? Miss Frigid Goody Two Shoes,' Maureen's voice was so loud that nobody could be in any doubt as to what had gone wrong in Peggy's marriage.

Peggy felt humiliated and cut right down to her very quick. She'd believed that she and Bill had enjoyed a mutually satisfying life in the bedroom, but being called a sack of potatoes in such a vicious way beggared that assumption (so publicly too!), and she dreaded to think what Bill might have said to Maureen about the most private areas of their marriage. There was a fleeting instant when Peggy wondered what the things that Maureen had taught Bill might be, and which he'd been so grateful for.

Then Peggy pushed these thoughts aside as she realised that what was even more disturbing about what she had just heard was that Maureen had said Bill still thought of her, and so maybe the personal side of things (between the sheets at least) hadn't been so bad. And in addition, Peggy found herself flooded by more complicated feelings threatening to surface to do with Bill still being sorry that their marriage had floundered. Even the mere suggestion of this made Peggy feel peculiar and as if she shouldn't think about any of it just now – Bill's letters had now dropped off and he'd not telephoned Tall Trees for a while and so she'd assumed he was making the most of his time with MaureenFromTheNAAFI. She hadn't allowed herself to think of how he might have been feeling, she was far too caught up in the mire of her own despondency, but this had probably been (another) mistake as she felt rather as if she had been punched anew in the stomach.

As the people from the other side of the street actually shuffled forward to stand on the pavement to watch the goings-on at the gate to Tall Trees more closely, Peggy's cheeks flushed and she didn't know where to look. It wasn't very becoming behaviour at the entrance to a rectory but she felt powerless to do anything about it.

'Oh, come now, I don't think there's any call for that sort of language,' Roger chipped in before Maureen could launch into her next tirade. 'And I don't think this particular conversation needs to be continued out in the middle of the street any longer, especially in front of the, er, children.'

The children had gathered in the short drive to Tall Trees and all looked disappointed when Roger swiftly held an elbow to walk a now-deflated Maureen hurriedly into Tall Trees and on into his study, as they'd been rather taken by Maureen's salty turn of phrase.

Roger asked Mabel to fetch a glass of water for both Maureen and Peggy, and then he told Maureen to sit down.

The last time Peggy had been in Roger's study was the day of the terrible argument that she had had with Bill, and as she passed through the doorway after Roger and Maureen, she shuddered. Right now it would be fair to say, she thought, that she would strangle Bill if she could get her hands on him. She had believed he had done his worst, but if this afternoon was anything to go by, evidently this wasn't the case.

Once Roger had made sure the two women were settled and didn't look like they were about to scream at each other again, or turn violent, he made himself scarce, shutting the study door firmly and shooing away the boys.

'Tommy!' said Roger, when Tommy didn't leave immediately.

'Pa, we want to see if we can listen through the wall with a glass,' said Tommy. 'We need the practice in case we ever have to spy on anybody. And it's Jessie's idea.'

'I don't care whose idea it was,' said Roger. 'It's over now so go back to the garden.'

Back outside the boys spent quite some time lamenting the loss of an opportunity to hone some real-life musketeer surveillance skills.

Inside the study Peggy and Maureen both seemed at a loss for how to go on.

Peggy sighed, and then listened to the tick-tocking of Roger's grandmother clock until the repetitive sound went a way to calming her.

'How did you get here today, Maureen?' Peggy asked after a while. She could hear the gloomy cast to her voice, and she wondered if Maureen could notice it also. 'And how did you know where to find me?'

'That was easy – I bribed somebody on the camp who hands out the post to let me know your address as Bill had let slip you were sending his letters back unopened,' said Maureen wearily. 'And then I just had to look up the train times, and I walked from the station as everyone seems to know about the clergyman who's taken in a host of evacuees.'

'What I don't understand is what it is that you really want from me?' Peggy took a sip from her own glass of water. She couldn't imagine humiliating herself by travelling to a strange place just to have a showdown with another woman, no matter what a man had done to her. But maybe Maureen's depth of passion was an indication of how much she, Maureen, cared for Bill; and could it be that Peggy's inability to think of herself ever acting similarly was in fact a sign that deep down she had always known that she wasn't in a perfect marriage? Peggy didn't know, but she guessed she would be mulling all this over at length once she had got rid of Maureen.

Maureen had taken off the second of her gloves and was now anxiously twisting and pulling the pale kid pair this way and that.

'Have you any other children, Maureen?'

Maureen shook her head, and Peggy realised how very pale she was looking. The foetus would be taking what sustenance it needed from Maureen, but Peggy thought she'd very likely have been in too much of a state to make sure she'd had enough to eat or drink while on the way to Harrogate, and this wouldn't be good for mother or baby. 'You look as if you need to refuel. Have a drink, and I'll see if there's anything left in the kitchen,' she heard herself saying.

Maureen reached for her glass of water, and Peggy got up to see what was in the kitchen. But as she opened the study door it was to find Mabel just about to knock as she had thought ahead and was carrying a couple of tinned pilchards on a slice of bread and butter, and a knife and fork, ready for Maureen.

This was why Peggy loved being at Tall Trees so much; it wasn't perfect by any means; it was noisy, the sleeping arrangements were a bit sardine-like and it was a squeeze cramming everybody around the kitchen table at mealtimes, but somebody was always looking out for somebody else, and this made the best of even totally horrible situations.

Peggy smiled her thank-you to Mabel, and was told in a whisper in return that Roger was tacking up Milburn and he would drive Maureen to the station in the trap. The next train out of Harrogate went in just over half an hour.

'I can't eat that!' Maureen was looking down her nose at the pilchards, and Peggy's shoulders tensed as Maureen still had that really annoying and grating tinge to her voice.

Peggy felt affronted on Mabel's behalf – it was a modest meal, but it was what everyone at Tall Trees had been quite happy to eat for tea. She gave an audible sigh of displeasure.

'Well, I think your baby is telling you to finish it up, whether you want it or not. And you've a fair way to go home tonight, so I suggest you tuck in now as you might not be able to get anything on the way back,' said Peggy peevishly, hearing her own exasperation in her voice.

Maureen pulled off a dainty corner of the bread and butter, and chewed it in an extremely picky manner.

There was a soft knock at the door and Mabel interrupted with two cups of tea, and by the time Peggy looked at Maureen's plate again, half of the food had already been scoffed, as Maureen was clearly starving and she was now tucking in like a proper trencherman. Peggy didn't like anything about the woman, but she couldn't have lived with herself if she hadn't looked after her properly when there was a baby on the way, as it wasn't the baby's fault that his or her mother was so irritating, although it was an inescapable fact that Maureen was a very, very irritating woman indeed.

Peggy waited until Maureen had finished and was reaching for her tea, and then she said reasonably, 'I don't think there is anything I can do to help you, Mrs Creasey. I'm sure Bill will come around when your baby is here and he can touch him or her, but you must realise that I really can't bear to have any contact myself with him just now. And I think if I did say anything directly to him just at the moment, then there's a possibility he might feel then that he's in with a chance with me, which he isn't, or to be more exact I don't think he is, although I'd be less than honest not to admit it does give me a pang to hear about him wanting us to be a family again, and I realise that now I've had time to think about it carefully I see increasingly quite what a large step divorce is for someone like me, and how costly it could be in terms of fees. I have to remember that Bill is Holly's father, after all, and that I mustn't do anything to hurt Holly's future. It's all very complicated, and anyway the immediate point is that Bill wouldn't understand if I told him you had been to see me and so the upshot could well be in that case it would make things worse for you. Ultimately I think you have to look after yourself and your own interests, and to sit tight, trusting in him wanting this baby at some point, or at least hoping that he will do when he sees it.'

All of Maureen's fight had dissipated and she looked deflated and tormented. When Peggy saw how diminished the older woman looked at that particular moment it was an image that was hard to square with the furious harridan who'd attacked her outside the gate at the end of the drive.

Nobody said anything for a while.

Then Maureen asked quietly, 'What was it like?'

Peggy looked confused before she realised what the other woman meant.

'The birth. Was it painful? I didn't think I'd have to go through it on my own.' Maureen sounded scared and alone.

'Neither did I,' said Peggy, who found herself softening a tiny bit towards Maureen. 'And yet I managed, and I'm sure you will too. I was poorly right before the birth, and so I can't remember very much about the actual birth itself, I'm afraid. But the moment I saw Holly I do remember that it all seemed worth it, although sometimes even months later I would find myself feeling blue and out of sorts. And when I found out about Bill and you, I knew I would never be without Holly, not for a single instant, even though I dare say it will be difficult to bring her up on my own. I'm sure that when you hold your own baby you'll feel the same sense of love and purpose, whether you have Bill at your side or not.'

Maureen looked back at Peggy with an expression that was almost impossible to read, and then she pursed her lips and reached for her handbag to get out her compact and lipstick to make herself presentable again.

Roger put his head around the door and said, 'Ladies, are you ready?' And with no real conclusion to what had gone on between them, Maureen and Peggy both stood up with uncertain expressions.

Maureen gave Peggy the briefest nod of acknowledegment as she passed her to go with Roger, and Peggy gave an equally small nod back. Then she experienced a stab of frustration with herself for even acknowledging the woman who had caused so much heartbreak over the past couple of months. And then Peggy felt even more frustrated with herself for being cross about giving Maureen the very tiniest of nods. She was a bigger person than that, surely, she admonished herself, and to not have done so back would have been diminishing and a sign of a wanting nature, wouldn't it? Peggy thought about it, and she couldn't decide.

Goodness, and damn and drat, Maureen had gone away although her distinctive and now headache-inducing overly flowery scent lingered, and yet here she was *still* spoiling Peggy's evening.

As Roger and Maureen drove out of Tall Trees, Peggy went to find Holly. Her head was aching with the effort of it all, and so she felt very much in need of a cuddle with her own dear baby.

Chapter Seventeen

Understandably Ted didn't find Jessie's letter to him about wanting help with fighting techniques very reassuring to receive, and he and Barbara couldn't quite decide about the best way of handling this. It was very rare for Jessie to ask for anything, as he was naturally quite a reserved and shy boy, and as he had been badly bullied when he was at the Bermondsey school, anything that would help give him a bit of confidence might be good. It sounded as if something had most definitely spooked Jessie, and that it was probable that the 'something' wasn't very good, and so neither Ted nor Barbara wanted Jessie to worry himself into believing that dealing with something by fists was necessarily the right or indeed the most appropriate first course of action.

One thing they did agree on though (well, Barbara did the agreeing, and more or less told Ted what he should be thinking) was that Jessie's spelling was coming on. While his letter was by no means perfect in the grammatical sense and there were some spelling mistakes, nevertheless it was a vast improvement to the letters he'd written before Christmas.

Ted had never enjoyed his lessons when he was a lad and he'd been proud to be a docker, following his father and big brother Jessie (the family tradition being that in each generation the oldest Ross boy was called Jessie) into the trade. While Ted had never wanted for more than to wake up each morning in the grubby narrow streets of Bermondsey and, when the wind was in the right direction, the wafting smells from the Peek Frean biscuit factory nearby that would drift over Jubilee Street, he now wondered if he'd be the last Ross to feel like this. During reflective moments watching the refuse barges navigate the Thames on the way to dump the city's waste in deeper waters, he would sometimes look down at his own work-worn hands and feel the ache in his shoulders from pulling chests and crates this way and that, and find it impossible to imagine Jessie following in his own footsteps on to the docks, or Connie being happy with working for somebody else like her mother did.

Indeed on their last visit to Yorkshire, Barbara and Ted had noticed how much time Roger and Mabel spent encouraging all the children to read. Jessie mentioned Peggy and Mabel had even taken the children to see a play one afternoon – it had been an amateur dramatic musical that one of Roger's parishioners had written, and although not very good, the children had enjoyed it (a lot more than Mabel and Peggy had, Mabel had whispered later to Barbara), and on another day there had been an outing to a museum that had an exhibition of bones that Roger had told the boys about.

Ted and Barbara often talked of the twins when hard at work on their allotment near Jubilee Street. The government was encouraging every square inch to be used for growing vegetables, and so six plots had been squeezed in following the demolition of a couple of stables – harking back to when there were more dray horses in the area – to allow the exposed earth to be dug over for planting up. Several months later the summer crops were verging on the bumper, which Ted said must be down to years and years of manure being piled up when the stables had been cleaned out,

As they hoed and weeded, Barbara and Ted talked over the quite different problems the children presented, Connie being too inattentive at school and too bold, and Jessie looking set to be something of a cuckoo in the nest, bookish and a deep thinker.

'I find it hard to credit them as ours,' said Barbara. 'Connie's so knowing, and I don't know where Jessie gets half his ideas from. He spent a good quarter of an hour when you were talking to Connie, telling me about codes and secret messages, and how they can be sent. It all sounded very clever.'

Ted didn't say anything, although he nodded. He'd expected the twins to turn out to be quite like him and Barbara, and that they would go on to live similar lives. But the war was altering things, he could see, and now none of that could be taken for granted.

'It's so difficult when we don't know what's going on,' Barbara continued as she pulled up some potatoes. 'I don't like that letter Jessie wrote. And I miss them, frankly.' There was a pause, before she added, 'Are you sure we shouldn't bring them home, Ted? Lots are, you see.'

Her husband stopped what he was doing and leant his elbows on his spade. 'I know, Barbara, I know,' he said gently. 'But we've been through this, an' jus' think what you'd feel if we brought 'em back and then the bombs come.'

'You're right, but at this rate they'll be all grown up before we're all together.' Barbara sighed with petulance, and then ground a cabbage-hungry caterpillar deep into the sod with her heel.

Ted nodded morosely with eyes that were just a bit too bright, and then he said, 'Why don't you go home, love, and 'ave a bit of a rest? You look done in.'

Back at Jubilee Street, Barbara allowed herself a cry, which wasn't at all like her, although she had to acknowledge that afterwards she felt more composed.

When evening opening hours came around, she put on her headscarf and headed to the Jolly to make a long-distance call to Tall Trees to see if she could find out a little bit more about what was going on. The plan she had discussed with Ted was that once she had scoped out the lay of the land, then Ted would write back to Jessie, seeming to keep it strictly a manly conversation between father and son.

Roger picked up the telephone, and told Barbara that he had no idea why Jessie had written this letter as he'd not noticed anything especially untoward, although Mabel had commented earlier that morning that she thought the children had in general seemed a little preoccupied. He added that he didn't think it was anything too much to worry about though, but he and Mabel would keep an eye on things, and he'd have a word with Peggy too to see if she were aware of anything that they didn't know about. If he didn't get back to her, then Barbara was to assume it was business as usual and that as far as anyone could tell, everything was all right.

'Actually I've just had an idea about something else that could help, but leave it with me, Barbara, as it might not come off,' Roger added as the conversation was coming to a close.

'But don't you worry about anything in the meantime. It's all under control here, and I'll let you know toot sweet if not.'

Jessie was less convinced than Roger about things being under control, however, as in the wee small hours of the night he'd started waking suddenly, with his heart beating furiously and with an ominous sense of dread sweeping over him. He'd tried telling himself that this crippling sense of fear was a bit irrational as the Hull lads seemed to have slithered back into their hole as neither hide nor hair of them had been seen since that time they had stood in silence sending the unmistakeable 'fucker' message to the Tall Trees boys that a fight wasn't going to be far off.

As battle tactics go, Jessie recognised, the major spear-rattling and then a long period of nothing either good or bad happening, was almost definitely more unnerving than if an ambush had been laid for the very next day, or there had been a physically aggressive-seeming and immediate blatant call to arms. This was because the period of waiting allowed one's imagination to work overtime, and Jessie found it very disturbing the longer the period of waiting lasted.

It struck him early one morning when he'd not been able to get back to sleep after waking with a start when it was still dark, that it was a little like the Phoney War the journalists were sometimes talking about and that Roger, Mabel and Peggy were often to be found discussing after their tea; once hostilities with Germany had been declared the previous September, other than a lot of men leaving to fight, and their own experience of being evacuated from London to Yorkshire, it was true that Hitler didn't immediately attack Britain, and so wartime life had quite soon gone on with a new sense of normality, a normality made twitchy with everyone being jumpy, waiting for something to happen. As far as the children were concerned the Hull boys had issued a challenge, but then done nothing further, and Jessie thought this might be worse than if they'd set a trap the very next day.

Tommy must have felt similarly as he suggested the boys hold a powwow in their bedroom at Tall Trees to discuss what they should do.

Larry and Jessie kicked all the clothes and towels on the floor aside, and the snakes and ladders, the Happy Families cards, and the try-outs for the latest code Jessie was working on, and then they all sat cross-legged in a square on the floor. Dusk was drawing in and so the boys used their torches to light the room, casting long shadows onto the unmade bunk beds and the blackout curtains.

After Larry had held the torch upwards under his chin and made the obligatory 'oooooh' ghost noises, Aiden gave a signal for quiet by miming his throat being cut, and then Larry reminded everyone they must remember their musketeer pledge of 'all for one and one for all'.

First of all, they decided, it would be good for morale to call themselves a name, and eventually they voted in Larry's suggestion of dubbing themselves the TT Muskets, the TT standing for Tall Trees and the Musket bit having the advantage of being both a gun and a shortening of their musketeer bonding.

On a piece of lined paper they'd scavenged from Roger's office and later tacked to the inside of the door to the cupboard where they kept their shoes and clothes, they listed then what Aiden called the 'debits' and 'credits' of the situation. Jessie couldn't help but smirk at Aiden sounding so grown up, but Tommy and Larry both had to be talked through what Aiden meant, and Jessie had to be most careful to explain the debits and credits in such a way that neither boy was left feeling stupid.

The debits were easy.

Jessie ticked each debit off on a finger as he said, 'There are more Hull lads than TT Muskets; they're bigger; they look used to a scrap; an' they look as if their fathers know how to make their fists do the talking…' Jessie shut up abruptly when he caught a look of Larry's perturbed face and he realised he'd strayed onto territory that Larry was all too familiar with.

Aiden raced to Jessie's aid. 'They look as if they're used to doin' things together – I bet this sort of silly act was first begun back in 'ull before they were even evacuees.'

'Pa and Ma, and Peggy too'll larrup us to Leeds an' back if they catch us squarin' up,' Tommy said reflectively, and Jessie ticked this off as a debit too.

'An' we'll be sitting targets on the paper-collection days,' said Larry, 'specially as we've told everyone where we'll be.'

'Yikes, that's true,' admitted Aiden. 'We'd best talk of our credits to cheer ourselves up.'

The credits took more thinking about, but eventually they managed to come up with some:

Jessie: The TT Muskets had the advantage of living
           together, which meant:

1. Ease of careful strategising and planning (and if necessary re-planning things, should the situation suddenly change), and

2. There was little danger of one TT Musket being caught on his own without the others. In theory there would at least be a little safety in numbers.

Larry: While every one of the TT Muskets was smaller than their Hull adversaries, being small might have advantages such as nippiness, as they could be in and out of an attack very quickly, and they'd be good at hiding, i.e. doing a stake-out, as they could squeeze into tiny and unobtrusive places to watch what was going on unseen.

Jessie: Tommy and Aiden had been born in Harrogate and therefore would know the lie of the land better – the Hull boys didn't seem to have anyone from Harrogate in their gang that they had made friends with.

Tommy: The TT Muskets had Milburn, and a pony had to count for something.

Larry: They could practise their own routine of moves.

Tommy summed it up by pointing out that none of the Hull lads would be as clever as either Jessie or Aiden. 'Beef usually beats brains, but the 'Ull lot don't know yous. But yers goin' ter need a gud plan…'

Jessie looked around at his pals. It needed to be a very good plan indeed, he concluded.

A week or more later, after the boys had been trying to come up (not very successfully, it had to be said) with their own routine for when they next saw the Hull boys), there was an argument over whether it was time that they should include the girls as honorary members of the TT Muskets – Tommy claimed girls were better at country dancing and maypoles, and so were used to this sort of thing – but all the boys were surprised when the motion was carried unanimously that they stay boys-only for now.

Rather to everyone's surprise, Jessie had probably swung it in the boys' favour by pointing out that, although Connie was incredibly suspicious about what they were up to and undoubtedly would be most cross not to have been included, it was an unavoidable fact that Angela wasn't going to be able to join in, given her wheelchair, and so it was only fair that Connie be allowed to spend time with her and not feel guilty that she wasn't with the boys.

Jessie was pretty sure that Connie might not see it like that at all, as she always baulked at the notion of 'boys' things' and 'girls' things', and he was in no doubt that her nose would be severely out of joint when she discovered what was going on, even though she was very fond of spending time with Angela. But he didn't want to go into all this with the others as it might make Connie lose face with them, although privately he thought her a little too hot-headed to be relied on in any tense or dangerous situation that they might be going to face. And while he didn't want to embarrass his sister by suggesting this, Jessie could see it being disastrous if Connie said something silly in a moment of temper and the TT Muskets had to look after her and concentrate their efforts that way, rather than putting everything they had into taking on the Hull lot. And, Jessie knew, neither Ted nor Barbara would approve of him being in a gang, added to which they *really* wouldn't like it if Connie were also a member, as both of them believed in 'boys' things' and 'girl's' things, and girls in gangs wasn't one of them.

Contenting himself to exhaling through vibrating lips, as Jessie said 'No girls', he tried not to think too much about Connie's wrath that would surely be directed at him at some point, as it probably wasn't going to be a pleasant few minutes.

Tommy nodded approval as he didn't like to think of Angela being exposed to danger, and Larry seemed to think no girls was a good idea too. While not obviously quite agreeing or disagreeing, Aiden (who was probably weighing up mostly the pros and cons of getting on the wrong side of Connie) had just opened his mouth to say something when Gracie tapped at their bedroom door to say that they were wanted by Mabel.

They raced downstairs with Larry shouting 'motion carried' and Aiden replying only a little grudgingly 'oh, all right then', and when they went into the kitchen Mabel was making pastry at the table and she gave a nod of her head towards Milburn's stable across the yard.

There, a surprise was waiting.

James was showing Connie how to tack Milburn up with a proper riding bridle, complete with a shiny bit and plaited webbing reins of the right length for riding, and a pony saddle. Both bridle and saddle looked as if they had seen better days, and the saddle, rather than being a leather saddle with sprung tree, was instead a rather moth-eaten thick felt pad with a leather bit sewn to the front on to which the stirrup leathers were attached, as well as the straps which the webbing girth buckled to. The stirrups were rusty in parts, and the saddle was thickly embedded with grey hairs from the back of the previous owner, but to all the children both it and the bridle seemed like manna from heaven, and they all shared a moment of grinning at each other.

'Hello, lads,' said James. 'I couldn't bear the wait for one of you to come to me with a broken arm or worse through riding bareback, and so I asked my patients if they had anything at home that would do for you to ride Milburn a bit more safely, and when Private Smith's parents came to see me, this is what they brought with them. You'll be pleased to know Connie is stealing a march on you with the tacking up, and so she'll be able to teach you how to do it.'

The last sentence had a deliberate tinge of irony to it, but seeing how Connie had just been voted off the TT Muskets membership roll, tactfully the boys let her get away with thinking they were happy that she really could instruct them.

'I've only just been able to do up the bit that keeps the saddle on, the girth I think it's called,' said Connie, who, aside from looking a bit quizzical at her pals for their lack of ribbing her, was a bit hot in the cheeks as she had been engaged in a manful tussle with the size of Milburn's tummy and quite a short girth. 'They puff themselves up when you are trying to tighten it, and she's a bit too fat, James says, well, a lot too fat actually. We need to cut her food back a little, and remember to check the saddle is on properly before we ride as Milburn will have let her breath out by then which might make the saddle slip around. If it's tight but we can just get three fingers under the girth, then it is done up properly. And we need to put the front of the saddle about a hand's width behind where her mane ends.'

'Well remembered, Connie, very good,' said James, 'now, who's for the first ride?'

Tommy went first and they headed to a patch of rough ground up the road and James, who had done quite a lot of riding as a child, called out instructions. The saddle and bridle made it much easier, and when it was his turn Jessie was able in just a few minutes to master rising and falling to the trot, and even had a short canter, while everyone else showed an immediate improvement from their bareback riding.

Milburn was very stoic about the children all taking it in turns, and although now and again she would dip her nose to the ground to grab a sly mouthful of grass, she stood there patiently while James taught each of them how to mount properly with a foot in the stirrup, and then to adjust the stirrup leathers either longer or shorter.

After they had all ridden and Connie had moaned about not having any shorts to ride in, not that anyone paid her much attention which put rather a grumpy look on her face, James turned to Angela and asked if she wanted a go.

'Can I? Oh might I? Oh *please*!' she said, clearly excited. James lifted her straight from the wheelchair onto Milburn and then he led her about. Milburn seemed to understand that she had a very precious cargo on board, and so she walked very smoothly and obediently.

'You've learnt what people say to Milburn when they are driving her, Angela, and so you could try that as you don't have enough movement in your legs to use them to control her. We'll make you a neck strap to hold on to, but I think that as long as you stay in walk you'll both do very well,' said James, as he quietly let go of the bridle and stood back so that

183

Angela was riding the pony under her own steam with the biggest grin on her face imaginable, the other children raising their hands in a silent air-punch of celebration.

Back at Tall Trees Milburn was given some carrot tops as a reward, and then James skulked around in the kitchen talking to Roger until Peggy came downstairs from having put Holly down for the night. Roger had had to hang about talking to James even though he'd really been itching to go into the parlour to put his feet up for a while as he listened to the wireless, but he was too polite to say so (plus Mabel had given him The Look which he translated as meaning that he was to keep the doctor talking), so the minute Peggy walked into the kitchen Roger made his escape.

It was Peggy's turn for concocting something that could be popped into the oven at lunchtime tomorrow and so she and James chatted about this and that as she parboiled potatoes and then sliced them into a huge greased baking tray, adding some fried pieces of crumbled sausage and an onion, and then she covered it with two damp tea towels and placed it on a marble slab in the cool walk-in larder, telling James that in the morning she'd add milk and some breadcrumbs as a crust that she would dot with margarine, and then it could be baked.

Peggy started on the washing-up, and James got up from where he was sitting and picked up a tea towel so that he could dry the pans and cutlery that Peggy had just washed and placed on the wooden drying rack. Then she put everything tidily away, the kitchen at Tall Trees now having much more organised cupboards and drawers than when Peggy had first arrived in Harrogate.

'Would you like a cup of tea?' she asked. 'I'll make some for everybody.'

Everybody else seemed to be gathered in the parlour now, ready to listen to the BBC news, but Peggy discovered that she'd rather sit in the kitchen chatting with James as they drank their tea.

At one point Connie popped into the kitchen to give the doctor a thank-you letter she had just made to say how pleased they all were, now that they had the saddle and bridle for Milburn.

'It's my pleasure,' said James, and then he patiently answered Connie's questions about the technicalities of Private Smith's artificial legs and the operation that had removed his injured ones. Connie nodded seriously when he had finished and went to find the other children.

James shook his head and smiled at Connie's retreating back and at her rather good likeness of Milburn in her new saddle and bridle that adorned the top of the page, but then Peggy saw his brow wrinkle when he began to read the thank-you note and was confronted with the poor state of Connie's writing and her terrible spelling, all of which was squished towards one corner of the small piece of paper.

'We just can't understand it,' said Peggy. 'She's as bright as a button, yet the schoolwork lags far behind, I'm afraid. It's quite another story with Jessie, but then it always has been as he's found schoolwork much easier – for him it's like a duck taking to water.'

'I wonder whether Connie needs to find something where her

attention is really captured,' said James. 'Private Smith was very impressed at her interest in what happened to him when he was taken to hospital and the intelligent questions she asked, and she was as quick as anything learning how to put the saddle on Milburn. Those things she asked just now, well, in fact I wouldn't be exaggerating to say that I've worked with doctors in training who haven't asked such intelligent questions.'

'Yes, she was the same when I was in hospital,' said Peggy, 'and once Holly and I were well enough to come home – all thanks to you, James – she then grilled me lots about feeding the baby and nappy-changing. And she's been very useful helping me with Holly as you only have to explain something to her once and she's got it, and she's been the best of all of them in the practical sense when helping Mabel with Angela. To be honest, I think Connie has really encouraged Angela to come out of herself as she just doesn't seem to see that the wheelchair may give Angela problems in any way.'

'Perhaps a career in nursing beckons for Connie – if this war drags on, I think we'll be taking them younger and younger. That reminds me, Peggy – I put Angela up on the pony earlier, and I think if she takes to riding and Milburn seems safe, then that might give Angela a sense of proper independence and will mean that she can go out and about a bit more,' said James. 'I don't know what you think about this idea, but on the days the girls are riding it might be a good idea to let Connie and Angela wear old pairs of the boys' shorts, as that's going to be a bit more dignified than them riding in their dresses.'

Peggy smiled at him and then shocked herself by saying completely out of the blue, 'Well, what a good idea, James, about Angela riding Milburn, I mean, although the shorts idea is probably sensible too. I'm sure being able to ride the pony under her own steam will mean the world to Angela, as long as you are sure that Milburn seems safe, or at least as safe as ponies ever are. And if we were in a public house right now, I would treat you to a drink for being so thoughtful about sorting out the saddle and bridle for the pony. In fact I probably should treat you to a drink or two sometime anyway as you've done such a lot for us evacuees.'

Up until that moment the conversation had flowed pleasantly and very naturally between Peggy and James, with their awkwardness of the afternoon at the first-aid demonstration forgotten. But Peggy had unintentionally overstepped and blundered across an invisible line of propriety – bang! – and suddenly they were back to where they had been that day, with them each feeling embarrassed and unable to think of anything to say.

And once her words had sunk in, both James and Peggy went a little hot and bothered at the boldness of what she had actually said.

Peggy couldn't think what had come over her as she always liked to think she thought first and spoke after. She supposed the reason for her unlikely impetuousness was that she was still all over the place following Bill's bombshell about Maureen and the hideous shock visit from the dratted woman. And now within only a matter of weeks following Bill's confession to his lack of fidelity on the telephone, when Peggy had screamed about his inability to remain true, here she was almost flirting with the doctor. Oh bother, maybe she spoke first and thought second, after all, Peggy had to acknowledge.

James wasn't any better either, his uncomfortable expression seemed to flag, as simultaneously he and Peggy remembered that she had been his patient, and weren't there rules about that sort of thing? Neither seemed quite sure of the exact technicalities of this, but still it all felt very tricky.

After a pause that was too long to feel anything other than clumsy and uncomfortable, James jumped up and announced as firmly as he could, given that his voice had a nervous tremble, that it was high time for him to go as he needed to get back to the hospital to make sure that the evening rounds were going off without any drama.

Although Peggy said hastily, 'Of course, yes you must, we've been monopolising far too much of your time here when you've been so kind to the children,' nevertheless her tummy did a little lurch of disappointment as he picked up his hat and strode swiftly towards the back door.

James opened it and then turned to her with an expression that could now only be described as self-consciousness giving way to something verging on the coy. 'I might just hold you to that promise, Peggy,' he said with a sudden twinkle in his eye and an uncharacteristically raised eyebrow.

Had they both taken leave of their senses, Peggy wondered, but she didn't need to think of a retort because James hurried off before he could see Peggy's deep blush of confusion and her hand reach to her chest to fiddle with the front of her pretty cotton blouse that had been made from the leftover material that Barbara had brought to Harrogate for Connie's dress, and which Peggy had changed into after putting Holly in her crib when she realised the young doctor was still somewhere downstairs after being out with the children and the pony.

Chapter Eighteen

Roger and Ted had been in touch once more over the letter that Ted had been sent by Jessie. Roger had thought for a while after Ted had read it out and then he said that many people would be feeling anxious as regards their personal safety these days, as he had noticed a creeping anxiety growing in the minds of some of his parishioners. He added that it was hard not to when the papers talked constantly these days of unpleasant things happening to ordinary people in Europe and further afield, with the implication that Jerry might invade, or hidden away at the bottom of the middle pages of the newspapers in an attempt to keep public morale as high as possible, that some hooligans were taking advantage of the blackout.

Ted agreed, and the upshot of the conversation was that a few weeks later a series of self-protection classes were going to be run at the church hall, which would overlap with both the advice the police were giving the general public because of the rising crime rates, and also what the Home Guard were doing in case Jerry invaded.

Roger had popped into the local police station and, as he suspected might have happened to judge by what he was hearing when he was out and about on church business, there had been an (some would say) inevitable rise in petty crime during the blackout, with burglaries and thefts up and rather too many people having had purses and wallets snatched in the dark, or worse. There had also been a rise in traffic offences and accidents as driving in the blackout was fraught with problems, especially as road signs and place names had been taken down to make things as difficult as possible for Jerry should there be an invasion, and so if somebody wasn't sure where they were or where they had to be, there was lots of room for error, both from drivers and pedestrians.

In short, there was an uneasy sense of distrust and cautiousness growing in the town, and this had translated to some women and the elderly feeling wary about leaving their homes at night. So although privately Roger felt there wasn't really much that could be done to deter someone who was clearly out for causing trouble, he was going to host a series of what would hopefully be reassuring meetings on how to look after oneself and one's property for anyone, grown-ups or children, who wanted to go. He hoped that would make people feel a little more active and in control of their own destinies, rather than them being stuck just waiting for something nasty to happen.

A PC Danders had been volunteered by the local police station, and he would offer some advice; and James said he was sure that one of his recuperating servicemen would be happy to help as well, which was indeed the case, in addition to the offer of running some elementary boxing lessons for boys.

A day or two later Peggy was talking about it to June Blenkinsop, who replied, 'You know my father was an ex pat in the Far East where, aside from his export business, he studied martial arts, so I can rope him in to demonstrate some moves.'

Peggy immediately imagined the extravagantly moustachioed and very proper gent who she knew from taking his money when he visited the café and who proudly had what could only be described as a military bearing, demonstrating a few karate moves. It sprouted such an incongruous image of dear Horace in Peggy's head that she had to quickly smother a rising chuckle in case June would be offended, although not before Peggy spied a look on June's face that suggested she had been struck by the same thought.

Jessie and the other boys perked up a bit when Mabel mentioned the classes to them one morning over breakfast. There had still been no sign of the Hull gang, although the children from Tall Trees had been sticking close to home when playing, and had mostly been practising their riding on the nearby patch of waste ground where James had schooled them. What had also helped them was that Milburn's food had been cut drastically in order to slim her down a little, and so she wasn't being grazed as much in hand. A vote had been taken about the newspaper collection, and they had decided to go ahead with it with the proviso that at the first sight of trouble they could, if they so wanted, knock the collection round on the head.

The boys had felt very concerned the day of the first collection round, a feeling which they tried very hard to hide from the girls, who they had still not mentioned the animosity of the bigger Hull evacuees to. Connie twigged something was up but, despite grilling both Jessie and Aiden, she had to content herself with sulking and then pointedly talking only to Angela when she couldn't get to the bottom of why the boys seemed so serious and wrapped up in each other. The round had, however, gone off without a hitch, and as time passed over the next few weeks and there was still no sighting of the Hull lads, the TT Muskets gradually began to relax.

In the evenings the children were kept busy cutting out and then sewing the cloth bags that James wanted for his patients at the hospital so that they had something to keep their bits and pieces in, as the TT Muskets were determined that one of their members would win the prize for the highest number of cloth bags made and donated to hospital. Connie and Angela were eyeing up the trophy for themselves too, and so there was a lot of friendly joshing and banter as the children cut out and stitched, and as Peggy commented to Gracie, quite a prodigious output, before realising by Gracie's blank face that she had no idea what prodigious meant, and so Peggy quickly said, 'They've made a large number,' to which Gracie nodded gratefully.

Gracie was now volunteering in the evenings at a third depot that was quite near both the paper-collecting and the scrap-metal depot, although the one that Gracie helped out at was mainly used in the packaging of weapons for sending abroad to the troops. Some of the new guns – usually Webley or Enfield pistols, although sometimes there were Lee-Enfield rifles or Thomson submachine guns to deal with, and once even Sten guns – arrived with a hardened amber waxy surface on their metal parts as protection in transit from the factory. Gracie's job was to scrape this off gently with a piece of wood to prevent scratching or denting the metal as far as possible, and then she had to polish the weapons with an oily cloth ready for them to be packed into new crates for shipping abroad. She said it was very hard work as the wax was difficult to budge, especially around the tricky bits where there were more fiddly crevices to dig it out from, and that it played havoc with one's hands. But Gracie also claimed it to be good fun more often than not, and that the other lasses there were full of life and cheekiness, and so Peggy thought she was enjoying her time at the depot, rough hands or no.

All in all, life felt pretty much in a pleasant enough routine at Tall Trees for now.

For everyone except for Peggy, that was, who realised she was the most unsettled one of the bunch. In fact she still felt out of sorts and, as Mabel described it, mardy. The brief excitement of almost suggesting – or was she imbuing what she had actually said with too much meaning? – as bold as brass to James that it wasn't beyond the realms of possibility that they could, at some unspecified time in the future, share a drink in a public house hadn't lasted long, and if she thought about what she had said now, she would berate herself for being so forward.

The result was that most days, Peggy found herself feeling in the doldrums and she realised that although she enjoyed helping June with the till and the cashing-up at the teashop, she felt a bit bored.

Lurking just below the surface as she went about her day-to-day life, Peggy found herself totally unable to shake off a depressing sense of failure about the end of her marriage, feelings intensified by the thoughts she'd had of all persuasions since Maureen's visit. More than once Mabel caught her sitting at the kitchen table quite late at night, with Holly sound asleep in her arms, and with Peggy staring morosely at a cup of tea that had gone cold and unappetising without Peggy once having raised it to her lips to take a sip.

Peggy had thought deeply about whether she should make a move to instigate a more formal end to her marriage, although every time she considered even talking to someone like Roger as to how she might go about this – as she knew he must have had experience of discussing this sort of situation with his other parishioners – she felt overcome with such a wave of exhaustion that she couldn't face it, at which point she would then tell herself she would think about it again, and tackle it another day.

Once, when Peggy was the only adult in the house, she had had to answer the telephone, which she had completely avoided using since the day of the terrible discussion with Bill. She felt queasy and breathless as she walked into Roger's study where the ring was clanging insistently, as she knew she had to pick up the receiver in case it was someone ringing for Roger with an emergency for which he would be needed. Sometimes a parishioner would call with the distressing news that a family member was close to death, and Peggy would never have forgiven herself if she hadn't stepped up to the plate when somebody else was having a much more traumatic time than she, even though there had been a discombobulating instant when she had contemplated pretending that she hadn't heard the ring of the telephone.

Luckily though, as she reached for the handset with a sense of dread and trepidation, this quickly gave way to a feeling of relief that flooded through her when she discovered after her greeting of 'Tall Trees Rectory' that it was Barbara who had telephoned.

'I thought I'd make a telephone call to give you a surprise,' her sister told her.

'For a terrible moment I thought I was going to be picking up the receiver to find Bill on the end of the line,' said Peggy. 'And so I can't tell you how happy I am that it's you! But nothing bad has happened, has it, as it's not like you to telephone? The children are out with the pony at the moment, but they'll be sorry to have missed you.'

'No, no, nothing out of the ordinary is going on here. All penny-pinching and making-do, and trying to get used to the rationing, but that will be the same with you up there, and so that's not really news, is it? And I've now got only the one pair of stockings left that aren't darned to pieces. I've just posted long letters to the children, and so you can say that although I'm sorry I've missed them, I'm sending love and they'll get my letters soon.'

'That reminds me, Barbara – James Legard read some of Connie's writing the other day, and I could see he was shocked at what he saw. Now that school has broken for the summer it's probably not worth bothering her too much, but they'll be up at the big school next term, and so I think our Connie is going to have to try a lot harder there,' said Peggy.

Barbara signalled her agreement with a heartfelt sigh, and the sisters talked for a while about 'the conundrum of Connie', as they called it, but as usual when they spoke on this subject they weren't able to draw any conclusions. Then Barbara quizzed Peggy about Milburn and whether she seemed safe for the children to spend so much time with, seeing as both Connie and Jessie had mentioned her often in their letters home.

Peggy said she didn't want to tempt fate and, while she

hesitated to describe Milburn as 'bomb proof', the little mare really didn't seem to be scared about very much, and then she enquired about her own and Bill's cat Fishy, which Barbara and Ted were now looking after. Barbara made Peggy laugh by telling her that with a flurry of people late to digging out their yards in Jubilee Street to be ready for their self-constructed Anderson shelters (Barbara and Ted having installed theirs the previous summer), this was disturbing a depressing number of rat nests, and Fishy now had a growing reputation in Jubilee Street as a pretty good ratter. That had led Ted to mutter the cat should really be called Ratty, given her penchant for dragging back heavy brown corpses to number five, a habit which he and Barbara had tried (unsuccessfully) to dissuade her from. However, there was an upside, as it meant that Fishy was getting quite a lot of odd titbits as a reward from various neighbours, and so she rarely mewed at number five Jubilee Street for anything to eat, which was very helpful.

Barbara changed the subject to what she had really telephoned about, and Peggy could tell this by the more workmanlike cast to her voice. 'I've been thinking about you a lot, Peggy, and I want to know how you are, how you *really* are. Your letters don't feel quite the ticket at the moment, it seems to me. I hope you don't mind me saying this, dear.'

Peggy sighed, and then she confessed to Barbara that she felt very up and down, and as if nothing – other than Holly – could quite please her.

'Well, I don't know how you'll feel about what I'm going to say, but we had a knock at the door last night, and Bill was standing there, as large as life,' said Barbara. 'He had a forty-eight-hour pass and of course he wanted to plead his case with me, so that I could try and persuade you to take him back. I told him I didn't think you'd be swayed, but I would say to you that he had visited, although that was all I was going to say, and I wasn't going to pass on to you any of his excuses as whatever he had been thinking about, which he didn't look too happy with.'

'Too bloody right I'm not going to be swayed, and I think we both know exactly what he was thinking about!' Peggy interrupted, and then harrumphed with feeling when her sister added that she'd also told Bill about Maureen's visit to Harrogate. It wasn't like Peggy to swear, and especially when she was speaking to Barbara, as Barbara could be sniffy about this sort of thing.

Barbara ignored the 'bloody', and went on, 'I don't think Bill knew about Maureen's visit, to be honest, as he went very pale which makes me think Maureen has kept quiet about going up to Harrogate, and then Bill had the gall to ask me what Maureen had wanted with seeing you. Luckily Ted stepped in at that point as I think he could see that I was getting a bit hot under the collar with Bill, and so Ted took him off to the Jolly, where he was a bit surprised to see that Bill proceeded to get in his cups, given that he's never been much of a drinker in the past. Ted told me that Bill had hoped, apparently, that he could stop with us, but Ted put the kibosh on that, thank goodness. So I've no idea where he ended up last night, although it wasn't with us.'

'Ugh,' groaned Peggy in such a heartfelt way that Barbara wished they were together so that she could properly comfort her sister, and that they weren't divided by hundreds of miles. 'Just the very thought of Bill is like a low-lying cloud hanging right above me, following me about and threatening to rain. I'm sick and tired of it. What am I going to do, Barbara?' said Peggy

The sisters talked for another minute or two, during which time Peggy told Barbara that if anything similar happened again then Barbara was to come right out and say it to her and not waste time or energy pussy-footing around in the way she had begun this telephone conversation. Barbara wanted to say she had been trying to see first how Peggy was feeling, but then she decided to keep quiet as Peggy had sounded grumpy and so her sister thought that to defend herself would only lead to more grumpiness. Nevertheless Peggy felt much better by the time they said their goodbyes, not least as Barbara had pointed out that Bill looked haggard and very wretched about the parlous state of his marriage and lack of contact with his baby daughter.

In fact Peggy's new-found feeling of being bolstered was still with her several hours later, and she awoke the next day in a stronger frame of mind.

Right after she had finished for the day at June Blenkinsop's she went to the post office to pay half a crown for a postal order to send to Barbara to cover the cost of what she would have had to pay the barman at the Jolly for the long-distance telephone call, and to send her as a small thank-you a bar of violet-scented soap she had bought in one of Mabel's bring-and-buy sales, and had been saving for a special occasion.

Peggy very much wanted Barbara to know that she had telephoned at just the right time, and that she had made her feel much restored – sisters were like that, weren't they? And this was a very valuable relationship, and a connection to be cherished. Peggy smiled at the thought of what she and Barbara meant to each other, and then her grin deepened as she thought of the tight bonds of affection that bound Jessie and Connie to each other too.

Family life had a lot to recommend it, she reminded herself, and more fool Bill for forgetting that in his haste to bed Maureen (from the NAAFI).

Chapter Nineteen

Unfortunately Jessie and Connie weren't feeling at all brotherly and sisterly right at that moment.

Connie was distinctly peeved at being cut out of whatever it was that was going on with her brother and his friends, and which she quite obviously had been excluded from. She'd had enough – more than enough actually – and she felt at the end of her tether. She pondered for a while and then she came up with a plan.

So she laid in wait for Jessie as he came out of the bathroom following his weekly bath – he'd drawn the short straw and had had to go into the now tepid and distinctly grey and murky water last out of the four boys – and, using the element of surprise as she knew that this would be Jessie at his most defenceless, she had sprung on him physically and had quickly pushed and bundled her affronted and complaining brother into her little box room, whereupon she had closed the door and quickly wedged her bedside table against it to prevent Jessie from making a run from her too easily.

As Connie had bargained – she was good at strategic planning, even Jessie had to acknowledge this – Jessie's cries that the boys should come and rescue him fell on deaf ears as the

Tall Trees grown-ups were all out and about on their daily business, while the other boys were playing a very noisy game of gin rummy in their bedroom. The door to their dorm was firmly shut and so their shouts and ribbing of each other made them quite oblivious to the predicament that Jessie now found himself in.

Poor Jessie quickly realised he had to handle this on his own, and he could only make a sound that was a bit like 'eek!', which he followed with a strong 'gerroff!' as he tried to clutch his damp towel more firmly around himself as Connie forced him onto the bed, before then backing a step or two away and positioning herself firmly between him and the door.

He gave a baleful look at his sister, and to his horror Jessie saw that there was one end of the towel still firmly held in one of her fists, and an extremely cross look on her face. This wasn't good, no, not at all.

'I've had enough, Jessie! If you don't tell me exactly what you are all up to, then I'm pulling this towel away, and pushing you out into the corridor and then chasing you down it to your room and then you'll have to explain to your pals why you are as naked as the day you were born and running away from me, and don't you dare think that I wouldn't,' Connie said to him, and then dramatically narrowed her eyes and stuck her head forward as if to further emphasise her point. Jessie's whole body quivered with tension. He'd never live this down if Connie actually fulfilled her promise. There was worse to come.

'*Then* I'll tell the others just what a sissy you are, not being able to deal with your sister or to keep hold of your towel, despite your sister not being thought good enough by you boys for whatever it is that you are all up to. And Aiden is just as bad, but I thought I'd get more out of ambushing you. And Peggy and Mabel would be very cross if I tried to pull away his towel,' Connie went on.

Jessie knew that 'very cross' would hardly have come close to what Peggy and Mabel would have had to say about it, should Connie have ambushed Aiden in this way. Aiden would have been furious too, and Connie would never have risked that, seeing how sweet she was on him. In fact Peggy and Mabel wouldn't be pleased either with what Connie was doing to Jessie, but he thought they'd put that down more to high jinx and sisters being sisters rather than anything malicious on Connie's part. But none of this was of the slightest help to him right at the moment.

He had no doubt that Connie meant every word of what she said – he hadn't been her twin for very nearly eleven years not to know that she wasn't fond of joking around like this. She hadn't seen him naked for three or four years, and that was fine with him and just how it should be, he thought. He hadn't seen her naked either, as although the Ross family weren't prudes, once the twins had got big enough that to bath them together was a bit more than the old small tin bath in front of the hearth on a Sunday evening could stand, they weren't the sort of family to encourage the type of behaviour that was anything other than deeply respectful of one another's privacy, and nudity definitely came under personal privacy. Indeed the thought of either his father, Ted, or his mother, Barbara, without their clothes on was simply impossible for him to imagine, and he suspected that Connie would feel similarly.

But only that very morning in the boys' bedroom, Jessie

and the three others had deepened their TT Musket vows by pricking their thumbs with one of baby Holly's purloined curved safety pins, and then the four of them had stood close to each other as they took it in turns to nick a finger with the pin, forcing a drip of ruby blood onto the tip. They said a new promise to each other, which Tommy insisted was an oath and that they should repeat to each other every day to remind themselves of the enormity of their musketeer pledge to one another, and pressed their four bloodied fingers together. The new promise was, 'TTs against the HBs; musketeers to the end'. HBs stood for Hull Boys, and the fact that they were musketeers meant that the others didn't want girls in the TT Muskets, Jessie knew.

'Um, er, um,' stuttered Jessie before he ground to a halt in front of his infuriated sister, his eyes bright and looking ominously close to tears, and his hair still dripping from the final dunk he had given it in the bath water. Connie had never attempted to get him to do her bidding over anything important like this before, and so he wasn't sure of the best way of handling it, nor what he should say to mollify her.

'I'm warning you, Jessie…' said Connie.

And then she gave a tug to the towel. It was a tug that was designed to be just sharp enough to worry Jessie more than actually to wrench the towel away wholeheartedly, but it was a reminder of what could happen to him if he kept the musketeers' counsel and Connie followed through on her promise. The towel was worn and threadbare, and Connie's fingers went right through the thinness of the material.

Rattled, Jessie groped around for what he could snatch to cover his modesty should Connie swipe the towel totally off him or rip the towel into an inconvenient hole that would expose him. He deeply regretted leaving his pyjamas on top of the pile of dirty clothing in the bathroom where on Peggy's instructions the boys had piled everything that needed washing as she was going to get the washing copper going later.

All he could see nearby that might help him in his predicament was Connie's black and white knitted panda Petunia, the sister to his grey bear Neville, but he thought that if he were to grab Petunia away from where she was nestled on Connie's pillow and thrust it against his privates then that would *really* incense Connie and make her most unpredictable, with the real possibility that something even more horrible might happen than being chased naked back to his bedroom and called a sissy.

'Jessie!' Connie warned again, her voice now edged with a low throb of menace, and he tore his eyes away from Petunia in case this was to madden his sister further when she realised what he'd been staring at, and (horror!) why.

He looked at his sister. It was almost as if he were seeing her for the very first time.

Connie's pupils were glinting from the light coming in from the window; they contained what looked like a starburst of excitement that was a shade too close to pleasure at his predicament for Jessie's liking. The summer-lightened golden hues in her thick tawny hair, roughly tied back into a messy pigtail that had strands leaping from it willy-nilly, her purpled-flowered cotton dress tucked into an old pair of Tommy's shorts with one of Roger's belts wound twice around her waist to make sure the shorts didn't fall down, a checked neckerchief knotted around her neck and a grubby pair of plimsolls worn without socks, all combined to give Connie a renegade, slightly pirate-like look. In fact, to Jessie's mind, his sister's practical, rather daring get-up embodied more of the sensibility of the TT Muskets than he could have imagined any of the boys achieving just by the way they dressed. Barbara would have thought her daughter to be scruffy if she could have seen Connie at that moment, but Connie was dressed for being able to do whatever the boys were doing, and with this in mind, it was a successful outfit.

Jessie dared to glance back at Connie's face, and her bold, unfrightened eyes staring back at him with curiosity as to what he was going to do sealed it.

Jessie made his decision. The others wouldn't be happy, but Connie would find out anyway at some point and they had all kidded themselves that they could keep the TT Muskets boys-only long-term, he told himself. Tommy and Larry would be cross, no doubt, but Jessie was pretty certain that Aiden would side with him, bearing in mind how much he liked Connie. Once Connie was subsumed into the gang, then of course there would be the question of Angela, who was much harder to make a case for as a musketeer, given her wheelchair, but Jessie supposed they would have to have her too, once Connie had been initiated into the TT Muskets as he was sure was going to happen now. He'd had too much bullying and being left out of things when he was at school in Bermondsey to want to wish on his worst enemy, let alone one of his best friends, that they were pushed into the outer reaches and left out of whatever larks were going on. Even if Angela were a girl.

'We're called the TT Muskets…' Jessie began.

By the time he had explained everything to his sister about the posturing of the Hull evacuees, and had even confessed that it had been he who had led the voting regarding no girls, Jessie's hair was almost dry.

'You lot are twerps, complete and utter twerps,' Connie cut in a strident tone, clearly having grasped the whole situation. 'Girls are your assets, dummy, your *assets*!'

With that, Connie pushed the bedside table back to where it belonged and with her brother clutching his towel so tightly around his thin body that his knuckles showed white, she marched Jessie back to the bedroom that he shared with the others.

'Right!' she said firmly the moment she was inside the door, and Jessie could see by the looks on the faces of Aiden, Tommy and Larry that they all guessed immediately that the TT Muskets were about to have a new membership of two.

To Jessie's surprise, no one seemed to mind very much about Connie and Angela joining their gang as not much of a fuss was kicked up – not that Angela knew anything about it yet. Nor did his friends dare laugh outright at Jessie's predicament, having instead to content themselves with the odd unsympathetic chortle in his direction when they thought Connie wasn't looking, which wasn't nearly often enough as far as they were concerned, although distinctly too often for Jessie to be comfortable with as he shuffled himself into his clothes behind Connie's back as she held the other three firmly in her gimlet gaze.

Twenty minutes later Connie had them all out in the garden, with Angela sitting in her wheelchair alongside Connie, having been told to make detailed notes, as Larry described the moves that the Hull boys had made before them.

Connie walked to and from the pigpen that Roger was

slowly constructing, her hands in her pockets and staring at the ground, being obviously deep in thought. At last she announced, 'Right, you musketeers, *this* is how we're going to do it', and then she went to stand in front of the boys in order to give a demonstration of what she wanted.

With their babes in their arms, both Gracie and Peggy were standing next to each other watching what was going on below Peggy's bedroom window, which overlooked the garden.

'Whatever are they up to?' wondered Gracie.

'I've no idea. But it seems to be Connie's show, and the boys are looking happy enough to go along with whatever it is that she is saying,' answered Peggy, 'especially Aiden.'

The women watched as Connie shamelessly bossed the boys into doing her binding and replicating her moves. She was very pernickety as to where their feet and hands had to be, and nobody seemed to be mastering precisely what Connie was asking very quickly.

'Well, maybe "happy" was an exaggeration, but whatever it is Connie is demanding they are trying their best,' Peggy added after a while. She had noticed the expressions on the boys' faces, who were clearly struggling with the intricacy and the timing of the moves that Connie was forcing on them.

'Bless 'em!' said Gracie. And then the young mothers chuckled, before giving in to the sort of belly laughs that made both Jack and Holly laugh too as their mothers pointed out to the babies what was happening below and how silly it all was.

Chapter Twenty

It was just as well that Connie had muscled her and Angela's way into the TT Muskets when she did, as the very next time that all six children were out together, as luck would have it they ran slap-bang into the Hull evacuees.

Or, to be more precise, the Hull contingent ran into them.

There was a muggy, overcast feel earlier that day as Milburn was tacked up and carefully backed into the trap ready for the children's latest newspaper collection. It was going to be a biggie as this time they had a couple of new streets to go to, while Mabel had given them a longer list of people they needed to call on to run errands for too.

Angela was hoicked up onto the driving seat by Tommy and Aiden, who then jumped back down to the ground, after which they passed the reins and the driving whip up to her. Beside her on the seat was a clipboard with the various streets of their route, and a list of all the additional houses they had to call at and the other errands they had to run.

The boys had, daringly, taken a vote and then a leaf out of Connie's book, and so they had copied the way she was dressing as far as they were able.

All six children were wearing grubby plimsolls with no

socks and, for the boys, rather than having their shirt buttons done up right to the collar as was usual, they had all left several buttons open so the top of their chests and their scraggy collarbones were exposed. They had each tied rolled hankies (the brighter the better, Tommy's being a particularly vivid orange) as neckerchiefs around their necks with the knots to the front. Their sleeves were folded up as high as they could go, and they each had their shirts tucked in on one side but not the other. Everyone was wearing the baggiest shirts they possibly could, Tommy having borrowed two of Roger's tatty gardening shirts for him and Aiden to wear, with their usual shirts being passed on to Larry and Jessie, both of whom were quite a lot smaller.

Connie was wearing the same outfit as on the day of 'Jessie and the towel' as it was now known to the children and, exactly like Connie, Angela had also tucked her dress into an old pair of baggy shorts, this time ones that Tommy had played football in (and although Mabel had said they were clean, the previous evening Angela had given them a good scrub as they had looked a bit mucky to her still, and then she'd left them on the soap rack on the bath to dry), and she'd tied her hair back like Connie's. Angela had wondered aloud to her friend that wouldn't it be more sensible for them to just wear their blouses with the shorts rather than their dresses? Connie was persuasive though when she insisted that it gave them extra opportunities for employing different identities should they need to follow anyone, as they could quickly untuck their skirts to reveal they were wearing a dress, and if they tugged their hair free from their pigtails too they could dupe whoever it was they were tracking into believing that they were several different people. Still, Angela doubted that anyone would be fooled by her having a variety of identities, no matter how dim they were, seeing as she would be sitting in the trap, or on Milburn, or else in her wheelchair. But Connie was clearly excited by the whole thing, and Angela didn't want to dampen her enthusiasm and so she didn't say anything.

In fact Connie had had a brainwave a day or two earlier. She had been determined that all six of them would wear something that was identical to identify them easily as members of the TT Muskets, and so one afternoon early in the summer holidays she humped Angela along in the wheelchair, with Angela complaining that Connie was nearly tipping her out at the kerbs, so bumpy was the journey, but Connie insisted she needed Angela's opinion. With a new respect for Tommy who would usually push Angela, Connie's face was florid from the effort of dealing with the chair by the time that she and Angela let themselves, in secret, into the dank and slightly musty-smelling room at the back of the church hall where Roger was storing all the jumble that parishioners had delivered for the next fundraising rummage sale, as Connie was convinced that she could come up with something there.

It took some rooting around, and quite a lot of delving into the piles of clothes and whatnot on Connie's part as Angela kept watch from the doorway back to the empty hall to make sure the coast was clear, as both girls knew that Roger – while he wouldn't have exactly told them off should he have discovered what they were up to, even if they had offered to pay for anything they took – would nevertheless have looked at them with the put-upon, slightly wounded expression he'd employ in situations like this. It was a look that all the children hated to see on his face and which would always make them promise to themselves that they wouldn't do again whatever it was that had caused Roger to look this way, or at least until they forgot that he had looked at them like this.

'Hallelujah!' cried Connie after what seemed an age, at which Angela beamed and then said an echo 'Hallelujah!' before she and Connie both clapped a hand to their mouths, in case they'd been blasphemous. The hall wasn't exactly church, but it was church property and the jumble stashed there was there for church purposes, while they were, in the technical sense, stealing, even though Connie had made a spirited argument that in fact what they were doing wasn't exactly theft, but was more 'working towards the greater good'. Angela hadn't been quite convinced, but she already knew that she was going to do Connie's bidding, and so in the grand scheme of things, their precise level of wrongdoing was somewhat academic as it wasn't going to stop either of them anyway.

What Connie had found were four lengthy ropes of thick twisted-silk cord, with two hefty thistle-shaped tassels on one end of two of the ropes. They were extravagant and luxurious curtain ties that must have held back huge heavy curtains to judge by the weight of the cord (very heavy) and its length (extremely long, certainly long enough to make into six belts to unite the TT Muskets).

'I wonder what big house this all came from,' said Angela rather dreamily as she ran the tips of her fingers along the slippery surface of the cord's silk, but then the more practical Connie took it from Angela's hands and wound the ruby-coloured cord into four skeins which then she hung on the back of the wheelchair.

'No idea, but let's skedaddle before anybody finds us,' said Connie as she quickly pushed Angela back through the hall and out onto the street where they headed home in what they hoped was as insouciant a manner as possible.

Later that day, Connie borrowed (without his knowledge) Roger's Stanley knife to cut the cord, which was as thick as her thumb, into appropriate lengths so that everyone had matching belts.

The next morning, each of the Muskets then wrapped the cord twice around his or her waist and used Roger's book of knots to decide what the most appropriate knot would be (sheet knots turned out to give the least trouble), or it was wound round just once in the case of Tommy's middle, as he had a bit of a tummy. As the only girls, Angela and Connie were allowed to add the thistle-shaped tassels as adornment to their belts.

Mabel had stared at them when they came down for breakfast for a few long seconds, although she contented herself with a mere 'um, a very, er, *casual* look, I must say', and then she went back to doling out boiled eggs to everyone without further comment. She clearly thought the children were playing some sort of game, which was fine with the Muskets, and so they all tried to keep their faces as innocent as possible in order to not arouse further suspicion.

Peggy was more direct. 'Why are you dressed like that? You look like urchins.'

Luckily the children were saved from having to lie outright by Holly getting a bad case of hiccups and giving such a wail of discomfort that Peggy had to attend to her immediately and so she wasn't paying much attention to Connie's fudged answer and just nodded along without listening, after which the children wolfed down their eggs, bread and margarine as quickly as they could and then made themselves scarce pronto as they rushed off to get Milburn ready for their newspaper-collection round.

The children had just got to the end of their round when they were about to pass the churchyard of the neighbouring parish to Roger. The trap had piles of paper in it, as well as some old scrap metal and items like worn-out rubber boots that all combined to make quite a Krakatoa of waste items, and in addition, several people had donated holey pillowcases full of old clothes for Roger's next rummage sale that the children were to drop off at the church hall. Angela was sitting in just about the only space that was still left, but the sun was beating down and it was hot up there on the driving seat, so she was looking forward to when they would get back to Tall Trees and could have a drink of water and spend some time cooling down in the shade.

The other five children walked next to the trap, saying only the occasional word once they had congratulated each other on how successful this particular round had been in what they had been able to pick up, their earlier energy having dissipated in the heat.

Then, just like the other two times, somehow the Hull evacuees did their stealthy and now-familiar blood-chilling trick of silently snaking over the stone wall and lining up in front of those from Tall Trees, although a fair way down the road still. Again, as one, they moved their feet apart at the same time as they inclined their heads towards their right sides and jutted out their jaws, before taking two large steps forward very quickly, and then suddenly standing completely stationary. Then the Hull boys rolled their shoulders backwards slowly and switched the angle of their jaws from their right side to their left. Not for a moment had they seemed to blink or taken their eyes off the group making their way cautiously towards them.

It was just as threatening as the previous time the Tall Trees boys had seen it, Jessie thought, and he was sure that everyone felt the same surge of adrenalin as he had. It seemed more of a danger this time around, thought Jessie and his friends.

But watching the routine rather than hearing about it second-hand was a new experience for Connie and Angela. Connie had already stipulated that no matter how threatening or dire or spectacular it was when she and Angela saw it in the flesh for the first time, the important thing was that that they looked as bored as possible and treated it as not very much at all, as the fact it didn't impress girls was likely to be very irksome to the Hull boys.

With this in mind, and while the Hull lot gave it all they had, the girls merely looked at each other and then both gave an exaggerated and very dismissive shrug, with Angela daring to say, 'Am I supposed to be impressed?' the implication being that she was distinctly *un*impressed.

· Then, as rehearsed, Angela pushed Milburn forward alongside the others, and sat up as straight as she could, sporting a deliberately grumpy frown on her face and slowly (as practised already to check that Milburn didn't spook by having the whip waved around above her back) bringing the long driving whip upright and then gently moving it from side to side.

Meanwhile Connie snorted contemptuously at the Hull evacuees, and marched forward to stand out on her own, which was quite a way in front of Jessie and the others. The Hull boys stared on with what seemed like a smirking amusement. To them, she appeared isolated and alone, skinny and small, and very vulnerable.

'What yer got fer us, bonny lass?' one said, and the others laughed. 'Come ter show us yer dollies?'

They obviously didn't know Connie.

There was an instant as the Tall Trees boys looked at each other and then they each gave three small nods to get their timing right, and then as one, they lined up behind a now stony-faced Connie. Taking the lead from Connie they began their carefully choreographed routine, which involved everyone, even Angela (though she had to prop the whip beside her) holding their hands together in front of them with their fingers interlinked so that each TT Musket had a clasped pair of hands held high in front of their chests as if in a prayer of supplication designed to appease the Hull lads, then they all looked down demurely right down to the ground for three long seconds.

Jessie risked a look at their opponents from beneath his eyebrows while this was going on and he could see them staring on in puzzlement now. Connie had moved a step or two nearer to them and this muscling in on their personal space was obviously unsettling them. The Hull boys were also rattled by this first stage of their routine as it clearly wasn't at all what they had been expecting, seeing as it looked at first sight to be the Tall Trees gang giving in.

This was a deliberate strategy though, Jessie knew, and he

glanced across at Connie, whose right heel was tapping out the beat for those behind her, and all of a sudden any sense of fear or trepidation left him – things were about to get interesting, and he felt brave and indeed as if he had never been more alive. It was a wonderful feeling, and he fancied he was standing taller, with much more of a dangerous cast about him.

As part of what they'd practised, the next bit was that the TT Muskets looked up properly at the Hull lot, and then obviously down at their still-almost-praying hands. Making faces and giving a single shake their heads as if to say a firm 'No', they then broke their hands apart, and stood sideways on punching their tightly-fisted left hands across their bellies, their heads tilted and their right hands stroking their chins, with their eyes almost closed above as they gazed over at their foes.

Then, very slowly they advanced sideways towards the Hull evacuees, doing four smallish steps with one side leading and then in unison turning and doing four steps with the other side in front.

'Dollies, my arse!' said Connie, which was equally shocking to those from Tall Trees as it was to the Hull boys, as she'd never given a hint before that she even knew such language. 'My ARSE!' she shouted at full voice again as Angela pushed Milburn forward.

There was the first sign of a breaking in the Hull ranks, with eyes starting to be flicked from side to side as they tried to work out what the other members of the gang were thinking about what was going on before them. They hadn't expected the pony to be so close to them or a girl to take the lead, and in fact Connie had had to do a lot of work to get the Muskets to agree to either of these strategies, as the boys had made it clear they felt it made them look feeble quite aside from the fact it was possible Connie, Angela or Milburn might get hurt. But Connie was relentless in trying to get her way, saying that in view of the Hull lot being bigger there could be an advantage in wrong-footing them with surprise moves, and eventually her insistence won the day.

The Hull boys weren't sure where to look, as they hadn't expected anything like this. Jessie knew that they must be weighing up the situation.

There were five boys from Hull, which would ordinarily give them a huge advantage, especially given their size and physical maturity as they were all at secondary school. Compared to these six primary schoolchildren in front of them, two of whom were girls (and one of those unable to walk, although their challengers were unlikely to know that), they had weight and brute force on their side.

However, aside from Connie seeming a demon, Milburn's head was raised and she was lifting her hooves high with each step, making herself seem as big as possible in an approved TT Musket manner, and she looked much more mildly curious than concerned about what was going on in front of her.

Then, quick as a hungry otter sliding into a river after a fish, Connie darted forward and grabbed caps from the heads of three of the Hull boys, which then she threw expertly one by one to Angela, who managed to catch them all single-handedly (Connie knew that Angela had been a two-ball champion at school back in Bermondsey, and they'd practised this, unbeknownst to the boys, just in case it was to come in handy, which it obviously had), and quickly Angela leant down to secrete the caps under the bench on which she was sitting.

The Tall Trees boys stood frozen for a second, and they looked at each other quickly to see what they should do, and in order that they didn't spend too long frozen lemon-like in inaction, Aiden hastily led them in mirroring their pose, swapping their arm across their stomachs and their hands on their chins.

Connie meanwhile jeered with a toss of her head, 'Arses!'

Her vocabulary was limited, but now the Hull boys were in no doubt who she meant. And although they muttered under their breath and flicked the vees, Connie's smiling face somehow dampened their attempts at intimidation.

And then Milburn stuck her nose forward, opened her mouth and snapped her teeth together a mere inch or so in front of the face of one of the lads – Connie hadn't bargained for this, but it couldn't have worked more effectively if she had, as suddenly, like a will o' the wisp disappearing, the posturing of the older boys from Hull dissolved completely. It was all too strange and unpredictable for them, and the result was that they started to edge away backwards, and after retreating a safe distance they turned to jog – well, it was more of a run really – a little further down the road before heading towards the stone wall surrounding the churchyard and vaulting over.

Once they had a wall between themselves and those from Tall Trees, the leader of the Hull gang looked relieved as he turned around and stared back at the Muskets, and in order that they didn't lose total face for being bested by girls and a mare, he leant across the top of the wall to shake a fist at them all as he shouted sharply, 'Bugger off! Do you 'ear? Piss off before we larrup ye! An' yer lads, yer sissies, hidin' behind those skirts.'

Connie kept her silence, as did the others, and then she gave a sweeping bow in the direction of the Hull boy staring at her, her right hand sweeping in an extravagant circular motion almost right down to the ground.

In response the lad hanging over the wall tried a louder bellow of 'Bugger off!'

But when the only response back to him from out in the road was Connie cupping a hand behind her ear and inclining her head with her eyebrows raised dramatically as if she hadn't heard him, he almost did a jig on the spot in frustration as he shook again one fist and then the other as he stared deep into her eyes.

Unperturbed, Connie tipped her head to the other side and merely raised her eyebrows.

'Sling yer 'ook,' called Larry, 'if yer knows wot's gud fer yers.'

'Yeah, piss off,' added Tommy.

Defeated, the Hull leader gave a shaky Heil Hitler salute at them, and then quickly flicked all of the Muskets a final flurry of vees at which Connie turned her face into a smouldering frown and took a threatening step forward, which caused him to jump back with alacrity, before he yelled a quivery 'Fuck off, fuck you!' And then he turned and sidled off in the wake of his fast-disappearing friends.

The TT Muskets slowly let out their breaths and allowed their tense shoulders to relax. And then there was a wonderful moment as Connie and her friends turned towards each other in victory, as they smiled broadly at each other while relief surged through their bodies that a potentially horrible situation had been seen off with such brio, and even Milburn gave a happy-sounding snort at the non-violent outcome of that particular encounter.

The silence now broken between the TT Muskets, they headed back to Tall Trees agog with their nerve, and chattering furiously about what had happened, reliving what they had done and how it had happened time and time again, telling each other excitedly how it had gone more in their favour than they ever could possibly have imagined.

As Milburn was put back in her stable and given a drink and a couple of carrots sneaked from the vegetable plot by Larry as a reward, Tommy hung each of the three purloined caps from rusty nails that were poking out from the wooden rafters high up at the back of her stall.

As trophies go, the caps, two tatty grey tweed and one holey navy twill, didn't look particularly special lined up like that, but none of the children were in any doubt of the huge victory they signified.

The children stood outside the stable, looking at the caps. But it was Larry who brought all of his friends back to reality with a bump. 'That was just fer starters. They'll really be after us now.'

There was a pause as they all pondered this.

And then Connie said, her eyes sparkling at the mere thought, 'I know. Isn't it exciting?!'

Chapter Twenty-one

There was a run of hot days, and then the weather broke with thunderstorms and bursts of rain that was so heavy that nobody fancied going out much.

It was now well into July and suddenly the war stalemate on home shores ended with a bang between Britain and Germany, and with the Luftwaffe beginning a series of daylight raids. The newspaper headlines screamed that fifteen people had been killed at an aerodrome in Wick, Caithness, and a week or so later heavy loss of life was incurred in Norwich, this time as factories and iron works were targeted. Not long after that, towns on the South Coast were attacked, especially the Channel ports and their defences. Coventry was bombed, as was Southampton, Liverpool, Bradford and Birmingham. It was hard for anybody, adults or children, to think of a single positive thing to say about this latest turn the war with Germany had taken.

More so than ever before, the BBC news was the focal point of everyone's days, and the general mood at Tall Trees among the adults grew increasingly sombre, and nowhere in the country seemed completely safe.

Barbara telephoned Roger and asked that the twins be kept

close to home, and he was able to reassure her that this was already happening. Barbara then spoke to Jessie and Connie, who were both a bit upset and told their mother in great, sometimes teary detail how very much they were missing home, and her and Ted. Barbara's voice had a distinct crack in it as she told them that she and Ted were missing them too and she wished she were with them right at that moment as she'd love to envelop them in the biggest and beariest of bear hugs, but it was much better that they were up in Harrogate rather than down in Bermondsey as it was going to get dicey in London before too much longer, she was sure, although of course she and Ted would make sure to take good care of themselves.

Angela and Larry both had letters from their mothers saying much the same, and so the victorious mood of the children from the afternoon of the cap trophy-snatch dissolved quickly into one that was much more thorny and low-spirited.

As Connie said ruefully to Jessie one morning as they went to collect the eggs from the hen coop at the bottom of the garden, 'All that work to get the Hull caps, and now nobody gives a hoot. I just wish we were back in Jubilee Street, and that the war had never happened.'

'I know what you mean,' answered her twin. 'Ma and Pa seem a long way away, and the other day I couldn't remember everything that was in my bedroom at number five and I never thought I'd not be able to do that. It's nearly our birthday too, and I don't think we'll be able to see them or get any presents.'

He and Connie stood and looked at each other. Jessie's words had hit a real chord with both children, and for the first time in months they gave into bitter sobs.

Mabel saw what was going on, and she called Peggy to see too. The twins looked lost and desolate, but they also seemed to be comforting each other.

'I'll keep an eye on this,' said Peggy, and then Mabel nodded in agreement and touched her comfortingly on the arm as Peggy added, 'Lovely as it is here with you and Roger and everybody else, and I'm sure Connie and Jessie would agree with that, it feels very strange that we have no idea when we will be able to go back home, or indeed even if we will have homes to go to when this is all over.'

As far the children were concerned, the concept of them being TT Muskets increasingly seemed childish and out of kilter with the real life-and-death attacks on British people, and so they tried not to think too much about the Hull boys after Jessie reminded everyone that they were probably feeling just as apprehensive about the outcome of the war as they were at Tall Trees.

However, there were only a limited number of days where playing snap or gin rummy, or reading or listening to the wireless, held everyone's attention before normal bickering turned heated and from there into full-blown arguments. A day or two's grace was won when it turned out that Gracie and Mabel both knew how to play whist, and so they taught this card game to the children in an effort to give them something different to think about, but this new-found enthusiasm soon began to pale along with all the other games that Mabel and Peggy tried to come up with, especially as Roger vetoed the children gambling with used matches or IOUs from their pocket money, which had livened things up between them for a while and made the games very energetically fought.

There was one excitement that did lift spirits though, which was the arrival of a tiny piglet that was going to be fattened up before butchering ready for Christmas. It was another extra mouth from Mr Ross, Milburn's official owner, as a young gilt (this was, Jessie informed everyone, a sow who'd not given birth previously, but the other children couldn't be bothered to rib Jessie or make cat-calls, which had become their usual response when Jessie shared unasked-for information on something he knew about but they, with the possible exception of Aiden, didn't) had had a litter of thirteen piglets but she had proved to be a poor mother, being too restless to feed them all properly and actually killing three of the piglets by either standing or lying on them. This latest member of the Tall Trees coterie was a sugar-mouse-pink sweetie who had been the smallest surviving piglet. He had an endearing frill of ginger hair edging each ear and the sweetest little piggy trotters. He was the runt of the remaining litter, given to Tall Trees for hand-rearing as he had already been trodden on once, although not too severely, but Mr Ross didn't think he would survive if it stayed with the gilt.

The quite large pigpen Roger and Ted had finished constructing on Barbara and Ted's last visit to Tall Trees had, so far, remained empty as Roger secretly had got cold feet about letting everyone getting fond of an animal that was not technically a pet but a prospective source of food, as this would ensure that there would be a high level of upset when the time for butchering came.

But the piglet – a little male who was soon named Porky Pig in honour of the Looney Tunes children's favourite, although this was quickly shortened to Porky – was too little to be left outside on his own in the pen, and so he was placed in a large wooden tea chest close to the range to keep warm, with an old woolly of Mabel's to snuggle in, that had been deemed too ratty for it to be unpicked and knitted up into something else.

Porky quickly snuffled his way into everyone's hearts, causing Roger to say to Mabel, 'I don't think he'll be making our pigs-in-blankets come Christmas', to which Mabel answered, 'Lawks a mussy! Don't say that, Roger! 'E'll eat us out of 'ouse an' 'ome if 'e don't go fer sausages.'

'Don't say I didn't tell you, when you are feeding him his own little Christmas dinner,' said Roger with a twinkle in his eye, and then he spent quite a while tickling Porky under the chin until the piglet's boot-button intelligent eyes drifted shut.

Porky was fed milk every two hours from a rubber-teated dolly's bottle that Mabel, who had grown up on a farm and therefore had experience of dealing with abandoned baby animals, had mixed with a beaten egg and a few drops of cod-liver oil.

The children were warned there was a high chance that Porky wouldn't survive as pigs tended not to do well away from their mothers.

'We mus' remember though,' Mabel told the children, 'that where there's life, there's 'ope, an' so we mustn't gi' up 'ope on this little one jus' yet. Now, who's goin to 'elp wi' t' piglet's feedin' an' gubbins?'

Everyone was going to chip in with this, it seemed, and so an hour was spent at the kitchen table after tea one day with the children dividing their duties between Porky and Milburn, and allocating who was doing what.

Porky turned out to be quite the little trooper though, and

he thrived on his bottle feeding, and soon learned to give a snorty call to arms when he was hungry and wanted some more. There had been a debate between Roger and Mabel over whether the children should get up to feed him during the small hours of the night. Roger's feeling was that they should be allowed to give it a go as it was probably time the children started feeling responsible for somebody else, and in any case they needed something to distract them from the grim news headlines on the progress of the war, won out over Mabel's insistence that the children were too young to carry such a heavy responsibility and they slept too deeply to be easily roused in the middle of the night.

Roger spoke very seriously to Tommy and his pals, saying this night-time feeding wasn't anything they should undertake lightly as Porky's life depended on them living up to their promise to look after him. And they would be tired the following day if they had been on night-time duties although they weren't to moan about feeling sleepy or allow themselves to act grumpily. Larry pointed out that with six of them to share the feeds across each week, it meant that they could catch up on their sleep before they had to do it again.

To Mabel's surprise and Roger's delight the system actually turned out to work surprisingly smoothly, and Porky never missed a feed. The children tried not to give Mabel I-told-you-so looks, but it was hard not to gloat.

Gracie told Connie and Angela that looking after Porky was a bit like her own duties looking after her baby, although it was harder with a baby as Gracie had to do her own night-time feeding with Jack each and every night, whether she were tired or no. 'So if yer don't like feelin' tired, then you'd better watch what you get up to with t' lads when you're older,' she ended darkly, and both Connie and Angela looked as if they really meant it when they assured Gracie that they were never ever going to kiss a boy, let alone do anything that might lead to a baby, whatever that might be.

Peggy caught Gracie's eye, and they shared a smile over the look of horror on the girls' faces, and Peggy thought she'd try to find an opportunity to say something similar to the lads. They were a bit young maybe, and she wasn't quite sure who knew what about how babies were made as some of their fellow pupils came from farms and so presumably would have much more of a biological knowledge that they had most likely passed on. Anyhow, in a mixed household of largely unrelated children perhaps it was sensible to start mentioning this sort of thing, as they wouldn't be children for ever and, heavens above! Peggy absolutely didn't want to break the news a few years down the line to Barbara and Ted that one of the twins was about to become a parent.

There was a balance to be struck, perhaps, about not giving the children too much information and therefore making this sort of thing sound inviting and something they should experiment with as soon as possible, and neither Connie nor Angela were developed enough to have started their menstruation yet, and so there probably were some months of grace. Still, Peggy inclined more to Gracie's view which was that she, Gracie, would never have fallen pregnant at just fifteen had she known a bit more about the birds and the bees before dabbling with Aiden's older brother Kelvin, which was clear proof that ignorance was no preventer of pregnancy.

In an attempt to lighten the mood at Tall Trees a little, Roger buckled one day after the children had been particularly tetchy at breakfast, and he promised a day out to the seaside at Withernsea as it seemed to him to be about the least likely place to attract the attentions of Jerry. As he said to Peggy, he thought the children were going a bit stir-crazy as they had been cooped up too long and that they needed to go somewhere where they could see something a bit different and run off a bit of energy.

The children were thrilled about something as carefree as a visit to the coast as they felt that, although Roger sometimes organised afternoon outings for all of them, arguably he was slightly too keen that what they actually did during those hours en masse away from Tall Trees should be 'self-improving'.

However, two gravely poorly parishioners and a broken water pipe that flooded the church hall meant that the trip to the coast had to be abandoned as Roger couldn't be spared, and neither could Mabel who had an important week filled with a lot of ATS organisational responsibilities, which disappointed everybody as Roger and Mabel were the only people in the household who knew how to drive. Peggy was cross with herself as she had never had the need to learn, and this made her think that she really should put this right at some point soon.

None of the London children had ever been to the seaside and so they were especially disappointed that their day out had been scuppered, while Aiden and Tommy, who had both been to Withernsea several years earlier on a school trip, looked almost as dejected.

Egging each other on to even lower ebbs and becoming more down in the mouth, later in the day when Roger had broken the news to the kiddies about the cancelled trip, Connie and Aiden had trudged over to the hospital to drop off the latest batch of homemade bags for the patients' possessions, and when James noticed their long faces and unusually quiet demeanour, he asked them what had happened.

The result was that later that evening James telephoned Roger, and offered his services as driver and host for the day out. James said that he was owed a day off, having worked for three weeks solid without a break, and so he'd love to have a blast of sea air, and as luck would have it there was an old charabanc that a friend owned and that he could borrow if Roger could siphon off some of his own petrol to help with the fuel, and provided Peggy would come to help him chaperone the children.

'I doubt we'll be able to get onto the beach itself,' James pointed out, 'as there's likely to be a variety of defences laid in the sand in order to hinder any attempted invasion on the part of Jerry. But it will be a nice day out and pleasant walking, and the smell of salt air and raucous seagulls. We can take a picnic and have fish and chips on the way home.'

'It'll give the children change to let off some steam and do something different,' agreed Roger. 'I might be able to help a little with the petrol.'

When Roger told Mabel, she agreed it was a good idea, and then before speaking to Peggy, Mabel telephoned June Blenkinsop to mention that Peggy would be needed for one day for a trip with the family, if that was all right with June. June twigged immediately that Mabel was trying to cheer up a still downhearted-over-Bill Peggy, and so she agreed immediately, and even offered to provide some of the food for the picnic.

And so the trip out was rearranged for the next Friday, with

Peggy and Holly to go, along with all the children. Gracie and Jack were invited too, but Gracie couldn't get cover for herself at the nursery, her daytime stint at the greengrocers, or for her evening session at the gun-packing depot.

Peggy was the last to know, and surprised and then a bit irritated about the way everything had been arranged without her say-so – 'Well, I think that's a bit of a liberty, and I'm not sure I do want to go,' she bridled – but then quite snappishly Gracie told her to 'gi' over' and that she and Jack would take Peggy's place if that was going to be her attitude.

Peggy's stomach did a little flip, and she realised that she really did want to go, rather a lot in fact, and she was going to be distinctly peeved if it were Gracie who went in her place, and so then Peggy had to bite a bit of humble pie and cut in quickly with, 'Let's not be too hasty, as I think I might be able to squeeze it in.' She had to look down then as she found her cheeks flushing on the cerise side of rose-pink, which had the advantage that she didn't see the look that Mabel and Gracie exchanged that was very clearly a private acknowledge-ment between the two women that Gracie knew all along she couldn't get time off work in order to muscle in on the day-out action but that she had thought that Peggy had needed a nudge in the right direction in order to buck her ideas up. And so in fact a rather successful ruse had been carried out that Mabel secretly applauded Grace for.

Chapter Twenty-two

On Friday morning the weather wasn't brilliant when James tooted the charabanc's horn outside Tall Trees. The sky was full of grey clouds, but it wasn't yet seven in the morning and so Peggy hoped the weather was going to perk up.

As Roger went to deal with the petrol situation, Mabel broke from giving Porky his bottle, at which he squealed in disgust, to give Peggy a hand putting mackintoshes, gumboots and umbrellas in the charabanc in case of rain, as well as calamine lotion and sun hats if the sun started to blaze, a number of towels (just in case) and several tartan woollen rugs for them to sit on when they had their picnic. They weren't able to fit the perambulator into the charabanc no matter how hard they all tried manoeuvring it in and moaned about it not folding up, and so Peggy resigned herself to spending the day holding Holly, which was a nuisance, she sighed to herself, as Holly was getting quite heavy these days.

The children clambered on board, and Mabel (who was now holding a peckish Porky in her arms as he greedily guzzled the last of his morning bottle) and Roger waved them off, with James peeping the horn in reply.

'Yes, the neighbours are going to be most delighted with all this commotion first thing,' joked Peggy, and she was pleased to see that she made James laugh. She remembered very clearly how peevish the neighbours had made her when they'd been all too ready to come out and watch her barney with Maureen, and so Peggy thought the noise they'd made cutting through the early morning was their just desserts for being nosy. Then she had to admit to herself that if she too had heard such a commotion coming from somebody else's driveway, then she'd have been right out too to see what was going on.

A couple of minutes later they pulled up at June Blenkinsop's and June ran out with several wicker baskets of food that she had got ready for them and, as a surprise for Peggy, a huge square of material that she told Peggy a customer who had spent time in Africa had seen women using to carry their babies in a sling, as June had never thought for a moment they'd be able to take the pram with them in the charabanc given how boxy and unwieldy it was, and so this could be a useful alternative. June gave Peggy a quick demonstration of how the woman had shown her the square of material should be knotted, and although Peggy felt a bit dubious about whether it would be secure enough to support Holly's weight on its own, she thought she might give it a try if they were going to take the children for a walk as she could support Holly in the sling with her arms.

It took about an hour and a half of chugging up hill and down dale to get to the coast (and they'd only needed the one stop at public conveniences on the way), and once they were there, the weather couldn't have been more perfect. The sun's heat was quickly burning off the cloud, but there was a gentle breeze and so the temperature felt pleasant rather than sweltering, while the smell of the sea was invigorating.

James made sure the food was in the coolest place in the charabanc, and then, while Peggy breastfed then changed and popped Holly into a clean terry nappy square, he took the children to find the public conveniences (again), which turned out to be mercifully close. Next he escorted them on a short wander so that there could be a bit of running around after being cooped up in the charabanc and he could get his bearings of what Withernsea, which he'd never been to before, had to offer.

After about half an hour they came back to collect Peggy and Holly, and there was a slightly awkward minute or two as James tried to help Peggy put Holly in the baby sling as per June Blenkinsop's instructions. There was a moment when he was standing right in front of Peggy and was support-ing Holly's weight while Peggy knotted behind her waist the ends to the portion of material that would wrap over Holly's bottom; it was a moment or two that felt to Peggy as if James were standing very near to her indeed, a feeling sharpened when he then reached up behind Peggy's neck to help her securely tie the top two bits of material. Peggy felt peculiar at his close proximity, awkward but also full of a not unpleasant heightened awareness, with her skin fizzing at the slightest of his touches, as he gently turned her around so he could check that all the knots were secure and that Holly was in no danger of tumbling to the ground.

James, however, gave no sign that he had even noticed he had been standing very near to Peggy as then he concentrated with what looked to Peggy like exactly the level of attention he'd shown when giving the children the blankets, a couple of umbrellas, a cricket set, and the baskets of food to carry.

They set out, with James pushing Angela, and Peggy making sure she was hidden away at the back of the group while she regained her composure, although her skin felt as if it was repeatedly imagining James's touch.

As they strolled along in the soothing sunshine Peggy began to calm down. She realised how nice it was to be on a day out, even if nearly everything was closed and there were lots of depressing signs of it being wartime about, with signposts having been cut off close to the ground and rolls of barbed wire hooked on to wooden frames across the beach as far as the eye could see.

The boys were fascinated with the technicalities of the defences, and kept a watch out for gun hides, while Angela and Connie wondered what it felt like to live so close to the sea.

They kept more or less to the edge of the coast as they meandered along, and after quite a long walk they turned a little inland and found some shade under which they spread the blankets.

'Let me take Holly for a while,' James said, and Peggy gratefully handed her over, and then turned away to reorganise all the blankets as James told Holly what a clever girl she was.

The boys started a game of Spies, and as James looked happy enough keeping Holly amused, Peggy said to Connie and Angela that if they wanted, the three of them could go for a walk all on their own, with no boys allowed. She remembered how at their age she'd loved to do something with her mother or indeed any older woman who was showing her a bit of attention, and so she hoped that the girls would feel similarly, which they seemed to as they chatted quite happily about all manner of things as Peggy pushed Angela's chair.

Later, after they had returned to the others and everyone had sat about in the sun for a little, James told Angela and Connie to set out the food and then he told Peggy he'd be just a few minutes, and he got up and walked quickly off. When James came back he was clutching some lemonade and four small dark bottles of Mackeson stout, all of which he had got from the hole in the wall at a public house that he'd noticed a little way back.

Peggy had laid Holly on one of the blankets, and Larry and Jessie had constructed a little frame from the cricket stumps wedged into the ground that Peggy was able to sling the piece of material between in order that Holly could be further protected from the rays of the sun by having her own little shadowy shelter within the shade that they were already sitting.

It was discovered that nobody had thought to pack any drinking vessels, which meant their only recourse was that they all had to swig directly from the lemonade bottles. The children thought this to be a total riot, with a cheery Tommy leading the shanty chanting of 'Yo ho ho, and a bottle of rum' that soon everyone joined in with as each new person took their drink. Peggy didn't like to think of what Barbara would have had to say had she seen Connie and Jessie supping straight from a bottle, but as she saw how much fun this was giving all the children she thought that maybe it wouldn't hurt too much, just this once.

To her surprise, as ordinarily Peggy was the sort of person who was always able to eat something, she discovered that she wasn't hungry. But she sipped her Mackeson with relish and contented herself with smiling now and again at everyone, and then she stretched out luxuriously and kicked off her sandals and raised her skirt to just above her knees so that her legs could catch a little sun. Then she closed her eyes, enjoying listening to the children chatter away as they ate their picnic and her eyelids felt heavier and heavier.

When she woke up for the first time she could hear there was a game of cricket going on not too far away. The sound of leather on willow and of James coaching the children with Angela calling out the scores from where she was sitting beside James, sounded such a quintessentially British, pre-war past-time that it quickly lulled Peggy back to sleep, after she'd made sure that a still-napping Holly was fine, which she was, having had the baskets propped beside her by the others as a break should an errant cricket ball roll in her direction.

Peggy's next doze was deeper and more restorative and when she started to come to, Peggy realised that the game of cricket was over and the children had gone off somewhere. She turned to look at Holly, who was still fast asleep, flat on her back under her small cloth tent with her two plump fists stretched out on the ground above her head, and Peggy realised that while she was asleep she had turned over and laid a hand protectively on her daughter's tummy.

Peggy smiled and put her head back down and closed her eyes. She couldn't remember the last time she had had a sleep in the daytime like this. But for the moment it was sheer bliss not having to be anywhere other than where she was, with nothing to do other than look after Holly when she woke up.

A shadow fell on her bare legs, and she opened her eyes to see the outline, stark against the blue sky above, of James standing beside her with the bat, ball and stumps in his hands.

He crouched down and began tidying away some of the picnic debris.

Peggy made as if to get up, but he said, 'You're all right. You've got at least twenty minutes more before everyone gets back. I sent them about a half-mile up the coast to work off a bit more energy, especially as they'll have to take it in turns to push Angela along. I gave them a list of things they had to see or find before they come back, and Angela is going to keep score of what everyone manages.'

'They'll love that – they're still at the age where they're really happy to be in friendly competition. They'll be at secondary school soon, and then it won't be long before they'll go all sullen and grumpy. What a lovely old-fashioned jaunt out we're having, and I mean old-fashioned in a good way. Why don't you come and talk to me?' she urged, 'I want you to tell me about driving and whether you think I could do it.'

Peggy had assumed previously that if she did get a mobile canteen going one day, to provide refreshments for the helpers who'd be clearing up after any bomb damage, that she would work in it alongside somebody else who could drive. But on the way to the coast that morning she had watched closely what James had done as he'd manhandled the charabanc, and she didn't think it looked too difficult, so she thought that if she drove the mobile canteen, then that would free up an able-bodied person to work elsewhere on something useful.

She told James now that she thought one of the disadvantages of growing up in a city was that one tended to get buses, or the occasional train, which meant there was very little reason for anyone to own a car. And actually she'd only been in a private vehicle on a few occasions.

James laughed at this, and said he loved driving and having his own car, not that he got to drive it very often these days, and he thought that one day nearly everyone would want to have a vehicle to call their own. He doubted she'd find driving too difficult and said that lots of women were now learning how to do it because of the war. Peggy said how Barbara was always talking about the women bus drivers and ambulance drivers in London, and James said he thought they'd be switching to women drivers for the hospital's ambulances too.

With the last of the picnic debris now tidied away, James stopped what he was doing and went and plonked himself down on a spread-out blanket near to Peggy, who now sat up and put a sun hat on as the sun had moved around. It was shining down, and after a while James stretched extravagantly and then lay back, almost horizontal but with his weight supported on his elbows and he closed his eyes for a minute or two. After a while he turned onto his side, facing Peggy, but with his head propped on his hand as he listened to her chatter on about what a nice thing it was that he was doing for the children, and that she was sorry that so far she had been absolutely no help at all in looking after them and had been leaving everything to him. And so on. Peggy suddenly felt nervous – she wasn't sure why – and so it seemed easier just to keep on prattling away about not very much at all.

After a while, and just as Peggy was suggesting that James tell her the story of his life, he leant across and, with a small smile, briefly touched a finger to her lips to stem her chatter.

She stopped what she was saying immediately but then James didn't say anything, as Peggy fought to steady her erratically thumping heart.

She looked at James again and she noticed that his face had caught the sun and that his brow was beaded with perspiration from running about in the cricket match. But Peggy didn't have more than a moment to think about this as then he said quietly 'May I?' causing her to move her head a little in his direction to catch his words, and when she had, she wasn't sure what he meant.

Then he leant over and kissed her softly on the lips, and she understood what he had be suggesting. Oh, how out of practice she was with all of this! she thought.

The feeling of James's lips on hers was a shock at first, although almost immediately Peggy gave herself up to the exquisite sensátion that set every cell in her body jingling.

Then the spell was broken as James wrenched himself away as if Peggy was on fire.

Abruptly he sat up, and shuffled his bottom across the blanket so that he was positioned well away from her. Looking anywhere but at Peggy, James began to apologise profusely as he tucked his shirt back under his belt where it had ridden up a little, and then he made to re-tie his shoelaces, saying quickly a flurry of things like 'I'm so sorry, Peggy', 'oh my goodness', 'I do apologise, I don't know what came over me' and 'please accept my apology, it won't happen again', at which Peggy's heart plunged in disappointment as it was clear to her that he had enjoyed the kissing, brief as it was, a whole lot less than she had.

Just for an instant Peggy stretched over as if to touch his arm, although she kept it hovering a few inches above his elbow, as she said, 'James', followed by another 'James', this second time more softly when she could finally get him to look at her.

'I'm not sorry, James. Um. Er, I haven't been —' Peggy began, although with no clear idea of what she should say as with a jolt she realised that she hadn't once thought of Bill as James had been kissing her, or indeed at all that morning that she could remember, apart from a fleeting moment when she was having a sponge wash before breakfast, and she certainly hadn't felt as if she were a woman still legally married to somebody else. Peggy wasn't at all decided as to whether this feeling of abandon (what else could she call it but that?) was a good thing or a bad thing.

Then Holly woke abruptly and began to cry insistently, clearly feeling that she'd been missing out on a party for far too long, and Peggy distracted herself by kneeling and leaning over to her daughter in order to pick her up, and James sighed in a way that Peggy was unable to fathom any meaning.

And so whatever had been going on (or *almost* had been going on) between James and Peggy in their few minutes in a bubble of a perfect afternoon was rudely ruptured into smithereens, leaving both feeling assaulted by a huge gamut of feelings.

Chapter Twenty-three

There must have been something in the air at Withernsea Sands that day because as the children reached the point along the coastal path that James had sent them to, after which they had larked around there for a while before they turned to head back to where James and Peggy and Holly were, Tommy volunteered to push Angela's wheelchair even though it was Connie's turn. Connie didn't mind at all as this meant she could walk side by side with Aiden.

Tommy pushed the wheelchair very slowly for fifty yards or so, and then he pretended that something was making one of the wheels drag but he insisted that the others should head on back to James and Peggy without waiting for him to sort it out in order that James wouldn't be cross about them all not returning to the picnic area at the time they'd been instructed. Tommy promised that he and Angela would catch up with everyone once the errant wheel had been sorted.

Aiden and Larry made a move in his direction as if they were going to help him, but Tommy made a snarly 'get lost' face at them from where he was now crouching behind Angela's back that brooked no arguments, and they quickly cottoned on that their services were not required and so they made themselves scarce.

As Aiden and Larry caught back up with the others, and several seconds later there was a loud gale of laughter from them, Tommy huddled down even further as he fiddled about with the inside of one of the back wheels. Although Angela tried to see what he was doing to the wheel, she couldn't quite peer far enough over to glimpse exactly what it was that he was up to.

Once he thought he had spent long enough doing this as the other children were quite some way away by now and their chattering voices and happy sniggers could no long be heard, Tommy said a firm 'that's better', and that they could get going now. But then he shuffled forward and stayed squatting as he began instead to talk to Angela and point things out to her such as the white-horse waves that they could see cresting the gunmetal-grey sea and the harsh calls of the ever-circling yellow-eyed seagulls who were flying above, carrying on their normal scavenging obviously unaware that the country was at war. And at long last Tommy finally risked snatching a kiss from a most surprised Angela, although whether it was from the kiss itself or because of Tommy talking about, as she saw it, not very boyish things like waves and birds, it was hard to tell.

It was the first time either he or Angela had ever kissed or been kissed, but then they were both only eleven and so it wasn't surprising, even though with each week that passed, Tommy was getting more of a shadow where his moustache would one day be. They both reddened profusely when they realised what they had done. But then they did it again, just to be sure that it hadn't been some sort of mistake earlier, before Angela muttered regretfully that they'd better rejoin the others or otherwise Peggy and James would be sending a search party out, and they didn't want to be caught like this.

'But maybe we could risk just one more before we go off to find everybody?' she said finally, and Tommy thought that she had probably had a good idea. A minute later he thought that in fact Angela had had a very good idea indeed.

It was an oddly subdued journey home from the seaside. Tummies were full of chips and garishly coloured boiled saveloys, and the children were feeling much more sloth-like than when they'd been driven the other way. It felt to all of them as if it had been a long day and that they had all had more than their fair share of fresh air and sunshine.

Peggy had been looking forward to eating some plump and juicy fried cod with her chips, but when they had got to a fish and chip shop it was to learn that sea fishing had now virtually stopped because of the danger to the fleets posed by German U-boats.

Peggy slapped a hand to her brow and then told James that she should have realised this would be the case as June had been muttering about the scarcity of fish for her fish pies, but she hadn't thought it through and she was sorry. Then James said no, it was his fault as it had originally been his suggestion, at which point they looked at each other slightly askance as, although their words had been to do with fish and chips, somehow it felt like they'd been talking about something else, and that something else was unspecified but all the same, quite, quite awkward.

Despite having gorged themselves with the picnic sandwiches earlier, the children were hungry again as they had done a lot of haring about, and so Peggy insisted that she should buy some food for them all anyway. Aiden chose a saveloy to accompany his chips, after which all the other children copied him, and then Larry wanted a pickled onion as well, which of course meant that all the others wanted pickled onions too. Peggy paid for everyone's food, insisting it was her treat, although it turned out to be quite a tussle to do this as James tried very hard to pass a note or two from his wallet over to the chip-shop owner before she could take the money from her own purse.

Then, as they waited for their food to be sprinkled with salt and vinegar and wrapped in individual portions in cut-up newspaper for them to eat outside straight from the paper, Peggy surprised herself by suddenly having to blink away a tear or two as the familiar smell of the fryers in the fish and chip shop reminded her with a painful whump to her chest of her dear puss Fishy, who was still with Barbara and Ted back in Jubilee Street.

Peggy's chest ached with missing her cat as she remembered how the tabby had always sat up and begged like a little dog by lifting her two front paws up and down together whenever Peggy and Bill had enjoyed some fish and chips. Fishy knew Peggy would soon be giving her a saucer onto which she had put some prime flakes of fish from Peggy's own portion and so this begging motion was to hurry her mistress up.

Peggy had noticed that, just like on the day of the twins

being overcome while collecting the eggs, her bouts of home-sickness would come out of the blue and would hit hard when they struck. In general she had thought herself lucky that she was an adult and therefore (she told herself firmly) less prone. But Barbara had told her on her last visit to Yorkshire when Peggy had talked about them, that Peggy was forgetting that she was a recent mother and so it was to be expected that she would be feeling emotional as she had a small baby to care for. Barbara advised that Peggy should remind herself that wherever Holly was would therefore be home as far as Peggy was concerned, at least for the moment.

And so it turned out to be, Peggy thought, as her thoughts of Fishy and her begging turning out unexpectedly to be the agent for making her realise that while there were positives to being in Harrogate, there was quite a large part of Peggy that was yearning for her old life, although these feelings were muddled as she knew too that she had enjoyed her kiss with James, which of course would never have happened had she stayed in London.

Wishing she could have Fishy in Harrogate with her, as the small kit's purrs were so comforting of an evening when they'd sat nestled together in a chair as they listened to the wireless, Peggy remembered then with something approaching affection just what a softie Bill had been for Fishy when she had been a wee kitten. And then it all felt a bit too much for her again, and her chin began to dimple with the effort of holding back her tears. Peggy looked downwards and stared morosely at her startlingly pink saveloy and the golden chips peeping out at her from the folds of newspaper she was holding. Holly had been left safely swaddled on the charabanc parked outside the chippy with its door open to encourage a breeze, and in a trice Peggy found that her appetite had withered away again, although she tried not to draw attention to this but she wasn't able to do it quickly or convincingly enough to stop James looking at her seriously. While she was feeling tired and not like it at all, Peggy had to make a show of eating, after which she gave in with relief, and then the children were very happy to divvy up the rest of her unwanted meal between them, even though Peggy could see that James was still examining her with scrutinising eyes when he thought she wasn't looking at him.

As they lined up to climb back into the charabanc to make their way home to Harrogate, Peggy pushed her way to the front of the queue.

'I'll sit at the back so that I can see to Holly,' she said brusquely, not caring if James thought her rude. She felt unsettled and unable to concentrate, and it was as if her thoughts of Bill and tiny Fishy had further complicated what had gone on earlier when she and James had been sitting on the rug.

Perhaps it was all just as well she was sitting back where she was, with no opportunity to talk with James as he drove, Peggy thought before they'd gone more than a mile on their way home. Now he didn't seem to want to look at her either, or to speak to her unless absolutely necessary, and he obviously didn't want to kiss her again. Bother. She didn't want to draw the children's attention to any of this in case they said anything to Mabel or Gracie (she knew Roger would never stray into such territory with her) but she didn't know if she was overcomplicating things and making a fuss about nothing very much that was merely indicative of a muddle in her head purely of her own making. Or maybe she was just overtired and had had too much sunshine, which was why she now could feel a headache coming on.

She should never have let James kiss her, Peggy admonished herself a few miles further on, and then felt worse when she remembered how regretful she had felt when James had pulled away from her after the kiss as if she were something unpleasant and as if for him to have made this move towards her was a huge mistake. That stupid kiss – she hadn't wanted it or asked for it (well, she didn't think she had, although she wasn't absolutely sure, as to be completely honest she doubted she would have lifted her skirt to just above knee-level if, say, she had been sitting in the sun with either Roger or Ted), but now that the kiss had happened she couldn't seem to stop thinking about it, no matter how hard she tried.

And as uncomfortable and squirm-making as part of the memory was, each time she remembered the sensation of James's lips on hers, her belly slid downwards with a lurch of pleasure that immediately made the secret places of her body tingle and do a different sort of squirm.

Holly had now finished her tea and so Peggy made sure her own clothes were back where they should be and then she placed her replete daughter over her shoulder to wind her, and she allowed Holly to fall asleep where she was as she seemed content and comfy.

Peggy had a lot of staring out of the window that she wanted to do as she tried to analyse the maelstrom of conflicting thoughts and emotions swirling busily around inside her. It was impossible for her to come to any firm conclusions, and she realised she must have been sighing in frustration with herself when Jessie looked over at her with curiosity, and she had to plaster on her face a cheery smile to encourage him to look elsewhere.

As Peggy mulled over her day, occasionally she turned her eyes towards the charabanc's mirror that the driver was to use to see the vehicles behind and which was positioned where the two pieces of glass that formed the windscreen joined in its middle. She could pick out James's face in it if she tilted her head just a little, and she saw that he appeared to be staring intently at the road which was what she would have expected, seeing as he was driving them all back to Harrogate, which was why she had dared to sneak a peek. But then James glanced into the mirror and they looked for a moment directly at each other, him frowning and turning away first. With a wash of perspiration down her back, Peggy made so sure that she didn't angle her head that way again that in tandem with her headache her jaw began to ache from being clenched with the effort of her only looking out of the window with feigned fascination.

Aiden and Connie had sat together just behind James, and Peggy could just about make out them asking the doctor a raft of questions about the hospital, and the sort of things James did there running his team of doctors. Above the noise of the charabanc's engine as it made heavy weather of going up a hill she heard James say, 'Aiden, if you come over one evening and it's not a busy time I'll show you around and you can see for yourself things like the operating theatre and the X-ray machine. I might be able to find a book or two that will tell you more.'

Connie had a slightly petulant tinge to her voice as she asked James what about if *she* were interested in medicine too and wanted something to read, and then there was a pause as both James and Peggy thought about a tactful way that he could deal with the fact that Connie's reading probably wasn't up to this sort of material just yet. But then James avoided this particular prickly issue altogether by saying, 'I meant both of you, of course.' Connie was mollified, leaving Peggy uncertain whether she was pleased or cross with James's diplomatic reply.

Oh dear, it seemed that neither James nor she could win, as far as her own thoughts were going that afternoon. They were damned if they did or said anything, and damned if they didn't, it seemed to Peggy.

Jessie and Larry were sitting in opposite seats, with their backs against the windows and their legs stretched out on the seat in front. They were silent for a while, but after that the tense atmosphere in the charabanc lightened as they led a round or two of singing, opening with 'Ten Green Bottles', and then Tommy, who had a lovely singing voice, and Angela, whose voice wasn't bad, joined in for a couple of verses each of 'It's a Long Way to Tipperary' and 'Good-Bye-Ee'. It was only when the children launched into 'If You Were the Only Girl in the World and I Was the Only Boy' that Peggy risked another look at the charabanc's mirror again, and her heart bumped alarmingly when she saw James steal a glance at her, and she had to turn her head obviously to stare out of the window and make it seem like she hadn't been looking at him, although she doubted he'd been fooled.

By the time they got back to Tall Trees Peggy felt quite worn out with the effort of thinking too much and trying not to look in the wrong place. Holly had picked up on her mother's now fractious mood, becoming quite grizzly, intimating with cries rising in volume that in all honesty she'd also had enough of the charabanc's noisy engine and a mother distracted by something that wasn't her, and so she was very much looking forward to her bath, supper and bedtime.

Holly's snivels gave Peggy a welcome excuse for slipping away with the minimum of fuss, ignoring James's outstretched hand he'd extended politely towards her elbow in an attempt to ensure she got herself and Holly safely down the charabanc's steps.

Once on firm ground Peggy made a show of keeping her eyes turned downwards in order to wrap Holly's blanket around the baby, and then called out in a falsely jolly tone, 'What a lovely trip, James, thank you so much, but I'd better get this little one inside right away, don't you think? And children you won't forget to say a nice thank-you and goodbye to James, will you? And if you can, everybody, just double-check that nothing of ours is left on any of the seats, as that would be really helpful. And Connie dear, can you bring me all of Holly's things please?' and without looking back, Peggy headed up the drive to the rectory.

She hot-footed it inside Tall Trees, bypassing with only a hasty smile in their direction in response to a 'hello there, have you had a lovely time?' from Mabel and Roger who were on their way out to help with the unloading, and who raised their eyebrows questioningly at each other in the wake of Peggy's hasty departure.

This, with the sound of the children saying in chorus 'Thank you, Dr Legard, for giving us a lovely day,' and James ignoring the children's thanks as he called to Peggy's retreating back a distinctly plaintive, 'But I was hoping…', made a cacophony of sounds that an overheated and overtired Peggy found stayed whirling in her ears as she heaved a still blubbing Holly up the stairs to their bedroom.

Chapter Twenty-four

My dearest Jessie and Connie,

How are you both? It's almost your birthday, and Ted and I can hardly believe you are going to be <u>eleven</u>! How exciting – and how big! Me and Ted are excited, that's for certain. And there's only a few weeks now until big school starts.

Did you enjoy your day out at the seaside? Peggy said it was lovely and sunny for the whole day you were out, and that everyone had a good run-around and a big blast of fresh air, but that there was no fish when you got to the chippy.

I promise you both, my darlings, that when this war is over and we are all back together in Jubilee Street, one of the very first things that we'll all do as a family is that we'll gorge ourselves silly on fish and chips until we just can't move. How does that sound to you, my dear Connie and Jessie? Is that a deal?

Daddy and me had a day trip out of London too. We went on the train down to the South Downs in Sussex, where there is some really good walking. (We honeymooned nearby, and so it is a place that holds very special memories for us, not least as the next year both of you were born!)

It was a beautiful sunny August day for us as well, and we both struggled to remember a better one. The air was clear and there must have been a shower of rain overnight that made the grass look very fresh, and greener than what we see in London around what hasn't been given over to food growing, and everything we could see was clean and almost sparkling, so much so that it felt almost perfect. It would only have needed the two of you there with us to be perfect, in fact!

We walked for two hours and we had just sat on some grass and were enjoying our picnic when we could hear aeroplanes flying above us. We looked up, and there in the skies very high up we could see all of a sudden our lads from the RAF fighting it out with what looked to be the same number of Luftwaffe planes from Germany. The sun was so bright that now and again we could see it shining off the metal of the aeroplanes, and there were so many aircraft up there that at times the sky looked quite crowded, can you believe?

Jessie, I'm not good at recognising types of aeroplanes but Daddy told me that he could see flying on our side mainly Spitfires, although he thought he might possibly also have seen a couple of Hawker Hurricanes up there for us too, with the Germans mainly in Messershmidts (not sure how to spell that – I should have checked this earlier!), I think he said.

The planes dipped and rose, and chased each other. I can't pretend it wasn't exciting to see – the weather was so clear and so completely without any clouds that the sky was almost dark blue, a real azure, Peggy would have called it.

After a while there was something about it that brought lumps to our throats I'm not ashamed to say that we both shed a tear as it was such a beautiful day and a sight we won't forget.

I want you both to know how very, very much Daddy and me love you, and that whatever happens to us all during this dreadful *war, I don't want either of you to forget this one really important thing, that we love you and we think of you both all the time.*

I'll write again soon, but in the meanwhile remember to eat up everything that Mabel gives you, and not to do anything silly with Milburn that might end up with any of you getting hurt. Be good, and do everything that Peggy asks you to as well.

With all my love, Mummy xxx

There was an emotional silence when Connie finished her laborious reading out loud of the letter over the breakfast table, with both Jessie and Aiden helping her out at times with some of the longer words, and Peggy once offering to take over the reading from Connie, who just ignored the offer.

Peggy had to swallow and wipe under her eyelashes as she understood that Barbara had seen something that would be talked about for years, and that she had been shocked to realise that she was watching young men die.

Roger cleared his throat loudly and made a show of shaking out and then folding the newspaper to another page, while Mabel gave a trumpeting blow of her nose into a hankie.

This wasn't at all what Peggy had been expecting when she'd handed the letter to the twins, as Barbara's missives were normally positive and cheery, and sometimes even contained a joke that would make the children laugh. Peggy always encouraged Connie and Jessie to take it in turns to read their letters out at the breakfast table as she was surreptitiously trying to get Connie to be a bit more confident in this area, but this neatly addressed envelope hadn't at all contained what she had bargained for and unfortunately it had been Connie's turn to read, which had further dragged things out, which in turn had highlighted the emotion behind what was being said. Now, in the dank silence following Connie saying 'kiss, kiss, kiss', Peggy wasn't at all sure what to say to the children in the letter's gloomy wake.

The situation was further complicated as Peggy was aware too that Larry or Angela hardly ever got letters from home, and in the past she'd noticed how they also really enjoyed hearing about what was going on back in Bermondsey and so she always encouraged them to sit and listen to the twins' letters from Barbara and Ted, almost as if they were pretending that Barbara was writing to them too. Larry's mother Susan wasn't good with pen and paper, Peggy knew, and of course his father was a raging drunk who didn't pay any credence to reading and writing at the best of times. And Angela's mother Ethel had her hands full with being the family's only breadwinner, while she also had to look after Angela's heavily disabled sister, Jill, who'd had polio as a baby, and a father suffering very poor health with shellshock from the Great War and such bad seizures every day that he was unable to work.

But now neither Larry nor Angela looked as happy to hear one of Barbara's letters being read out as usually they did, while Peggy could see both Tommy, who of course saw his parents every day, and Aiden, who saw his parents often too as they didn't live far away, were looking anxiously in their direction, before switching their gazes back between them and the twins.

Awkwardly, Larry pushed his chair back with an ear-jangling scraping sound on the stone flags of the kitchen's floor, and he hurriedly left the room without looking at anybody. Angela looked down moodily into her lap, and picked at the hem of her skirt.

Barbara's unsettlingly confessional tone and her uncharacteristically insistent declaration of her and Ted's love for the twins had of course been lovely in many ways, and fortifying too, Peggy was sure, for Connie and Jessie to receive, but it must have highlighted to both Angela and Larry that their own family situations didn't provide anything like the same succour for them. All in all, it would have been a perturbing letter for all the children.

'I think Mummy must have been very upset when she wrote this to us at it didn't really sound like her,' unintentionally agreeing with her aunt, Connie broke the silence, her voice and her brow crinkled with thought as she had been so concentrating on saying the words as she read, that Peggy thought she hadn't until then had time to absorb what Barbara had been saying. Still frowning and looking at the letter, Connie hadn't seemed to notice that Larry had left the room so suddenly.

With a twist to her heart, Peggy saw how Connie's contemplative expression, just for a short while, made her look almost grown up. It was the first time Peggy had had a glimpse of the woman that Connie would become one day, but she could see this clearly now, and then Peggy thought of the inexorable way that time passed them all by and how time really did, as the saying goes, wait for no man. Trying to brush these philosophical thoughts aside, Peggy wondered then whether any of the others had also spied what she had just fancied she had seen in Connie, although she could see too that the moment had passed and Connie was back to looking just like any girl a week or two before her eleventh birthday, and actually nobody really seemed to be looking at her just at the moment as they all seemed lost in their own thoughts.

'Yes, I think Barbara was very upset when she wrote to you both,' Peggy agreed sadly. 'To me it sounds like by chance she and Ted saw something they'd never come across before, and then when they realised quite what it was they were watching, Barbara felt full of awe and also very sad, both at the same time. And I think these feelings have stayed with her. I expect Daddy is feeling a bit the same.'

'I can't imagine Daddy crying,' said Jessie loyally. 'I think Mummy made a mistake and his eye was watering because he'd got something in it, or because he had been staring at the shiny Spitfires for too long.'

To Peggy, Jessie appeared to be very young and very much a little boy still, experiencing nothing near the shift of physical development and hormones that Connie seemed to be just on the cusp of. Peggy's heart went out to Jessie and the way he was trying to stand up for his father in front of them all.

'Well, we all know how Ted is very strong and not overly emotional, a bit like your mother is usually,' said Peggy carefully, as it was important that she didn't make her nephew lose face, although she didn't want to allow Jessie to believe that boys always had to button bad things up, 'and it was very bright and sunny from all accounts, and my eyes water sometimes if the light is very bright, and so Barbara might have made a mistake if Ted were crying or not. But if Daddy did cry just a little when he was standing on the Downs with Barbara and watching the fighting, then you do know that is nothing to be ashamed of, don't you, Jessie? Some things in life are so sad that they would make *anybody* – simply anybody at all – have a quick cry.'

The boys looked askance and as if this couldn't possibly be true in any circumstances, and even Gracie seemed distinctly dubious.

There were unexpected repercussions to Barbara's emotive letter arriving at Tall Trees as it kick-started an obsession amongst the boys with the aerial dogfights now taking place over British soil and also over the English Channel. The newspapers were full of descriptive reports too, and following a speech Winston Churchill had made in the House of Commons the aerial offensive had now been widely dubbed as the Battle of Britain.

The boys became increasingly fanatical about paying attention to any reports of what was going on as regards British combat in the skies, and so on Roger's collection of ancient road maps of Great Britain, which had been put up on the long wall of the upstairs landing, they began to plot with drawing pins holding little stickers, various strategic events they heard on the radio or read about in the papers.

Aiden and Larry began bringing discarded newspapers back with them when they had finished their shifts at June Blenkinsop's, and the boys would scour the newspapers later in the evening, cutting out various stories so that they would then have to get the sticky pot of Gloy glue out in order to paste the cuttings into a scrapbook, and then put the remains of the newspaper in the stable where the papers and metals were being piled ready for the depot.

Pride of place in the scrapbook, on the very first page, was a *London Calling* story with the blousy headline 'The Fighting Spitfire', as this outlined all the attributes of the Spitfire and, fascinatingly, gave a detailed diagram of the craft, very neatly labelled, that showed all its features, both outside and inside. On more than one occasion, as Peggy went upstairs to put Holly down for the night, she heard the boys quizzing each other in the intricacies of this and other British fighter aircraft, or destroyers if there had been reports of something happening at sea.

The girls were less interested in the technicalities of the various aeroplanes or aerial strategy, but hours would pass when they seemed happy enough to allow the boys to show off to them all they were learning about a variety of planes, tanks and sea-going craft. And as a present for the lads Connie and Angela spent a whole two days making up a set of playing cards for Snap using carefully traced drawings of the various fighters, the cards then being used in some nail-bitingly lively games.

'I'm not sure I approve of this fixation the children have at the moment with the war,' said Peggy to Mabel a day or so later. She had been hoping that all this talk of fighting strategy and aircraft was going to be a brief craze that would blow over after several days, but it looked like the children's interest was much deeper than ideally she'd like and that in fact their interest was increasing rather than going the other way.

'Me neither. But it's only t' be expected, I supp'se,' Mabel pointed out.

It wasn't long before the children asked – no, they absolutely *begged* – to be taken to the cinema more regularly as Pathé

News was now starting to broadcast newsreel of actual fighting, and the children were desperate to see some films of real-life action. There was a debate between Peggy, Roger and Mabel as to whether this was a good thing or not, as Peggy was concerned that if not checked, the war would grow into a truly unhealthy obsession, while Roger felt that for the children to be informed sensibly of what was happening was the best way to stop them getting too imaginative as to what was going on elsewhere and perhaps frightening themselves.

Peggy thought overnight about what Roger had said, and then she decided that he had made a valid point, and that for Roger to accompany the children to the cinema as per his suggestion was probably the best option as otherwise the chances were that they would start to sneak in anyway on their own, in which case they wouldn't have an adult on hand with them to put into a wider context what it was that they were seeing, or to explain what the news broadcasters were speaking about if there was talk about political strategy. Still, Peggy decided not to consult Barbara as to what she thought any about this, as it might make things awkward if Barbara said a firm 'No' and then the twins disobeyed her by going to see the Pathé News anyway or refused to desist in their avid poring over stories in the newspapers of the course the war was taking.

The result was that the children were asked by Roger if they wanted to contribute their pocket money towards a weekly visit to the cinema to see the news broadcasts, which they did. Roger told them that he would be accompanying them, as chaperone.

'Pa!' Tommy's voice had a whine to it, 'the lads from school won't 'ave anyone wi' 'em. It'll make us seem like babies if we can't go on our own.'

Roger replied uncharacteristically gruffly, 'Well, the deal is that I come with you, so you must like it or lump it. And if that is a problem for all, or any, of you – Tommy, are you listening? – then the cinema and Pathé News, and putting pins in maps is off the agenda, I'm afraid. And I mean it.'

Chapter Twenty-five

With quite a lot of scrimping and planning, Jessie had saved a whole two bob of his pocket money to buy Connie a birthday present. One morning, not long after he'd fed and cleaned out Milburn, and given her a wash-down as the weather was so warm and clammy even right in the middle of the night that the pony had sweated up in her stable, he left the others to deal with the chickens and Porky as he wanted to walk to the shops with Peggy, who was on her way to her morning stint at June Blenkinsop's and who was pushing Holly along in the perambulator.

As they strolled along, Jessie told his aunt that he'd wanted to go to the shops on his own in order to choose Connie's birthday present as he didn't want to be distracted by the others as to what he might choose to get her.

Peggy told Jessie that he was a very nice brother for Connie to have, and that she personally was proud of him for wanting to get his sister something nice for her birthday. Jessie gave such a grin of joy at her compliment that Peggy gave him a shilling to add to his spending fund (thinking she must remember to do the same for Connie later) as she vowed to herself that she would tell the children more often when she felt they were doing something nice. It didn't cost her anything to do this in the emotional sense, and the rewards really seemed worth it as far as the children were concerned, to judge by Jessie's grin. And, Peggy admitted to herself, it was nice to make somebody else smile, as she hadn't been too good at this since the trip to the seaside, other than with Holly of course. But Holly smiled easily and could even find her own feet hilarious, and so Peggy didn't feel particularly impressed with herself for making her daughter chuckle.

At the shops Jessie enjoyed himself as he wandered about for an hour or more, and eventually made his mind up that his sister's present would either be two cinema tickets so that Connie and Aiden could go to the flicks on their own or a tube of pink Chapstick (it almost looked like a pale lipstick, although he knew it would be colourless on her lips as Aunt Peggy had one – but Jessie had heard Connie and Angela talking only the day before about how much they were looking forward to having their own lipsticks one day, provided there was still some left in the shops by the time they were old enough as they'd heard on the wireless that make-up was running out and was increasingly hard to find, and so this seemed a good compromise that Jessie could afford and that he thought his sister would appreciate). Jessie didn't think Connie and Aiden were necessarily girlfriend and boyfriend, but he knew they liked being together and so he thought Connie might enjoy the cinema tickets as a thoughtful present. This was a bigger gesture than it might have first seemed, as Jessie often felt a bit jealous of the way Connie looked at Aiden, as until they had arrived in Harrogate he was used to being the one she wanted to spend time with more than anyone else and so when she gave Aiden her special, conspiratorial look, it did give her brother a pang somewhere deep down inside him.

Jessie was standing on the pavement near the shops and, frozen in indecision as to which was the present that Connie would most enjoy, he had just tossed a halfpenny in the air to help him decide – heads for the Chapstick, tails for the cinema tickets – when he was unable to adroitly catch the coin in his right hand ready to slap on his left forearm, and with a sigh of frustration he had to watch it skitter off his arm and down onto the pavement.

But before he could lean over to pick it up, a mouldy old boot with the leather at the toe worn completely through, the tread of the heels ground down to nothing, and the laces so raggedy that they were long enough for only the top two lace-holes to actually be used, stamped itself down hard on the halfpenny as it was spinning, and flattened the coin into a mossy cleft in the pavement.

Jessie, who had been deep in concentration, jumped with the shock at what he was seeing. He had thought he was in a pleasant, dreamy world of his own, thinking about presents and birthdays. But as he looked up quickly, his heart sank. In fact he was in his worst nightmare.

He was alone, with none of his friends nearby, while standing directly in front of him were the five evacuee boys from Hull, oozing cockiness and delight at having discovered one of the TT Muskets hived off from the rest of the gang. He fancied he could smell their unwashed bodies, and sense them sidling around to circle him completely.

Jessie hoped one of them would be looking at least a little friendly, but no such luck as every single one of their dingy, blank-looking faces seemed nothing short of mean and aggressive, and clearly out for trouble.

As he felt the chilly shiver of somebody walking over his grave despite the heat of the morning, Jessie knew without a shadow of doubt that he was in for a drubbing. He was hopelessly outnumbered and, although he had assiduously concentrated during the self-defence lessons that Roger had organised in the church hall, he realised now that out in the real world events unfolded in a very different way to how one practised for it in a class and he, distressingly, had nothing in this particular situation to offer in his own defence. Jessie looked about wildly, hoping to see anything or anyone that might come to his aid, but in this he was defeated immediately, quickly concluding that there was precious little he could do to help himself. He would just have to face whatever was coming his way with all the bravery he could muster.

It was the biggest, the one who had told the Tall Trees lot to bugger off when he'd been leaning over the wall yelling at them just after Connie had humiliated them all, who had his foot on Jessie's coin. Of course it was.

Gone was the Hull boys' now silly-seeming routine of showing off and posturing. Jessie longed for it to be back, as in comparison with the brooding, hard, vindictive stares of these lads up close that he could see before him now, if they had employed their old series of moves perhaps it could have bought Jessie just a little time to try to think of a way out of his predicament. But there was no chance of that this morning, he could see.

''Ey up, that's t' little runt from t' gang wi' t' daft pony an' t' cocky bonny lass,' said one with a hideous inevitability.

265

The capless, big one in the middle replied significantly, 'Aye, yer right, bonny lad, so it is. An' wot a little runt 'e be', and then he stepped forward and began giving Jessie sharp pushes in the chest. This boy was strong, and with two of his compadres having moved behind Jessie to cut off any chance of escape, Jessie found himself being forced backwards into an alley. Each time his chest was struck Jessie felt a jab of pain that made him wince (not too obviously, he hoped), but he suspected that this was just a prelude to something much worse.

He was right, and the only good thing about it all was that he didn't have to wait too long for it to happen.

'I, er ... I ...' he tried, but his words were lost in a kerfuffle and suddenly Jessie found himself on the ground, bashing his hip bone and his elbow as he went down, as one of the lads behind him had stuck out a leg which Jessie had been pushed backwards against until he lost his balance and had tumbled down onto the cobbles in the alley. It was all happening so quickly that now he didn't even have time to be scared.

Then, without further ado, all these Hull evacuees pounced. They were full of bloodlust, Jessie thought, and he quailed as he heard them yell 'take that' and 'what d' yer think o' that, yer fuckin' jessie?' and 'yer bleedin' soddin' toe-rag', as viciously they repeatedly kicked and punched him.

All Jessie could do was to tuck his chin to his chest, and try helplessly to cover his head with his arms and hands as the blows and thumps and kicks rained relentlessly down on him although, oddly, after the first wincing jolts of pain, for a while he felt very little. As he lay on his side sucking up what they had to offer – which was a lot – Jessie drew his knees as close up to his belly as he could in order to make himself as small a target as possible as he just tried to get through the next minute or two.

'Yer jessie, yer little bleeder!' one yelled, but Jessie had already got the point.

The assault seemed to go on for ever although Jessie heard the breathing of the boys become more laboured as their initial enthusiasm dwindled, and gradually he felt a slight lessening of the power of their kicks and punches.

And then there was a slight pause.

The next thing Jessie heard was Tommy's strident voice shouting with – as Jessie thought to himself as he was now hit by wave after wave of pain sweeping over him – a depressing lack of originality in swearwords, ''E might be a right jessie all right, but he's our fuckin' jessie, d' yer 'ear, yer fuckin' maggots? Lay off 'im. 'E's *our* fuckin' Jessie, d' yer get it, yer fuckin' bastards? OUR fuckin' JESSIE!'

While correct in the technical sense, Jessie didn't think the Hull lads had any idea of his name, and so he couldn't help feeling that Tommy was perhaps not promoting quite the most sensible version of him, and it was an assertion that in all likelihood would lead to a greater flurry of kicks and punches on his prone body.

However, Jessie was wrong in this assumption, as then there was a different sound of hitting as the complexion of the attack altered and there was a flurry of faster-seeming whacks and blows, accompanied by somebody grunting with the effort of what they were doing. These were whacks and blows that weren't touching Jessie any longer as they were being targeted elsewhere, just above where he was lying in the dirt, and there was a long moment or two where time stretched elastic before the harsh, ear-piercing sound of a policeman's whistle interrupted whatever it was that was going on in the alley.

But by this point Jessie was oblivious and beyond caring, as he was no longer conscious.

Chapter Twenty-six

Her sandals making slapping noises on the floor, Connie barged into June Blenkinsop's where Peggy was sitting behind the counter taking the money from customers.

'Aunt Peggy! Aunt Peggy, come quickly, Jessie's been hurt! Hurt very bad. He's not moving and his eyes are shut, and I think he's dying,' Connie screamed really loudly as she pushed her way to the front of the queue.

The café sounds of pleasant chattering and cutlery on crockery fell silent as most of the customers were regulars, and so they knew Peggy and all the evacuees at Tall Trees, especially since the arrival of Milburn had made them such a distinctive bunch of children over the summer. Several of the customers had remarked at various times to Peggy that the Tall Trees children looked as if they were having a wonderful time larking around.

For an instant Peggy looked frozen in the dead still of the teashop as she stared uncomprehendingly at Connie as if she couldn't quite take on board what her visibly distraught niece had just said to her.

'Aunt Peggy – Jessie's *dying!*' Connie tried again, and this time Peggy understood her niece's desperate words.

June told Peggy to just go with Connie, assuring her that she could manage both the till and keeping an eye on Holly, who was happily snoozing the morning away in her perambulator that had been placed in the shade in the teashop's back yard, insisting that Peggy should hurry off and do what she had to do.

With this Peggy was able to put herself in gear. She gave the tiniest of grim smiles in her friend's direction and, wrenching off her pinny and throwing it towards the counter but it landing on the floor in her haste to leave, she fairly raced from the café with Connie at her side, followed by several calls of good luck from the customers. Hot on their heels was one of James's doctor colleagues, who'd been enjoying an early lunch but who had downed his knife and fork immediately when he realised a child was lying very possibly badly hurt.

The alleyway where Jessie's duffing-up had taken place was only a few streets away, and by the time a slightly breathless Peggy and Connie ran into it a policeman was there. He was holding with one of his giant meaty hands firmly onto the arm of the now chastened-looking ringleader of the Hull boys, whose knuckles were skinned and whose brow was sweating around a crop of angry-looking whiteheads, while the policeman was using his other hand to clasp the upper arm of Tommy, who was leaning forward to get a view of the Hull boy around the policeman's generous belly, staring at him furiously. The Hull boy was alone now as the rest of his gang had made themselves scarce at the copper's whistle but this one had been too shocked at what had happened to run away quickly enough and now he was making sure he didn't catch Tommy's eye.

Several members of the public were gathered around Jessie, who was still out cold, lying forlorn and bloody and completely motionless in the dirt and filth of the alley.

Peggy was horrified when she realised that the small bundle of crumpled clothes that initially she had taken for some tatty and ancient garment discarded in a heap by a lax owner was actually her nephew, when she peered more closely at what everyone was looking at. She was struck by how little and vulnerable Jessie looked lying there, deathly white, and with his mouth open and blood on his teeth.

Jessie's limbs were lying anyhow, his dark lashes feathered on an alabaster cheek as the young doctor kneeled on the cobbles to check that he was breathing. Then, the doctor gently turned Jessie onto his side and placed his own jacket under his head, after which he bent Jessie's top leg forward at the hip and then back at the knee so that he was propped up.

As Peggy saw the doctor carefully feel in Jessie's mouth to make sure there were no obstructions, she thought what a pitiful sight it all was, and she was really glad that Barbara and Ted weren't going to be seeing their dear son lying helpless like this.

Connie began to howl, spooked by how deathly still Jessie was, and Peggy pulled her close. Worried that more of the children from Tall Trees may have been set on by the gang, Peggy asked where everyone was and through Connie's sobs learned that Aiden had run to the hospital to see if he could find James, and that Angela and Larry were back at Tall Trees and so they had no idea that anything had happened. Connie had been going to the shops herself as she had wanted to buy her brother a present (just like he had been buying one for her, although Connie didn't know this), while Tommy had been with her as he'd been sent on an errand by Mabel, and Aiden had been there too as he was on the way to June's to take over from Peggy early as Mabel had thought she looked a bit drawn that morning.

The long and short of it was that the children had seen the last bit of Jessie being pushed into the alley as they turned the corner at the top of the road but they hadn't been able to get there in time to prevent him taking quite a pasting doled out by the five boys.

Connie was just starting to describe Tommy's lightning defence of Jessie when Aiden ran back to the group in the alley at this point, panting extravagantly and looking very worried, and between gasps wheezing out that he hadn't been able to find James at the hospital. However, the doctor who'd been looking after Jessie told Aiden he mustn't worry as somebody had just telephoned from a nearby newsagents to the hospital on his say-so to request an ambulance.

The doctor tried to reassure Peggy further by saying that James was an expert in head injuries and so it was best that Jessie be taken to the hospital as soon as possible, and to this Peggy could only mutter, 'We know, thank you, all about Dr Legard, as unfortunately we've already had experience of the extent of his skill as he's been looking after one of our other evacuees, Angela, and he also treated myself and my daughter.'

Then quite a lot happened at once. Another two policemen turned up, and both Tommy and the Hull boy were marched off to the police station. And the ambulance arrived, and Jessie was put on a stretcher and lifted into the back of it. His eyes started to flicker open at one point although alarmingly all Peggy could see was the whites of his eyeballs, and he let out a reverberating groan that sounded to her almost as if he were experiencing all the pain and distress there was in the world.

'Connie, you and Aiden run home now and tell Mabel and Roger what has happened and that Tommy is going to be at the police station – that's really important, as they must know where he is as quickly as possible,' instructed Peggy over her shoulder as she climbed into the ambulance after the stretcher. 'I'm going to the hospital with Jessie, and you children – listen to me, as this is important – I want you all to wait back at Tall Trees together so that we know where you are. Nobody is to leave Tall Trees, do you hear me? I will let you know as soon as I can when there's any news, and so try not to worry too much, Connie, as hospital will be the best place for him. And Aiden, can you pop into Gracie's greengrocers on the way and get her to pick up Holly from the café please and take her back to Tall Trees?'

The door to the ambulance was closed and Peggy caught a glimpse of Connie and Aiden's ashen faces as they stood side by side to watch the ambulance drive away.

Then Peggy turned to look at Jessie for what felt like a long while. He had an ambulance man taking his pulse, and then Peggy stared down at her own hands, which she saw with some surprise, as she had been oblivious, that they were shaking uncontrollably.

At the hospital James was waiting outside for them, looking very weary as if he had been working through the night. He'd just finished an operation by the look of it and he was still in his scrubs, but he jumped up nimbly into the ambulance to assess Jessie, crouching close beside Peggy as he did so. He had a word with the medic who had been looking after Jessie in the ambulance, and then James shone a torch into Jessie's eyes, after which he took his pulse and ran his hands swiftly over Jessie's head and then his arms, legs and ribcage.

James sat back on his heels and Peggy could feel the warmth of his body, he was so near to her.

Jessie groaned again, and Peggy caught hold of his hand and said, 'Jessie darling, it's Aunt Peggy and I'm holding your hand. You've been in a fight, and we're now at the hospital. James is looking after you. Jessie... Jessie?'

Jessie's eyes fluttered open and closed, and his body looked unbelievably tense. But then his eyes stayed half-open once more and his body seemed to sink back down into the stretcher. Peggy could see that one of his hands – the one she wasn't holding – was badly vibrating with an involuntary shudder, a horrible mirror image to her own trembling hands.

'His pupils are the same size, which is good, and I can't feel any obvious breaks in any bones or serious injuries although it might be some time before we can ascertain this for certain, but I don't like much that he's still unconscious. I want to X-ray him and he will need to be admitted for observation,' James told her. His tone was gentle but professional, and Peggy found the calm timbre of his voice made her feel just a shade less anxious.

Peggy turned to look at the doctor, and saw James's face close to hers, but he was observing Jessie with great concentration as he tried to work out the extent of his injuries, and he didn't notice her. Certainly, there was none of the electric charge between her and James that Peggy had experienced by simply being close to him during their day out to Withernsea, which although only a few weeks previously, seemed a very long time ago now, and Peggy chastised herself for even thinking about their day out.

Peggy nodded and then asked James whether Jessie's treatment would be expensive, and then he told her not to worry about the cost for now as they could think about everything like that later. She couldn't prevent her eyes filling; James's kindness following the shock of what had happened to Jessie was hard to bear.

And then it was time for she and James to clamber backwards out of the ambulance and stand uncomfortably side by side as Jessie's stretcher was heaved out and he was carried into the hospital.

An hour or two hour later Peggy felt exhausted. Jessie had regained a patchy consciousness, and although he had a headache and felt very tired, and he had been sick several times, James didn't seem to be excessively worried about him any longer which, of course, was excellent news. After a more thorough check-up James encouraged Jessie to go back to sleep, James saying then to Peggy that Jessie looked to have mild-to-medium concussion and that if she needed to head back to Tall Trees for a while to deal with the children and feed Holly, then now would be a good time, as Jessie would likely sleep for at least a couple of hours.

Obediently Peggy trotted home, where she found Connie very upset still, and Gracie looking quite fraught as besides four very anxious children in Connie, Angela, Aiden and Larry, she was trying to deal at the same time with two crying babies as both Jack and Holly had picked up on something being very wrong in the household, with the result that each of them was now egging the other on to greater and greater teary efforts.

Angela had gone very quiet, and although they tried to hide it when Peggy walked in, nevertheless Peggy noticed Aiden and Larry trying to conceal from her a piece of paper on which they were making elaborate plans of how the TT Muskets could teach the Hull contingent 'a lesson' for what they had done to Jessie.

As Larry tried to tell Peggy all about their musketeer pledge to one another and so it wasn't acceptable that Jessie had been hurt and Tommy arrested, Peggy forced the boys to hand the piece of paper to her and then she felt too tired to be diplomatic.

'Right, all of this silly gang stuff, this pathetic musketeer stuff, stops right here and right now, do you hear me? Larry and Aiden? There will be NO reprisals in any shape or form, I want you to understand this. Each of us grown-ups has got far too much to think of with this beastly war and with Jessie being hurt without worrying what daft thing you are all up to as well. You were asked by Roger a couple of weeks back if there was anything going on, and like butter wouldn't melt, you all said there wasn't – and that was obviously a lie. Big error. Make no mistake about this, if any or all of you dare to make any such plans for reprisals, then Aiden can right away go back to live at home, and Angela and Larry will have to find new billets with other families in Harrogate, do you understand? And it could be that the rest of us have to go elsewhere, and new people come here. I mean this, so just don't any of you test my patience on it, as I am absolutely serious and I've clean run out of patience. I am just about to break the news to Barbara and Ted that Jessie is in hospital and Tommy is at the police station – just think for a minute about this – and I want you all to understand how serious this situation is.' Peggy voice was firm in the extreme, and the children exchanged serious glances.

She allowed her words to sink in for a heartbeat or two, before going on gravely, 'It could be that Mabel and Roger will have had quite enough of all the trouble and disruption of having all of us evacuees here with them at Tall Trees, and that they will ask us all to move anyway, for which in that case all of you will have to shoulder some of the blame, as must I for not being stricter with you. *I* wouldn't want us all here if Tall Trees were mine, we've been so much trouble, and especially so when Roger and Mabel have gone out of their way to make us all welcome.

'So I want you all to think about this and what has gone on, and to very much hope that Jessie makes a full recovery. And if by some miracle Roger and Mabel *don't* want us all to go elsewhere, I want this to be the very *last* time anything happens while we are all here when either the police or the medical services are involved. I repeat, there are to be absolutely *no* reprisals for what has happened to Jessie. Do you all understand?'

Peggy stared crossly at each of the children, and Connie, Aiden, Larry and Angela responded by looking down with sullen expressions at the kitchen table.

'Have I made myself clear?' Peggy asked again, and then when nobody replied to her once more, she brought her hand down on the kitchen table with such a racketing whack that everybody jumped, and both Jack and Holly winched their cries up to howl level.

But Peggy had gone beyond caring as she yelled at the children who were all looking at her with dumbfounded expressions as they had never ever seen Peggy anything other than mildly irked previously, and certainly never for her to let loose anything like this display of temper, '*Children, have I made myself bloody clear*?'

Ignoring Connie's timid 'yes, very clear, Aunty Peggy', a clearly still fuming Peggy got up and marched to the study where she almost, but not quite, slammed the door behind her in fury. Then she made a long-distance call first to Mrs Truelove's haberdashers in Bermondsey where Barbara worked, only to discover that there was a fault on the line and she couldn't get through, after which she telephoned the Jolly public house, asking without going into specifics if somebody could track down Ted or Barbara in order that Peggy could telephone the Jolly at four o'clock to speak to one or both of them.

Finally she telephoned the police station, where a kindly desk sergeant allowed her and Roger to have a word. Tommy and the Hull lad were still being questioned but it looked unlikely that matters against Tommy were going to be taken further, Roger told her, although it was possible that the other boy from Hull and his friends might face some sort of charge.

'I'm so very sorry, so sorry indeed, Roger, as us evacuees have been nothing but trouble for you since we arrived, and now poor Tommy is in trouble for sticking up for Jessie, as I think that's what happened when Tommy saw the bigger boys pick on him, from what I can make out from Connie. I can only apologise for all the upset that we have inadvertently brought to your family,' Peggy said. She sniffed then, and swallowed down the painful lump in her throat.

Roger was uncharacteristically quiet and not very forthcoming, saying merely that she'd better get back to the hospital to see how Jessie was, and that they would all talk about it later when everybody was allowed home.

Peggy felt a tiny bit better when Mabel took the telephone receiver from her husband to say to Peggy that if Ted and/or Barbara wanted a lodging if they needed to come to Harrogate then that would be all right, and that the policeman had told her he'd learnt from the boys that apparently there'd been some simmering trouble between the Hull evacuees and the children at Tall Trees for a while, although it didn't sound, so far at least, as if Tommy or any of the others in their group had in any way been the instigators of what had gone on earlier in the day.

Peggy was somewhat reassured at what Mabel said, but she knew she'd be kidding herself if she thought everything was going to snap back to normal as far as their generous hosts were concerned as when they were speaking just now, Mabel had had none of her normal jolliness about her, just like her husband hadn't either.

Without talking to the children again as she was still furious with them, Peggy gave Holly a quick feed and put her down for her afternoon nap, leaving her in Gracie's charge, and she then stalked quietly out of Tall Trees as she still felt too cross with them all to have anything pleasant to say to anybody, and worked off a bit of her temper by striding out on her way back to the hospital with as much speed as possible.

Her feet felt hot and tired by the time she got there, and her brown leather sandals had rubbed quite a large blister on one of her heels.

She noticed the clock high on the wall in the corridor was saying it was almost two o'clock as a ward sister escorted Peggy into a small room where Jessie was now lying in bed. His soiled clothes had been removed and he had been cleaned up from the grime of the alley.

He looked virtually unrecognisable as his face and head were badly swollen where he had been kicked, and one of his eyelids was really puffy and a deep palette of blackberry-coloured hues. His lower legs looked to have a frame over them as there was a boxy shape under the bedclothes that was suspending the sheet and blanket, preventing them lying on his legs. The bruises on his body and arms were starting to come through now in a variety of blackberry and liver colours. He had a hand bandage, covering what looked like a small splint on two of his fingers. As her eyes travelled across Jessie's battered body, carefully heeding each injury he had, both big and small, Peggy couldn't stop herself wincing when she saw the punishment Jessie had taken.

She sat down in the chair that had thoughtfully been placed beside his bed and then she reached for Jessie's unbandaged hand and stroked it gently. Peggy looked for something positive in the pitiful sight in front of her, and eventually the best she could do was to decide that Jessie looked now as if he were asleep, rather than unconscious, and she supposed that to be a good thing.

A nurse came in to check Jessie's vital signs but she didn't say anything to Peggy other than a nodded 'good afternoon'. A long while after the nurse had gone, James came in and stood behind Peggy.

'I can't stay long, as I have to be back in theatre in a little while,' he said. He sounded exhausted.

Peggy didn't look up at him, but she nodded to show that she had been listening as she leant over and smoothed Jessie's fringe to one side on his forehead.

James added, 'Jessie has had quite a time of it, and he's going to feel very sore. Not only was he kicked and punched but I think he was stamped on too, and he's had some of his fingers dislocated. I think we'll have to keep him in for a few days as, while there's no sign that he's going to be permanently disfigured, I think he'll need us to give him some pain medication. And by then we'll have a better idea if his head injury is serious or not, although I am banking on it being concussion rather than anything more worrisome. He was quite lucid when he came to, and could remember who the prime minister is and what day of the week it is, although he couldn't remember anything beyond walking to the shops with you.'

'The poor little tyke,' Peggy said after a while as she watched the gentle rise and fall of Jessie's chest as he slept. 'What a time he's had. And whatever am I going to say to his mother and father about this? I'm a terrible guardian for these children, any fool can see that, and Barbara and Ted are going to be beside themselves. Connie is beside herself too as she is worried for Jessie, while Aiden and Larry are on the warpath and want to get the gang of bigger boys back for what has happened to Jessie, although I've more or less given them an on-pain-of-death ultimatum that no such thing is to happen. Oh, I don't know, I think sometimes we'd be better off back in Bermondsey, threat of bombs or no... And I'm in no doubt that Tommy won't have enjoyed his visit to the police station, and neither would Roger and Mabel who, incidentally, could barely talk to me when I spoke to them earlier. I thought that after the damn apple incident last autumn that all the children were a bit more sensible now, but it doesn't seem like it, does it? It's all such a mess.' She tried to bite back an aching sigh.

'Don't be so hard on yourself, Peggy,' said James, as he laid a hand on her shoulder. 'I think you're all doing pretty well up here, taking everything into consideration.'

She stayed still and didn't say or do anything. James kept his hand where it was, and Peggy had to tamp down an almost overwhelming urge to lean her head against his arm.

Peggy could hear the sounds of the hospital in the background, and Jessie's occasionally uneven breathing. And still neither she nor James said anything to each other, or adjusted their positions.

And then, feeling like she was at last stepping off the edge of the terrifying abyss that she had been teetering on for months, Peggy reached up to her neck, not daring to look up at James, and after a final moment of indecision, she clasped the doctor's strong and reassuring hand that was resting on her shoulder, and his fingers interlaced themselves with hers.

The clicking of the second hand of the clock hanging in the corridor just outside the door to Jessie's room seemed very loud to Peggy as the tableau of herself, James and Jessie stayed as it was until a nurse came to collect James for scrubbing up, and by then the shadows had shifted in the room quite considerably as the sun slowly inched across the sky. And Peggy knew she had collect her scattered thoughts as it was high time she had to telephone the Jolly to explain to Barbara and Ted what had happened.

Chapter Twenty-seven

If Peggy had felt tired before, it was nothing to how shattered and at the end of her tether she felt by the time she got back to Tall Trees in the early evening. Her dress was creased, and damp with her perspiration and now and again she could detect a sharp whiff assaulting her from under her arms, while she was limping as the blister on her heel had ruptured painfully.

Holly was fractious about the unexpected change to her routine and she was demanding attention. Thus Peggy had to feed her before she did anything else, thinking glumly to herself that she must make more of an effort to get Holly fully onto solids, as a day like they had just had highlighted all too clearly how difficult it was with a baby who wasn't weaned. But breast milk was free and in Peggy's case, abundant, and Holly always seemed content to suckle and she rarely grizzled for something more substantial as Jack had done, meaning that he was more or less weaned already even though he was younger. Peggy couldn't stop soul-searching – it had been a day for it – and as she watched Holly's lips suckle, she wondered if she'd breastfed Holly just as much for herself as for what was best for her daughter. If she were honest with herself she thought it all too likely that in the wake of what had happened with Bill, Peggy had found tremendous, or even too much, comfort in feeding Holly herself as it created such a life-enforcing feeling, and Peggy had appreciated feeling needed by her daughter when it was quite clear her husband didn't feel similarly.

Peggy had a top-to-toe wash and changed her clothes. She went downstairs and plonked Holly down on a rug on the lawn in just her clean nappy in order that she could have a good wriggle and work off a bit of energy by kicking her legs in the air, with Jack beside her in his clean nappy too, and Angela and Connie keeping an eye on them.

This was because Roger, Mabel and Tommy came back about an hour after Gracie had given everyone something to eat and drink before leaving for her nightly shift repacking the guns, and Peggy wanted to give them some time with herself so that they could say to her whatever they needed to.

Tommy was passed a drink and a sandwich and then, unusually, was allowed to take both with him as he was sent to find the other children, after which Peggy insisted on making tea for Roger and Mabel.

They were all very polite with each other, which was fine as far as it went, but it did feel oddly clipped and formal, and Peggy missed the easy camaraderie of only yesterday between her and their evacuee hosts.

Peggy had sent the boys out to see to putting Milburn to bed for the night, and to pop Porky into his pigpen in the garden for twenty minutes so that he could start to get used to it as he was putting on weight with such alacrity that he wasn't going to be able to sleep in his packing crate by the kitchen range for very much longer.

To avoid any awkward silences in the conversation now, Peggy busied herself with the teapot and moving things around in the pantry as everyone listened to Porky's increasingly loud and indignant squeals from his pigpen, calling to let everyone know that a terrible mistake had been made and somehow he'd been left somewhere he shouldn't have been, and this needed putting to rights pretty damn quick as he had lots to do back in his spot in the kitchen. Porky's cries set the chickens off, which roused the cockerel that was being kept several houses away, which set next door's dogs barking furiously, and then Milburn gave a ringing neigh as if to say 'flipping heck, do be quiet all of you!'

'I expect you're glad to be back in the peace and quiet of home,' said Peggy wryly.

Roger gave the tiniest snort of mirth at this but he couldn't disguise his mouth twitching into a smile, and so Peggy wondered if it might be going to be all right between them after all.

She put the teapot down in front of her hosts, and Mabel organised the teacups.

'How is Jessie?' asked Roger.

'It's hard to say, but he looks quite badly hurt as he's covered head to toe with bruises and cuts, and two of his fingers have had to be splinted; he's concussed too. That's what we know about anyway. But at least he's stable, and James thinks it more a case of superficial injuries and that he needs time to recover and for the pain to lessen, rather than there being anything seriously wrong. The poor love, his head is swollen though almost to the size of a marrow, and his eyes are slits. If one didn't know that was our Jessie lying in bed, then I think he would be impossible to recognise,' said Peggy.

She added that she had spoken to both Barbara and Ted, and so if it was all right with Roger and Mabel, then they would come up in a couple of days for just a single night, timed to coincide with the twins' birthdays, although if Jessie's health deteriorated before that, then of course they'd like to come sooner.

'Ted is training to be a river ambulance man, as every indication is that London will be targeted soon, Barbara told me, and ideally he needs to finish his training before he can come. And Barbara is doing a first-aid course tomorrow and the next day as there's going to be a system that if people are bombed out of their houses, then the walking and talking will be sent to reception centres by the air-raid wardens to be out of the way of the emergency services at the scene, and so Barbara is learning what might face her as she's going to be one of the people who will help out in the reception centres. As always seems to happen, Jessie's hospitalisation couldn't have come at a worse time for them,' Peggy explained. 'Anyway James let me telephone the Jolly from his office and fortunately he was on hand to explain to them that he'd given Jessie a mild sedative, and would do the same tomorrow as this will give Jessie's body a chance to start the recuperation process, and so for them to visit in a few days would give Jessie a chance to get over the worst and then he'd enjoy seeing them more when the initial pain has had time to lessen slightly. James did warn them that poor Jessie looked more badly hurt than he was, and they must be prepared for him looking quite shocking.'

Mabel and Roger asked quite a lot of further questions about Jessie, and then Peggy reciprocated by enquiring about Tommy and the police station. She realised how tense she had been when a feeling of relief flooded through her when Mabel reported that it seemed that, although Tommy had been kept there for a while, he had been (it looked like) exonerated of blame, and meanwhile the rest of the Hull gang had been picked up by the police. These lads were going to be held in custody until later that night, but really this was a bit of sabre-rattling on the part of the police, who wanted to give them a bit of a scare, as it looked like they'd get a caution rather than be sent to court, unless Ted insisted that they be charged.

The desk sergeant had told Roger that they all came from very difficult backgrounds, and none of them had been lucky enough to find good billets in Harrogate and so their evacuation had been a bit of a disaster really, even though it might well have given them a respite from worse conditions back at home in Hull. The sergeant didn't think they were bad lads as such but more that they hadn't had the benefit of parents who cared much about them, while their billets just wanted the money from the government for their keep, and for them to be out of the house all day.

'I said I wondered if there was a way where rather than giving them a police record, which won't help them get jobs when they are older, they could instead be instructed to do something for the community as punishment,' said Roger. 'That way something good would come out of what has happened, and perhaps one or two of them might discover that rather than always acting the goat and looking for the worst, there can be a good feeling to be got through doing something for somebody else. We left it that I would have a ponder about what sort of thing perhaps they could do, and I'm glad Ted is coming to see Jessie as I'd like to talk to him about it. But it's not easy to know quite what they could do, seeing as they're only twelve and thirteen.'

'Thirteen? Twelve… Goodness, is that all? I thought that lad looked older. But this means they're still nothing more than children themselves!' Peggy was shocked as she thought again of the horrific extent of Jessie's injuries that these boys had caused.

They all sipped their tea contemplatively, and then Peggy said, 'I do feel bad in general about what's just happened. We have so imposed on the kindness of both of you already, and yet while we try our best, all we seem to do is make trouble for you and cause you more work.'

There was a pause in the conversation, filled by a new burst of Porky's calling.

'I found some biscuits on t' way 'ome,' said Mabel then, reaching into her handbag for a brown paper bag. 'You'd best 'ave one before t' kids get wind. Or mebbe two.'

And with that Peggy knew that she and the other evacuees weren't going to be asked to sling their hook and leave Tall Trees. Well, not just yet, at least.

Chapter Twenty-eight

All things considered, the twins ended up having a surprisingly nice birthday, even though the children had discovered the day before that James had had to award the prize for the biggest number of bags for his patients' possessions to the local boy-scout troop.

Jessie had been allowed to come home from the hospital that morning, and Roger had gone over in the car to fetch him.

The sunny weather came back after a couple of muggy and grey days, and so Tommy, Larry and Aiden were allowed to lug the small sofa from Roger's study out into the garden for Jessie to sit on. James had been very firm that Jessie wasn't to run around or do much at all for the next few days, and he was to be in bed *and asleep* by eight o'clock – that was the deal if Jessie were to be allowed to go home, and there were to be no arguments about it, otherwise he'd be kept in hospital for a few days more.

To bolster James's point, Peggy reminded Jessie that school would be starting in a week and if he didn't take care of himself he might be forced to miss the start of term at his new school and so by the time he would be able to attend he wouldn't know where his classroom was, or what his timetable was, and so he'd feel on the back foot in comparison to his classmates. To judge by his frown, Jessie clearly didn't like the thought of this, and so Peggy thought he'd do his best to get better before the new term began.

Connie said she didn't want to celebrate her birthday until Jessie was back once more at Tall Trees, even if it meant she had to move her 'official' birthday to another day for this year. And to make sure Jessie got enough rest and could lie in the next morning, he could sleep in her room, and she could top and tail with Angela. Connie looked much happier when James announced that Jessie would be able to be at Tall Trees to blow out his birthday candles after all, although it had been close-run.

As Jessie wasn't coming home first thing, which meant that Connie's 'birthday' wasn't allowed to start yet, as a treat the others insisted that they did her morning chores for her. And then, they said, she was to be allowed to ride Milburn all day (if she wanted) without having to take it in turns with anybody.

Connie asked Peggy if she could go out on her own on the little chestnut – it was the first time any of the children had done this, and Connie was by no means the best in the saddle and so it was quite a big ask for her to make.

'Please, please,' Connie wheedled. 'I promise on Porky's life that I'll only go up to the top of the pretty lane and back again, and I won't go anywhere else, and I won't trot or canter. Please, Aunty Peggy.'

Peggy smiled as the 'aunty' was only employed when the twins had been naughty or they really wanted something. The 'pretty lane' as Peggy and the twins called it was one of Peggy's favourite places to be too and when Gracie was over at the packing depot of a summer's evening Peggy would often lay Jack and Holly side by side in the perambulator after tea and walk there, enjoying the dramatic countryside that dipped and rose on either side of the stone-walled lane, and, best of all, the gentle downhill slope almost all the way home. As it was Connie's birthday and because she'd been very good over the summer, Peggy agreed to her taking Milburn for a solo ride, even though privately she felt anxious about this as knowing their luck just at the moment Connie would probably fall off and injure herself, Peggy thought to herself gloomily. But it was also true that Connie was growing up and she couldn't be kept in cotton wool for ever, Peggy knew, and so this would count as one of the small but necessary steps of Connie gaining for herself a little independence on her road to becoming an adult.

Connie's ride went off without a hitch, despite Peggy's concerns, with both her and Milburn impeccably behaved. Connie's huge grin of achievement when she rode into the back yard exactly an hour after she had left, and Milburn's jaunty turn of her head to see if Peggy had a treat for her, made Peggy very glad that she had agreed that Connie could take the pony out.

Milburn had just been given a drink and untacked, when Roger edged the car slowly into the yard. He helped Jessie climb slowly out of the vehicle, and from there straight out into the garden where Jessie sat down cautiously on the sofa, which had been placed in the shade under one of the tall trees that had given the rectory its name.

Mabel and Peggy winced to one another when they saw how gingerly Jessie was moving, and how very bruised and swollen he still was with the white of one eye now revealed as a deep magenta, and what a pronounced limp he had. He did look much better than he had that first day in hospital, however, and so Peggy told herself to be thankful for small mercies. But it took him a terribly long time to totter his way over to the sofa, supported by Roger, and then carefully lower himself onto it.

As the children gathered around Jessie, soon sitting cross-legged on the grass before the sofa and excitedly chattering away and wishing him 'Happy Birthday', there was a demanding snort and a small squeal and Porky, who would now follow the children around very much like a little pink dog with russet-edged ears, asked to sit up on the sofa beside Jessie too, which made Jessie smile and pat the cushion beside him as encouragement to the piglet to climb up. Peggy could see the way this was going as it was hard to deny Jessie anything just at the moment, and so she had to run and get an old towel as although Porky was very clean, only doing his droppings in one corner of the yard when let outside and with the weather having been too hot for his trotters to be muddy, she didn't quite trust the porker *that* much. And even Bucky the cat, who was never particularly friendly with anybody other than Larry (although when Peggy had been lying ill in bed just before Holly was born, he had deigned to have the odd paddy-pad snuggle now and again), jumped up onto the back of the sofa. Close to Jessie's head, the black and white tom crouched down with his front paws tucked under, the soft fur on his chest vibrating with audible purrs.

All in all, it was a pretty formidable 'welcome home' committee, and although Jessie looked tired, his weary smile that he couldn't seem to lose showed that he was undeniably pleased that he'd been so missed by everybody.

The twins had been told that Barbara and Ted would be telephoning at five o'clock, and that they'd asked if Jessie and Connie could bear to wait until then to open all their presents, which they agreed to.

Of course, Roger and Mabel and Peggy knew that Barbara and Ted would, train delays notwithstanding, arrive earlier in the afternoon as a surprise, and so they were looking forward to seeing the look on the twins' faces when they saw their parents walk into the garden.

Dinner in the meantime was a sandwich picnic on the lawn, and then both Jessie and Connie looked up as they heard unexpected voices singing strains of 'Happy Birthday', to see Ted and Barbara walking around the corner with Ted carrying a string bag bulging with some wrapped presents and Barbara parading a birthday cake.

Connie leapt up, with a loud cry of 'Mummy! Daddy!' clearly forgetting to act as old as she could, but Ted and Barbara had to cut across her hellos when they saw Jessie trying to struggle painfully to his feet with, 'Don't get up, Jessie, we'll come to you.'

After Ted and Barbara had been hugged and kissed, at last the twins could have a proper version of 'Happy Birthday' sung, and everyone joined in quite raucously. And then, with all the other children doing a one-two-three to set them off, Jessie and Connie opened their presents.

Jessie went first. He was given a Frog Penguin model aeroplane kit of a Spitfire and some new larger plimsolls from Ted and Barbara; a selection of tiny pots of paint and a couple of small paintbrushes so that Jessie could decorate his model aeroplane to look as authentic as possible, from Peggy and

Holly (Peggy being rather proud of herself for tracking them down in these straightened times as they had proven devilish hard to find); a wall poster detailing the various types of aeroplane from Connie, with Peggy's help, and a pocket-sized thesaurus from James. Jessie had to take a breather at this point, as he was finding it all a bit much and his bottom lip was starting to wobble.

Then Ted said 'chin up, old man' and he rallied with a 'thanks, Daddy', and slowly a broad smile grew as Jessie opened the rest of his presents, which were a selection of boys' comics and some gobstoppers from the other musketeers; a jigsaw of a Hawker Hurricane from Gracie and Jack; a tin of toffees bought from a whip-round for Jessie's birthday by the patients on the corridor of Jessie's room at the hospital – none of whom would let on where the sweeties had come from, which made Ted and Roger mouth 'black market' and 'fell off the back of a lorry' to each other, as they tapped their forefingers to the side of their noses – and a new set of pencils, a fountain pen and some blue-black ink for 'Big School' from Roger and Mabel.

'Thanking you all,' said Jessie, and then opened his mouth to say something else, but nothing came out as he'd got too distracted by reading the assembly instructions on the box of the model Spitfire kit.

Connie had waited not very patiently for Jessie to finish with his presents before starting on hers, and naturally her present-opening was a much more hurried and businesslike affair but then that was Connie all over, in contrast to her brother's more gentle approach.

Peggy realised that Jessie was worn-out after his injuries, and of course he'd always had the tendency to get a bit overemotional when tired. Peggy glanced at her sister, who looked back with the sort of expression that suggested she was thinking the same, at which Peggy mouthed 'bless them', followed by 'shall I get a blanket and pillow', at which Barbara nodded in agreement.

Connie was also given the fountain pen, ink and pencils by Roger and Mabel, as well as Enid Blyton's *The Naughtiest Girl in the School* by James; girls' comics and gobstoppers by the musketeers; a wooden-backed bristle hairbrush and hair ribbons by Peggy and Holly; a jigsaw of children dancing around a maypole from Gracie and Jack; the Chapstick *and* the money for Connie and Aiden to go to the flicks together from Jessie, helped out quite a lot by Peggy; plimsolls and a selection of clothes from Ted and Barbara. Connie was growing more than Jessie just at the moment and so they had had to take more of a practical cast with her present, which Barbara apologised for, although Connie looked thrilled all the same, especially when she spied how enviously Angela was looking at some of the new garments.

'Come and have a look at what we got,' said Jessie to his friends, and Connie made room for them to gather round.

Once Jessie had had a blanket tucked over his knees and had been persuaded to shuffle down on the couch so that he was almost lying down, the adults left the children to it and got Mabel's ancient deckchairs out and sat in the sun. It was very convivial and relaxed, with somebody getting up now and again to have a sliver of cake, make more sandwiches or tea and homemade lemonade, Gracie having managed to scrounge a couple of lemons from somewhere (which caused black-market nose-tapping again), and with the babies on a tartan rug being encouraged by everybody as they were both doing their best to start crawling.

Ted and Barbara deposited Porky on the ground from the sofa – he wasn't a happy piglet – and spent some time perched next to Jessie, Barbara with her arm around him, as they asked him what had happened, after which they said they were going back to their deckchairs and that Jessie should try to have a snooze if he could manage it as he had to remember he was still getting better and so he needed lots of sleep as this would make him enjoy his birthday evening a bit more.

To everyone's surprise, and once Porky had resumed his rightful position at Jessie's feet, the pair of them did manage to doze off despite all the activity and chatter around them, although after a while the children got Milburn tacked up and backed into the trap, to take Roger and Ted on a Grand Tour. Gracie said she'd better get ready for the guns that evening, and so this left Mabel, Peggy and Barbara looking after Holly, Jack, and Jessie.

'How do you think he is?' Peggy asked her sister, nodding her head towards Jessie, who was now lying flat out on the sofa, sound asleep with his mouth flopped open.

'Well, I was glad I'd been warned how terrible he looks, as I'd have been truly sickened otherwise, and I admit there was a horrible moment that I thought I'd drop their birthday cake when I first caught sight of his injuries as it really made me catch my breath, especially that eye. But now that I've spoken to him, I feel a little reassured. He is worn out though, and so I am wondering if he ought to do half-days for the first week at school next week,' said Barbara keeping her voice very quiet.

''E's certainly been through t' mill, ain't 'e?' said Mabel. 'I think it best t' ease 'im back t' school gently.'

'Mabel, I want to have a word with you as Ted and I do appreciate more than we could ever tell you how understanding you and Roger have been over this whole sorry mess.' Barbara's voice was still low as she groped in her handbag and pulled out a small sheaf of the recently issued wartime blue and orange £1 notes, held together by a Kirby grip, which she now held aloft. 'Here's £10 from our emergency money that we keep by, and we'd very much like to donate this to the church funds, as a small sign of our gratitude. I'm sure Roger will be able to find a worthy cause for it.'

Peggy looked on in amazement. This large donation would go a long way to wiping out Ted and Barbara's remaining rainy-day money Peggy knew that Barbara had saved by squirrelling away every spare penny assiduously since she'd been married. A significant proportion of this fund had already been spent on getting the children ready to be evacuated, as they had been sent away with snazzy new clothes, after which, although Barbara and Ted could claim some travelling expenses from the government for going to Harrogate to see the twins, Peggy knew that they had probably had to dip into the rainy-day money for at least a proportion of their bus and train fares to get all the way to Yorkshire as often as they did. The fact that Barbara and Ted felt they should make such a huge payment to Roger was a sign of how terrified they were that Jessie and Connie would be asked to move, Peggy suspected, the more so as if Roger and Mabel decided that they wanted to billet other evacuees who were much less trouble than the ones they already had it would be very unsettling for the Delberts and all the Rosses. And of course if they were all sent away from Tall Trees then it was very unlikely that Peggy and Holly would be able to stay billeted together somewhere alongside Connie and Jessie.

Mabel looked flabbergasted when she saw the fold of bank notes. 'Oh! Barbara! I really don't know about this at all...' she began.

Barbara interrupted, 'I think you'd best take it, Mabel, and then you can give it to Roger either this afternoon or after we've gone tomorrow. Otherwise I'll have to give it to Ted to give to Roger, and Ted will have to insist that Roger accept it, and it will all be very awkward. And I don't want it to be awkward, as Ted and I just want you both to know how very, very grateful we are, especially when even with billets that do seem to work, as this one has been so wonderful most of the time for the twins – and I know a lot of the evacuees' billets don't pass muster at all, as Larry's and Angela's didn't – it's not always a smooth or happy process. And don't forget,' Barbara waved the bundle of money in the air, and then leant over and slid it onto the saucer of the cup of tea that Mabel was holding, 'Ted and I do very much want Roger and you to spend it on good causes or needy people, and these days who can afford to turn their backs on ten pounds when there are so many people waiting for the help that wonderful people like you and Roger can give them with a sum like that?'

Not long afterwards there was the sound of Milburn's hooves turning in at the gate, and as the pony and the trap were put away Peggy, Barbara and Mabel talked about evacuation, and the good and the bad things about it, from the perspectives of the evacuees and also the hosts, and the pressure the organisation of it all was putting on the government, and what was going to happen now that so many evacuees had returned to London with the long-threatened bombing poised to begin?

The women had rather depressed themselves talking this way as it was all very thought-provoking, but they pasted happy expressions on their faces as the children came back noisily into the garden, followed by Roger and Ted.

With the extra sounds around him, Jessie stirred and then sat up, yawning widely, asking if he had missed anything.

A lazy scavenger hunt was just being organised by Roger, when there was a cheery 'Is there anybody home?' and James popped his head over the hedge. He had come bearing gifts, in the shape of some ginger beer for the children, and two bottles of champagne for the grown-ups which he'd had the foresight to chill already.

'What a treat!' said Roger, and hurried off to find some glasses and to put one of the bottles of champagne on the stone floor of the dark pantry to keep cool.

Mabel organised a blue-and-white-striped canvas deckchair next to Peggy for James to sit in, and Peggy and Barbara shared a secret smile at this as, although she was trying not be obvious about where she was manoeuvring James, there was something about the way that Mabel moved and spoke that made this impossible, which was rather endearing.

Roger came back with a tray held high that even had an ancient ice bucket from happier times complete with cold water in it for the bottle of bubbly they were just about to open. The children were told that if they were careful they could take their glasses and the ginger beer and told they could sit further down the garden to share it if they wanted to play at being grown up, which apparently they did, and Jessie was allowed special dispensation to go and sit with them.

'I was given the champagne the other day by Private Smith's

parents, and so I thought this was a good day to crack the bottles open, and to toast Connie and Jessie on their birthdays,' James said.

'An' we've cause fer celebration too,' said Mabel, and went on to explain to everyone about Barbara and Ted's donation of £10 to the church fund. She had obviously decided not to wait for a quiet moment with her husband.

Roger went quite pale for a moment when he heard about the money, and then he thanked the twins' parents profusely for their gesture, adding, 'I won't make a show of not taking it, as it really will be a godsend.' He scratched his chin. 'Um, I wonder if this can be the start of a fund. I want to help boys like those Hull evacuees, who seem to have nothing and no one in their lives who gives a hoot about them. But—' Roger nodded towards Barbara and Ted, as he remembered that it was their son the Hull boys had attacked 'that may seem very crass and unpleasant to you, considering how our own Jessie has suffered at their hands, and especially so when it is your money that might start things up?'

Peggy tried to read Barbara's face. To her it did look as if her sister had taken umbrage at what Roger was suggesting, but that, for the sake of politeness, she was trying to bite any sharp response back, but then Peggy saw Barbara glance at Ted and immediately Barbara's expression softened when she saw Ted nodding in approval of what Roger had said.

'On the contrary,' said Ted, 'some help is what boys like this need. Somebody to show them the way into the working world, otherwise they'll be thugs all their lives.'

All the adults nodded agreement.

'It's funny you should say that,' said James, 'but I was

talking with Private Smith's parents, and they are also keen that something be set up to help injured servicemen feel they still have a lot to offer, and I feel they may also offer some funds as I don't think they are badly off and they are keen to support their son. Maybe we could use the soldiers, sailors and pilots who are recuperating but who won't be able to fight again in some way, even if it is only to help lads like those bad lads with their reading and writing.'

'Well, we'd better sign Connie up for any reading and writing,' said Peggy, and then she coloured and immediately had to make a grimace of apology to Barbara and Ted for speaking out of turn.

But although Barbara gave a tight-lipped look in her sister's direction, Ted said – he was obviously in a very conciliatory mood – that if something was organised then to judge by the letters she was sending back to Jubilee Street, then absolutely Connie should be involved as she wasn't trying her hardest, to judge by her writing.

'Shall we see if there are any raspberries in the fruit cage as I think we might have squirrelled away a little cream to go with them,' said Roger to change the subject, standing up to go and check, 'and then we can have a bit more of a think as to how we could organise something for underprivileged children to best help them with their reading?'

Peggy didn't dare say anything as she felt she had put her foot in it with her too-quick comment.

She turned to look at Connie, who was standing at the bottom of the garden with everyone other than Angela and Jessie, who were now deep in conversation with one another back on the sofa. In a patch of sunlight Connie was showing the rest of the children how she had taught Porky to sit down on command, and they were laughing at what she had done, as Connie boasted that within a week she'd have the piglet rolling over and playing dead.

Peggy couldn't help but wonder if it might be a very good thing indeed if Connie did have some more help with her schoolwork in order that this could, in some way over the next year or two, be brought up to match her quick and adventurous mind.

The summer nights were starting to draw dark earlier, and so by the time everyone had enjoyed a new potato and mince dish this late August evening (Mabel was trying a new recipe – *hachis en portefeuille* from *More Good Food* – that she brought to the kitchen table as if she were a French waitress as she said an 'ooh la la', and which was promptly declared 'delicious' by her diners), the men had moved the sofa back into the study and Jessie was ready to have a bath all to himself.

This was his very first bath ever when he didn't have to share the water, as even back in Jubilee Street he and Connie had always taken turns in the tin bath on the floor of the kitchen. It was just as well as the water had too much dried blood in it after he had got out for anyone else to be able to step into its murky depths after he'd finished, and it made him feel very grown up as he climbed into a set of clean pyjamas. Then his sister and parents joined him in the boys' bedroom for a hour so that the Ross family could enjoy a bit of time on their own, gathered around while Jessie lay in bed.

By then Peggy had put both Jack and Holly down for the

night after their suppers, Porky had been encouraged to get back reluctantly into his tea chest in the kitchen, and the children had tidied away everything in the garden. The shadows were long and the dropping temperatures meant that Peggy had had to shrug herself into her favourite cardie.

She came back down to the kitchen to find it empty of everyone (they were all listening to the BBC news on the wireless in the parlour) other than James, who then poured the last of the champagne into two clean glasses and handed one over to Peggy.

'Mabel's given me some carrot tops for Milburn,' he said, waving a green and orange bundle in the air and turning to go out into the yard.

Milburn called to them as they walked towards her. Carrot tops were probably her favourite treat, after sugar lumps of course, not that there had been any of those for quite some time, the pony's limpid eyes seemed to be saying to Peggy.

Sure enough, Milburn made short work of her scran, but then she stayed looking over the door, regally allowing James and Peggy to stand either side of her nose as they stroked its seal-coloured velvetiness, very occasionally and only for an instant one of their fingers grazing against the other's.

'Peggy, I forgot to mention earlier that one afternoon when he was at the hospital, I got Jessie taken into the recreation room, and he began talking to one of the patients about an idea that he had had that if he were trying to send secret signals to his side as to where people might be hiding or where enemy forces are, then he would do it through ploughing lines in fields, or planting crops in rows, marking directions towards the enemy that then could be seen from Spitfires flying high above but any such signals wouldn't be too obvious to those on the ground. Jessie had made diagrams and maps of how he might do this, and worked out some sort of semaphore, and it was all very detailed,' said James, to which Peggy laughed as she knew how involved Jessie became in something when he had an idea.

'Jessie does love to think up secret communications. Those boys have spent weeks learning all they can about the war, and they have invested simply *hours* every evening trying to work out dastardly ways to beat Jerry,' she added, with an affectionate chuckle lurking just beneath her words.

'Well may you smile, Peggy. But it looks as if Jessie may inadvertently have stumbled onto something rather important, as one of the other patients overheard this chat and then he had a look at what Jessie had done and then made a call to Whitehall, and this patient – he's very high up – mentioned to me this morning that they going to look into this, as there have been reports within the War Office, so I hear on the wards, since Jerry's occupation of France of there being too high a discovery of our spies already planted there. And so it could be that something like this is already happening but that nobody at the War Office thought of the possibility. I must tell Jessie, but I might wait until after today, as if he takes a while to heal he might need cheering up, and I thing this would give a boost to his spirits, don't you, Peggy?' asked James.

'I certainly do. Goodness me though!' Peggy's eyes were wide. 'Ask a ten-year-old, as they say. Er, I mean, ask an *eleven*-year old…'

'Here's to Jessie,' said James as he held up his champagne glass to clink it gently with Peggy's.

Milburn realised she was superfluous to requirements and

she moved to the back of her stable to investigate if there were any bits of hay left that by some miracle she had ignored earlier.

'To Jessie!' echoed Peggy, as she touched her glass to James, and then she took a sip. She couldn't tell if her heart was beating so rapidly because of the champagne bubbles sliding up the side of the wide bowl-shaped glass, or because of the light of the lustrous full moon that had already risen, although it was only dusk, and was painting the crystal of their champagne glasses silver, or because of the way James was looking at her, as he put a hand on her hip and slowly drew her towards him.

Whatever it was, as their lips touched, Peggy felt dizzy.

Then she told herself to live a little and that she wasn't doing anything wrong, at which point she gave herself fully into her first proper deep (much deeper than when on their day out) kiss in very nearly a year. It wasn't perfect by any means, but it was an exceptionally nice kiss all the same, even though she and James didn't seem to know quite where they should be putting their hands or if they should put their champagne glasses somewhere out of harm's way or just make the best of kissing while holding onto them.

It felt awkward – James was only the second man Peggy had ever kissed – but it was a pleasant awkwardness, and after they broke apart they stood there smiling at each other. Then, as Milburn noisily chomped her way through a mouthful of hay that she had indeed overlooked, and without breaking their gaze deep into the other's eyes, their smiles deepened into chuckles as they both realised they didn't quite have the words to describe what had just happened. They put their glasses down on the ground, and then stood close together to kiss again.

Roger and Mabel, who were peeping with interest at what was going on in the back yard between Peggy and James from their perch behind the landing window on the turn of the stairs, each gave a happy 'hmmn' at the sight, and Roger pulled Mabel close and gave her a quick kiss on the side of her forehead.

Mabel had been going up to check on Holly and Jack when by chance she had looked out of the window and seen the clinking of the champagne glasses, and so she had beckoned to Roger, who was just leaving the bathroom, that he should join her to see too.

As the long-married couple linked hands together on the stairs in silent support of Peggy and James below, they agreed the pair outside Milburn's stable made an extraordinarily handsome sight, the sort of pairing who looked as if they were made to be together.

Then Roger and Mabel's happy expressions turned to baflement and then something bleaker as a figure dressed in dark navy darted forward and punched James to the ground with a single blow to his face, as Peggy gave a heart-rending squeal of shock and, in response to the unexpected thud of James hitting the ground, Milburn neighed loudly in fright.

Chapter Twenty-nine

'Bill!' cried Peggy.

'Ger outta my way, Peg,' her husband yelled, as he pushed her away so firmly that she ended up on all fours on the ground, with some stray bits of straw from Milburn's bed pressed into her palms.

Bill ignored Peggy as he leant down and yanked James upright, only to knock him down again straightaway.

'*Bill*!' Peggy screamed as she tried to scrabble out of the way on all fours as Bill lurched backwards into her.

'Go an' stop it, quickly, Roger, but mind oot, I don't like the look o' 'im,' Mabel told Roger, and he clattered down the stairs at the same time as Mabel raced up the stairs and along the landing as she hurried to get Ted.

By the time Ted had got out to the yard, soon followed by Barbara and all the easily mobile children, who were in their bedclothes, and Mabel too only a fraction behind the others, Bill had hit James again and taken a swing at Roger too that caused the rector's specs to fly off, leaving him trying to move his jaw from side to side, gently raising his right hand to it.

Milburn was thoroughly spooked and was hurriedly pacing back and forth across the back of her stable, giving low rumbling whinnies of fear and furiously flicking her ears backwards and forwards as she svished her tail.

With a grunt James scrambled to his feet and suddenly he and Bill were really going for broke, James now giving back to Bill as good as he was getting. James had boxed at school and university, and it was evident to all that he was better able to look after himself than Bill had anticipated, to judge by Bill's heavy breathing and the sounds of hefty blows being traded. Both men were making horrible 'ooofs' and 'aahs' as they slugged it out, with Bill also repeatedly saying 'you fucker'.

'Stop, James. James! Bill! Bill, let him alone, you idiot – he's a doctor, a surgeon, and he can't afford to get injured. Bill!' shrieked Peggy as she scrambled to her feet and tried to pull apart the brawling men. It was to no avail as they dropped to roll on the ground together, with their feet kicking and scuffling against Milburn's stable door with thumps that made the wood judder as they twisted this way and that with no care to the racket they were making, and Peggy shuddered as she heard the champagne glasses being crushed to smithereens. But both men had gone beyond the stage of being able to listen to reason.

Roger and Ted elbowed past Peggy to wrench James and Bill apart but they weren't able to separate the sparring men quickly enough to prevent a final head-butt from Bill landing square on its target of James's nose with a sickening crunch that everyone could hear as his nasal bone splintered and dark blood splattered across the breast of his white shirt.

Mabel ran inside the rectory to telephone the police, and she called for the children to come with her back to the kitchen, but although they edged backwards a bit not one of them left the back yard. They all wanted to see what was going to happen.

At last Bill was dragged away from James by Ted and Roger, while Peggy stood in front of a heavily panting James, who stared over her shoulder, never taking his eyes from Bill.

Queasily Peggy glanced at her husband. He looked crazed and as if he only had eyes for James, although Ted – who was standing behind him, tightly gripping Bill's upper arms – was trying to calm him down, saying as firmly as he could (which wasn't terribly firm, as Ted was shocked at the sudden bad turn the evening was taking, and so his voice was a bit up and down), 'That's enough, Bill, pal. You've made your point, that's enough, pal. There are women an' children 'ere watchin' you. An' it's our Connie an' Jessie's birthday, an' you don't want ter spoil that, do you? Easy, pal. Easy!'

Ted's anxiety was evident in his cockney roots coming through now in his accent more than anyone was used to these days, as over the years he had picked up on Barbara's more proper way of speaking.

Bill ignored Ted's words completely, and instead he took a deep breath and then gave what could only be called a primeval snarl, as suddenly he tried to break free by wrestling himself this way and that and then trying to jump upwards, although when Ted held firm in anchoring him to the ground, he gave three earth-shattering kicks to Milburn's stable door as he vented his temper.

Barbara had gone to Peggy's side to stand in front of James, but he too was beside himself with fury, yelling at his rival Bill, 'Control yourself, man – there are women and children here, you blithering idiot,' cutting across Bill's garbled stream of blasphemy.

It was too much for the pony and, thoroughly panicked, she

squealed in terror and then forced first one small front hoof over the top of her stable door, and then the other and then somehow Milburn wriggled her big belly up and over the top of the door, knocking Barbara to one side as she raced out of the yard, and managing to clip Bill's thigh with a well-aimed kick as she pelted past, which made him yell in pain.

Sounds of a police car with its emergency bell ringing careering up the road could be heard, and then the dreadful drumming of Milburn's metal shoes on the tarmac as she ran out into the road.

There was a squeal of brakes and the sound of the car slewing around, and immediately a dreadful thumping noise, a sickening bang and a second bumping noise before the shatter of breaking glass, and the sound of metal sliding on tarmac.

Milburn gave a terrified bellow, and then there was a moment's silence, and a cascade of metal shoes as Milburn struggled to remain on her feet. Peggy's heart felt as if it had exploded, and her ears rang – and then she realised that was the sound of the pony's iron shoes crashing down the road now at full gallop.

'Milburn!' screeched Peggy and Roger together, and then Roger shouted, 'All you children stay *here*, do you hear me? I mean it – *here*!'

Peggy, James and Roger left the screaming children and raced to the entrance to Tall Trees, leaving Ted to hang onto Bill (he looked like all the fight had now left him), and Mabel and Barbara to make sure the children all stayed well out of harm's way.

Gracie, who'd been inside with the babies and Jessie and Angela, ran across the yard to get a halter, and with the back door open the distressed cries of Jack and Holly rang out in the night air, as she raced out to the road in pursuit of the bolting pony. Peggy remembered that Gracie wasn't fond of horses, and had never made a fuss of Milburn, and so she knew how much the quick-thinking Gracie was putting herself out, and she hoped that neither Milburn nor Gracie would come to harm.

Out in the road the police car was at an angle with a badly dented bonnet, one front wheel up on the kerb, a window smashed and a windscreen that was mostly missing. The white five-bar gate that was always propped open at the entrance to Tall Trees was hanging off its hinges, tipping askew at a ludicrous angle, and part of the police car's front bumper had tangled with it. A thousand little pieces of glass had scattered all over the place glinting in the bright light of the moon, a horrible parody of the shiny champagne glasses of only minutes earlier, Peggy found herself thinking and then she was cross with herself for such thoughts in the middle of a disaster.

One of Milburn's shoes had been wrenched off and was lying forlornly in the road, with the nails still attached. It looked to Peggy as if Milburn had run straight into the road and the police car had had to swerve to miss her.

A young policeman was dazed, kneeling in the road on all fours, his forehead pulsing with blood and with his arm at a horrifically strange angle as he kept repeating, 'I didn't see it, I didn't see it', while the other policeman, this time with a bloody nose and something unnaturally shaky about his movements as he stood beside the wrecked car, supporting himself by its open twisted door, repeated again and again, 'I know, I know.'

James ran to them. 'Sit down on the wall. You've head injuries and must be examined.'

Roger said he'd telephone the police station again, and James told him to phone an ambulance first and then to bring out blankets, as shock was a possibility for the two policemen, and something for the bleeding would be useful too.

'What shall I do?' said Peggy.

'Support the broken arm.' James wrenched his shirt off, and tore off one of its arms and passed it to Peggy. 'But also watch for any traffic and flag motorists with the shirt arm to make them slow down.

James began to rip up the rest of his shirt to use as bandages, and Peggy watched him expertly tend to the men, his own chest getting increasingly bloodied from the drips still coming from the injury to his own nose.

Roger hurried out with a sheet, some blankets, and several towels that James employed to staunch the bleeding, and then he used part of the sheet as a rudimentary sling for the broken arm. Roger's presence was calming to everybody and he actually proved to be much better at knowing what to do than Peggy, helping the policemen sit more comfortably and asking if they could remember what day it was and the name of the wireless station that broadcast the daily news, questions that yielded only vague and inaccurate answers.

Then quite a lot happened all at once. The ambulance arrived and soon the policemen were being helped into it, and then there was a tricky moment when James's grazes, his broken nose, and his bloody knuckles caused concern, but James insisted that the ambulance go on without him, saying he'd head over to the hospital later to be checked out, which the medic in the ambulance itself wasn't happy about.

A police car drew up meanwhile, and three policemen got out. Both the ambulance and the police car had to park well back because of all of the broken glass and the difficulties in replacing any tyres.

James, hobbling slightly, went with them and Roger back to the yard, as he said that he'd have a look at Bill to make sure he wasn't badly hurt.

Barbara came out to sweep up the glass, and Peggy found herself standing in the road, incapable of saying or doing anything.

It all felt too much, and suddenly she had an overwhelming desire for a stout in the Jolly back in Bermondsey, and a simple night in the Ladies Bar, rough round the edges as it was and sometimes stinking of fetid river smells.

'I miss London, Barbara, and I miss you,' said Peggy in a croaky voice, and Barbara stopped what she was doing and went to hug her sister, whose body sagged against her. 'Really nothing's gone right since we've been here, and just when I think we're getting back on the straight and narrow, something happens to tip it all upside-down again. I can't take it anymore.'

'Peggy, you've had a shock, and anyone would feel like you just at the moment,' Barbara replied. 'But none of this is your fault, you do know that, don't you?'

The sisters looked at each other, Barbara trying to bolster Peggy, but Peggy's eyes staring back, glazed with defeat.

At last there was the welcome sound of a faint clip-clop-ping, although the beat wasn't quite regular because of the missing shoe. Peggy felt a rush of relief and she realised she had become fond of the pony. She sped towards Gracie who was holding Milburn's lead rope very cautiously, although the pony looked glad to have found a friendly face, even if it was only Gracie.

'T' pony were down on t' busy road,' said Gracie, 'an' it's a miracle nobody 'it her or she didn't run into someone on t' way t' pub as there were a lot aboot, but a man caught 'old of 'er and then put t' rope on 'er fer me an' she came back as good as gold.'

'Give her to me.' Peggy touched Gracie on the arm and then took the pony and led her back into the yard. She felt too wrought up to thank Gracie properly for her quick thinking in giving chase, but she thought her friend would understand.

In fact everything that had happened in the last hour felt overwhelming, and suddenly Peggy couldn't hear properly and nor could she quite catch her breath, and she felt heady and faint. Milburn's nose touched her arm as if she felt the same.

Barbara and Maureen had bustled the children inside, and so the yard felt quieter even though there was the occasional burst of a raised voice from inside as clearly the children were upset.

For a few seconds Peggy, still clutching Milburn's lead rope, had to cling onto the top of the stable door to stop herself sinking to the ground. Then she forced herself to gather herself and turned to look at the pony. She couldn't see too well in the blackout but it looked as if Milburn had skinned her belly from going over the door, and there was an open gash on the top of one of her legs. Blood trickled down her shoulder, and the hoof that had lost the shoe seemed to be torn and badly split.

Milburn looked shocked and exhausted, and she was sweating freely with her nostrils flaring in and out much more rapidly than normal, but Peggy thought the pony's injuries didn't seem to be in any way life-threatening. She patted her damp neck and Milburn gave a grunt, although Peggy wouldn't have described it as one of pleasure. She leant over and gently stroked her ears, which were colder than Peggy would have expected. She tried to put her back in the stall, but Milburn planted her feet apart and rolled her eyes with her head high in the air, before turning to look at Peggy as if she were checking to see if Peggy was serious.

Peggy realised how terrifying the pony's last moments in her stable must have been, and she stroked Milburn nose and said, 'Quite right, old girl, not just yet,' and Milburn gently pushed at Peggy as if to say thank you for understanding.

'Aiden!' Peggy called.

'Only me?' said Aiden, poking his head around the back door a second later. He must have been right on the other side.

'Yes, just you,' Peggy answered. She thought Aiden the most reliable of the children and also that he would be very diligent in keeping an eye on the pony in case she suddenly took a turn for the worse, as Peggy wasn't quite sure if ponies could suffer from shock. 'Please come and take Milburn onto the grass near the veg plots. I need you to be very sensible now, so see if she wants a drink, and after that let her have a few quiet minutes and a mouthful of grass if she wants it until everything quietens down here and we can try the stable again. But before you take her go and find those blankets Roger took

315

outside – I can't remember them going in the ambulance – as we can put them on her back for half an hour with some straw underneath to make sure she doesn't catch cold as there's a slight nip in the air and she's been sweating.'

Aiden looked purposeful and very grown up as he went to do Peggy's bidding, and she could see why Connie was so smitten.

Chapter Thirty

The policemen were back in the road inspecting the damage to the police car, and Bill was in Ted's charge, although they had edged around the side of the garage.

James had given Bill a once-over to check he wasn't seriously hurt – how this must have cost him, Peggy thought – and now James looked to have disappeared somewhere inside the rectory, presumably to wash and to borrow a shirt from Roger.

Peggy went to stand in front of her husband. He looked filthy, and she could smell acrid sweat and more than a whiff of stale alcohol oozing from his pores.

Well, that explained a few things, Peggy thought sadly, but she had already suspected as much.

'However did you think this was all going to work out, Bill?' she asked quietly, as Ted tactfully took several paces back to give them a bit of privacy.

Bill refused to catch Peggy's eye, preferring instead to stare down as he flexed his hurt knuckles.

'Peg, I came to tell ye Maureen 'as 'ad the baby, but although I'm goin' to pay for 'im, I'm never goin' to see 'im. I told 'er that.' Although he had started reasonably enough, Bill's voice got more strident as he continued, 'It's your an' my 'Olly who's *my* girl, and I want us – us, Peggy! – to be a family agin. An' I come all the way 'ere to tell you this an' then the very first thing I see is you canoodlin' sumfing awful with yer fancy man. An', seein' that, what red-blooded man wouldn't 'ave acted as I did, 'is wife a whore and a 'ussy right before 'im? You tell me that, Peg, you tell me that.' He tipped his head to look defiantly at her, seemingly oblivious that it had been his seduction of Maureen that had fractured their marriage vows, and that this meant that many would feel Peggy was no longer bound to them.

Peggy stepped back a little and she didn't say anything as she took in the sorry state of her husband. He looked dreadful, indeed such a woeful sight that Peggy could hardly believe that she had ever thought him attractive.

In the background was the sound of another vehicle arriving, presumably a police car to collect Bill and take him to the police station, or a vehicle big enough to tow the wreck away.

'James is not my fancy man, Bill. He's, um, um, er well, he's not important, that's all you need to know,' said Peggy at last as, gravely, she held Bill's stare. 'He's not my fancy man.'

'I *saw* you, Peg!' cried Bill. 'Your tongue down 'is throat…'

Peggy felt a fury rising. This seemed unfair, and yet her feelings were complicated. What had felt in the moment as a special lingering kiss had now been described with a clinical accuracy that felt demeaning and embarrassing, and suddenly she felt wrong-footed by Bill. Perhaps it had all been too soon, and perhaps she had gone too far. Not that Bill had any room to criticise, but…

'He's nothing, you stupid man,' Peggy almost shouted, 'do

you hear me? What you saw is not important as regards you and me, not at all.'

Ted touched her elbow in some sort of warning, and Peggy swung around to see that James was standing in the yard.

She knew that he would have just heard her saying he wasn't important and that he was nothing.

And in that moment she understood with a fearsome clarity that actually James most certainly wasn't nothing to her. He *was* important to her, very important, although right now he could only be thinking exactly the opposite.

Peggy could have screamed in anguish, but all her emotions felt used up, and so she didn't say anything and could only stand dejectedly, her head angled downwards.

What she had been trying to get over to Bill was that James was nothing to do with how she felt about *him*, Bill. That whatever was going on, or wasn't, with James was happening regardless of the train crash that her marriage had become. But her words had come out wrong, and most hurtfully as far as James was concerned. It would be no exaggeration to say that Peggy wanted to curl up and die right at that very moment.

She looked up at Bill once more, and was surprised to see that the policemen were now standing around him, and that he was sneering in triumph in James's direction.

'Peggy? Peg!' Bill called in anguish over his shoulder an instant later as he was bustled unceremoniously away.

'Get out of my sight,' Peggy said softly, but only to herself. Her heart felt as if made of stone as far as he was concerned.

She looked towards James, his nose flattened and swollen, the side of his face grazed and what looked like a black eye developing.

Peggy's dejected heart slithered lower as his only response was to glower furiously at her for a long second with his lips pressed together in a hard line, and then pointedly he stalked past her and out of the yard without a word or a backward glance. He was followed by an awkward-looking Ted, as Roger came to Peggy's side to say that the police had said they wanted witness statements, and so James and Ted were to go to the police station too, with Roger to go tomorrow.

Peggy felt without a doubt that her firmness with Bill was also the death-knell as far as any chance of she and James being together was concerned. With a depressing tremble, she saw that her and James's best moment had already passed. His face thrown into relief by the moonlight as he'd refused to look at her, he'd seemed so resolute, so wounded, so unbending. She didn't feel she'd ever be able to breach his defences.

Suddenly she craved a new start, something completely different, far, far away from all this upset and strife.

Roger had a blanket in his arms and he gathered a bundle of hay to take to Milburn.

'I think this is the final straw, Roger,' Peggy said in a very low voice. 'I can see that you're just ordinary folk, Mabel and you, and the way you live your lives, it's a good way, I can see that, but no matter how much I try to be like you both, it's not how us from Bermondsey find ourselves living *our* lives. Every day there seems to be some new trouble we bring you, and it has all amounted to too much for generous people like yourselves. We've tried, and tried hard, and I know you have too. But I think we've all failed in stopping it being one drama after another, and it just can't go on. It's not good for any of us.'

There was a pause.

Roger said, 'Peggy, I think you might be about to say something you will regret, and so please don't feel you have to say anything at all, or even apologise. Certainly it's been, shall we say, *livelier* than Mabel and I had imagined it would be, having you all here with us. But it's not all been bad, has it? In fact I'd even go as far as saying it has been good for us all, really.'

'I think it would be best if we go back to London. The twins would like it as they miss their parents, and I think I need to have my sister and Ted close at hand. I can't do this on my own any more,' said Peggy regardless, her tone more resolute although full of abject dejection. She hadn't really heard what Roger had said, so convinced was she that what she was saying was the best option.

'Are you sure you're not saying this as a consequence of it merely being a horrid evening?' Roger asked.

Peggy shook her head. 'It's too unsettling and too difficult not being at home in Bermondsey, and I suppose I accept now that I am just not up to it.'

And so Roger added, 'Of course you must do what you think right, Peggy. But make sure your decision is thought through properly. Why not talk it over with Barbara and Ted?'

He laid a hand on her forearm, and she put her hand on his, saying, 'Thank you, Roger. I don't have the words to express what we all owe you.'

Roger sighed sadly and then filled a bucket with some water and shaking his head ruefully he went to the garden to check on Milburn, tactfully making himself scarce as he thought Peggy needed some time on her own to absorb what had just happened.

Peggy was left alone in the back yard. The moonlight was bright on her face still, which meant it was casting shadows that managed to seem somehow blacker than black, and she could hear what were presumably sounds of disentangling the car from the broken five-bar gate.

Peggy gave a small groan and then, exhausted, she slid her back down the stable wall until her bottom touched the ground, and there she stayed deep in the shadows cast by Tall Trees with her knees bent up in front of her. It wasn't a very ladylike position, and ordinarily she would have been worried about her knickers or her petticoat being on show. But she was beyond caring.

She was also beyond being able to cry, she discovered. She recognised Holly's wail, but in the knowledge that there were people with the baby, Peggy didn't even have the energy to go and see to her daughter.

She wrapped her arms about her legs and rested her forehead on her knees as she tried to comfort herself. She stayed like that for a long while, until well after the police had removed their vehicle.

Peggy felt worse than she could ever remember feeling, certainly even worse than after she had hung up the telephone when Bill had broken the news to her about his relationship with Maureen, which she had thought back then, more than three months earlier now, was a low point beyond which she could never plunge again.

How wrong she had been, Peggy thought now. She hadn't believed such pain and strife that she felt at this minute was possible.

But it was.

It was.

Peggy raised her head and looked up at the outline of Tall Trees' roof, where the people she loved were all inside.

She sighed.

It was going to be the most terrible wrench, and she would lose good friends in Roger, Mabel and June Blenkinsop, she knew. And if she left Harrogate she was also going to lose the possibility of anything wonderful happening between her and James, but that was her own fault and actually she had lost that already. And she could see that there were many arguments for concentrating on being a good mother to Holly, rather than trying to find a new love herself. But it hurt – oh, how it hurt! – the thought of how she had been so callous-seeming in front of James.

Miserably Peggy tipped her head to look up at the stars, and she saw Orion's belt twinkling directly in the darkness high above her.

A breeze gusted and Peggy felt her arms goose-bump. There was the faintest sense of the forthcoming crisp autumn nights in the air – and for a second Peggy imagined she had the smell of bonfires in her nose and the distinctive dull sound of footsteps on pavements on the first really cold morning in the winter echoing in her ears – but these sensations dwindled when she noted how the sky above her looked the most glorious she could remember, the velvety darkness majestically cushioning the mysterious dome of the moon and the stars sparkling just for her, it seemed, magnificent and awe-inspiring.

Peggy mused on how insignificant one person's life was when compared to millions of years the stars and planets had witnessed, shining down at her from the heavens across all those light years away. She felt very small, a mere speck of humanity. And then the sound of Holly laughing rang out, and as her eyes flicked towards the back door and the sight of Connie and a limping Jessie sneaking out to find Aiden and Milburn, she realised that although she, and they, were simply a miniscule part of a pattern much more complex than she could ever hope to grasp, nonetheless she had achieved something vital by bringing Holly into the world and she should be proud.

Peggy allowed her shoulders to relax and her breaths to deepen. She tried to think of her hurt and her frustration as something she could package up deep within her and then push to somewhere far away. But try as she might, she couldn't, and a fresh wave of despair engulfed her, dissolving the more positive feeling of a moment earlier.

She stared upwards once more, and saw something unusual shadowed in front of Orion's belt, and Peggy's brow wrinkled slightly in incomprehension.

A moment later she held her breath in trepidation as she realised she could hear now what was undeniably the drone of a bomber's engine.

And then there was a trembling flicker of subdued light and, a few seconds later she fancied, a faint and muffled sound of a bomb exploding many miles away.

With a tremble, Peggy realised that she had just experienced her first bomb, and no matter how life-and-death her own personal struggles might be, as the summer of 1940 drew to a close, she understood with a breathtaking clarity that the war itself might be about to make fools of them all and annihilate each of their private battles.

Peggy felt as if a chapter of her life had just ended abruptly.

She thought that for ever in her mind, even if she and Holly survived the war, it would be 'before the first bomb' and 'after the first bomb' as far as she was concerned. It felt a significant moment, and Peggy felt the hairs on her arm stand proud anew, although this time because of a charge of emotion and not through chill.

She discovered she'd been holding her breath and as she let it out Peggy put her forehead back to her knees. What a horrible world it was. A cruel, stinking, unfair, horrible world.

Now she found she could weep.

She let the tears fall unchecked.

She wept for all the children at Tall Trees and the precarious futures that were facing them, she wept for Holly as it wasn't Holly's fault she had a mother as hapless as Peggy, she wept for James's patients and what they had been through fighting for home and country, she wept for James's skinned knuckles as she hoped that he hadn't done serious damage as if he had then people might die who he could have saved on the operating table, she wept for the people who might just have lost their homes or even their lives in the explosion she had witnessed just now, she wept for Milburn being so unnecessarily frightened, and afterwards she wept for Maureen's baby boy, rejected by his father through no fault of his own, and even for Bill, and his failure to be as loyal as she had been.

There was a throbbing far above her that increased in intensity, and as Peggy heard more enemy bombers flying across Yorkshire, and as those inside Tall Trees spilled out into the yard to run to the road and stare at the sky, Peggy looked up to see these agents of death flying side by side, one line first and then a second line and even a third, as they crossed the shiny stars of Orion on their way to dropping their bombs on the cities of Britain.

And lastly Peggy wept for herself, and her fear at what might be her own – and her beloved country's – destiny in this time of war.

You can read more of Connie and Jessie's
adventures in the first book in the series

The Evacuee Christmas

Far from home, in the midst of war…

ONE PLACE. MANY STORIES

Bold, innovative and
empowering publishing.

FOLLOW US ON:

@HQStories